——————————— ★ ———————————

He was lying on his side, his face toward the camera. One arm, bent at the elbow, was half under his rib cage, the other arm was stretched forward. One leg was straight, the other bent at the knee. He was still wearing the black jeans and turtleneck. Behind him, out of focus, was a blocky white structure that looked like the base of one of Hannah's pedestals.

"Yes," she said. "Yes, that's Kent Reed." She drew a breath. The air smelled of wet city, a hint of garbage and exhaust underlying the scent of fresh rain. "He's dead?" Her voice rose at the end, but it wasn't really a question.

"Yes." Sharpman thumbed through the photographs again and held out another. "What can you tell me about this?"

It took a moment for her brain to interpret what her eyes were transmitting. It was the maquette. What was left of it.

——————————— ★ ———————————

Previously published Worldwide Mystery title by
GRETCHEN SPRAGUE

DEATH IN GOOD COMPANY

Maquette for Murder

GRETCHEN SPRAGUE

WORLDWIDE.

TORONTO • NEW YORK • LONDON
AMSTERDAM • PARIS • SYDNEY • HAMBURG
STOCKHOLM • ATHENS • TOKYO • MILAN
MADRID • WARSAW • BUDAPEST • AUCKLAND

To the beloved survivors:
Emily and Tim
and
Elmer

MAQUETTE FOR MURDER

A Worldwide Mystery/March 2001

First published by St. Martin's Press, Incorporated.

ISBN 0-373-26378-3

This book is a work of fiction. The cities and neighborhoods
mentioned in it do exist in the real world, although I have
changed the name of one small municipality. The people with
whom I have populated these locations and the institutions
I have placed in them, however, have no existence in the real
world. Neither, to the best of my knowledge, do the works of art
I have attributed to some of these fictional people.

Printed in U.S.A.

Acknowledgments

Thanks to Leah Fried, Andy Galler, Donald Glassman, Toby Golick, Edie Meeks and Timothy Sprague for providing information about things I didn't know enough about before I talked with them. Any mistakes are not their fault, but are, instead, the result of my still not knowing enough.

ONE

Love

THE TAXI STOPPED in front of a steel overhead door, half-way down a block of steel overhead doors. What distinguished this particular door from its neighbors were the brick-faced second story above it, the horizontal strip of security-wired windows, pale with interior light, cut into it, and the accumulation of cars parked along the curb in front of it. The cab had to stop in the middle of the street, but no honks or epithets resulted; at six-thirty in the evening, the trucks that frequented the working warehouses had retired for the day.

"This is it?" asked Joe Gianni.

"This is it," said Martha Patterson. Hannah Gold's studio, Williamsburg, Brooklyn.

Martha allowed Joe to pay their fare, accepted his offered hand, and with no more than a token protest from her aging knees, emerged into the showery, but not at the moment showering, May evening. A many-voiced babble drifted out to the street through an open, human-sized door to the left of the overhead door. The invitation had said 5-8, but they were not really late; as everyone knows, the stated hours for a stand-up reception amount to little more than a suggestion.

Inside, clots of people, wineglasses in hand and voices at New York volume, stood among a scattering of Hannah's works that were displayed around the room. While Joe wrestled their raincoats onto the rented coatrack, Martha watched Hannah excuse herself from one of the groups and bustle across to them. Her soft gray garment—certainly silk, for no other substance would flow so liquidly, and certainly designed and produced by Hannah herself, for fabric was her medium—fluttered with the breeze of her passage. The color matched her hair, the neck-to-ankle drapery camouflaged her grandmotherly figure, and the cut of the costume proclaimed her an artist as surely as Martha's tailored dress and Joe's suit and tie defined them as professionals.

Crying, "At last, at last," Hannah enfolded Martha in her arms, then released her and held out both hands to Joe. "And Mr. Gianni, of course. Lovely of you to come." Four months past her sixty-third birthday, she was as excited as a girl celebrating her sweet sixteen.

Martha, who had known Joe professionally for upwards of three decades, was accustomed to thinking of him as restrained beyond the average. But any New Yorker who has achieved a degree of worldly success has mastered cocktail party etiquette; Joe took Hannah's offered hands and air-kissed in the direction of her cheek. "Joe, please," he said. "It's very kind of you to have me."

"Oh, Joe, please, I'm the soul of kindness." The skin around her eyes crinkling, Hannah released his hands and linked arms with him and Martha. "Come, eat and make nice over the baby."

"The..." That did perplex Joe for a moment.

"The maquette," Martha cued him.

Earlier, when she'd granted his rather surprising request to accompany her to this reception, she had found it necessary to explain that a maquette was a small-scale model of a proposed large work of art. This one, whose display was the occasion for the party, represented the most recent stage of Hannah's autumn-blooming career: it was her entry in a competition for a large-scale sculptural work to be installed in a corporate space in Minneapolis.

"The maquette, of course," said Joe. "I'm looking forward to it."

The gray-painted concrete floor had been swept clean of the ravelings of thread and odd little fabric scraps that accumulated when Hannah was working, the industrial sewing machines at the side of the room were covered, and the caterer had disguised the big table on which Hannah cut out her patterns with a leaf-green cloth. They sampled properly runny Brie and trendily high-fiber crackers; then, carrying plastic glasses of better-than-tolerable wine, they began a meandering journey across the room, interrupted every few steps by introductions: two or three dealers; a writer from a slick-paper art magazine; a tall, fortyish man with a ponytail of gray-flecked mahogany-colored hair, who was talking with great intensity about the interplay of light and shadow to three women, two of them very young and very attentive, the third a stocky woman with Asian features whose smile said she'd heard it all before but didn't mind hearing it again.

The maquette, illuminated by a pair of spotlights on a ceiling track, stood on a blocky waist-high pedestal a few feet out from the far side wall. A bulky man in worn jeans and scuffed work boots was standing in front of it, his arms folded across his chest. Serious biceps bulged his T-shirt, and the overhead light created an aureole around his shaved brown scalp. It wasn't until he turned that Martha recognized him as a sculptor who, at his last opening, had been wearing an Al Sharpton haircut.

"Love," he said. He appeared to be addressing Joe.

Joe raised his eyebrows and sipped his wine.

"Joe Gianni, this is Dennison Simm," said Hannah. "Martha, I know you've met Dennie."

Martha nodded. Joe shifted his wineglass to his left hand, extended his right hand, and said, "How do you do."

Simm grasped the offered hand in a complex grip that

might have had some street significance. "Do?" he boomed. "About like everybody else, I guess. Eat, drink, fuck, work. How about you, man?" It wasn't clear that he expected an answer; as he spoke, his gaze slid away across the room.

Nevertheless, Joe responded. His right hand still imprisoned, he produced a cocktail-party smile and said, "Well, I suppose that about sums it up."

The answer reclaimed Simm's attention. "Good man," he barked. He released Joe's right hand and slapped his left shoulder. Joe managed to extend his arm far enough to let the jostled wine miss his trousers and splat onto the floor.

"Love?" This time Simm was addressing Hannah. "Like gettin' married?" His voice slid up the scale into an Amos-and-Andy parody. "Maybe one a them tents they put up for a weddin' down on the ol' plantation? Keep the sun off all the massas an' missuses scarfin' up the mint juleps 'longside the magnolias?" But again his attention wandered across the room.

This time Martha let her gaze follow his. He seemed to be watching a young woman who was standing near the back wall, partly concealed by an abstract metal sculpture on a chest-high pedestal. Dredging the depths of her unreliable memory for names, Martha came up, first with *Olive*, and then with *Quist*. *Olive Quist*, who would be Olive Simm if she had chosen to take her husband's name.

Was Dennison Simm watching his wife or assessing the art?

Martha's judgment declared the woman to be the more worthy of attention. Her skin was the color of milky cocoa; her hair was teased into a dark froth around her head; her body, inside a red minidress, was nubile; her legs below the abbreviated skirt were shapely.

Obviously unaware of her husband's scrutiny, she was gazing into the middle distance. Once more Martha let another person's concentration direct her own gaze. While Dennison Simm was watching Olive, Olive seemed to be watching the ponytailed man who had been discoursing on light and dark, his three female listeners, and a second man, younger and slimmer, who had joined them. With lowered eyelids and curved lips, this newcomer was directing a stereotypically seductive gaze, not at either of the young women, one of whom was smiling in his direction, but at the Asian woman, who was ignoring him.

"Well." Simm returned his attention to Hannah. "Guess it's 'bout time to be gettin' on. Thanks for the *in*vite, Miz Gold, ma'am." Once more he cuffed Joe, who this time avoided spillage altogether, and said, "Good to meet you, man."

When he had passed beyond earshot, Joe said, "Odd man."

"A good sculptor, though." Hannah spoke absently; most of her attention, like Martha's, was following Dennison Simm, who was heading for his wife. "Oh, child!" she breathed, "be careful!"

Olive had reached blindly toward the sculpture beside her and, still staring at the group in the middle of the room, was stroking a smooth area near its base. She was obviously unaware of Simm's approach until he was only a step away. He clamped his fingers around her wrist and jerked her hand away. The sudden motion rocked the sculpture on its pedestal. Almost absentmindedly, Simm steadied it with his free hand while with his other hand he twisted Olive's wrist at an angle that had to be painful.

Joe started forward half a step.

"Let it be," said Hannah.

Joe glanced at her and subsided.

And almost at once, the domestic drama turned anticlimactic. Simm transferred his grip from his wife's wrist to her upper arm; to anyone who had missed what had gone before, the grasp might appear as affectionate. Thus linked, they made their way toward the coatrack by the door.

The next act, if any, would take place elsewhere. Martha retrieved her attention and directed it to the maquette.

She had seen almost nothing of this work's progress, though she had heard much. Like many of Hannah's recent pieces, it was an arrangement of patterned fabric draped over a framework. What was new was its over-the-top lavishness. The maquette was much scaled down, of course; it measured about four feet high, three feet wide, and a couple of feet deep. The installed work was to be twelve feet high. The drapery would consist of hundreds of yards of hand-stenciled parachute fabric, whose folds would form passages leading viewers into a center chamber. There, a white linen cloth encrusted with embroidery would be draped over a lopsided structure resembling a misshapen altar. On this structure, securely fastened against pilferage, would rest a tattered stuffed object that vaguely resembled an emaciated teddy bear.

This creature, the altar cloth, and a scale model of the altar were displayed beside the maquette. A set of computer renderings that showed what a walk through the work would be like was mounted on the wall behind it, next to a blueprint of the armature, which was to be constructed of riveted and welded I-beams.

"Hi, Hannah, I'm sorry to be so late," said a voice behind them. "Hi, Martha." Wendy Kahane, Hannah's assistant until a few weeks ago, had arrived.

Wendy was somewhere between youth and middle age, thick-waisted and double-chinned, with a rebellious tangle of dark hair. Martha liked her a great deal.

"Oh, there you are!" Hannah said. Embraces were exchanged; Joe was introduced.

"So what do you think of *Love?*" Wendy demanded.

"Love?" said Joe.

"*Love* is its name," said Hannah.

"Oh. Yes. I see." Joe sipped his wine. "So if somebody wants to call it a wedding marquee..."

"Dennie is not stupid," said Hannah.

"Matter of opinion," said Wendy. Something behind them seemed to catch her eye; she said, "Oh, God," and began to sidle off. "I'll talk to you later, Hannah."

Martha turned. A young man—the one who had joined the group to which Olive Quist's attention had been directed—had left that group and was approaching.

"Don't run away," Hannah called after Wendy. "We're going to dinner."

Wendy looked back over her shoulder, glanced once more at the newcomer, and raised her eyebrows.

The snub was obvious, but the young man's smile did not waver, although his eyelids flickered for an instant.

Hannah reasserted control. "Martha, Joe," she said, "this is my new assistant, Kent Reed. Kent, my dearest friend, Martha Patterson, and her friend Joe Gianni."

So this was Kent Reed. Martha had heard a good deal about this beautiful young man (Hannah's epithet) who was Wendy's replacement, but this was their first meeting. She offered her hand and said, "How do you do." *Beautiful* was not an exaggeration; he was tall, loose-limbed, and high-cheekboned; his skin was a shade between café au lait and pale beige; he wore his hair in a neat modified Afro.

"Martha, what a treat," he murmured. He didn't exactly shake her offered hand; he gave it a squeeze that was probably meant to flatter with a hint of affection. Perversely, Martha was simply annoyed. He said, "I've heard so much..."

"*And,*" Hannah repeated, "her friend Joe Gianni."

Instantly obedient, he released Martha's hand and modulated his manner from charm to good fellow. "Mr. Gianni," he said. "Joe. How are you?"

Sepia. That was the word for the beautiful young man's skin color.

Joe's right hand had found its way into his coat pocket. He left it there, nodded, cleared his throat, and said, "Fine. And you?"

Kent nodded at the maquette. "Isn't it marvelous?"

Joe cleared his throat once more and said, "Impressive."

And there the conversation stalled; no one seemed to have anything more to say. As speechlessness engulfed them, Hannah stood with her hands folded loosely in front of her, a thoughtful line etched between her brows. She might have been conceiving a new work to be called *Awkwardness.*

And all at once an imp sprang forward from the lawless recesses of Martha's mind. "You must be an artist, Kent," she said.

"Ah, well," he said. "I aspire."

Ah, well? Good heavens. Martha looked across the room at the upright piece Olive Quist had been caressing. "A sculptor, perhaps?" prodded the imp.

The sepia skin flushed. "Well, I've made a few pieces," Kent said, "but lately I've been getting into the artistic potential of digital imaging."

Martha's interest in computer-generated art was less than minimal. She ignored this lead and said, "Might that metal piece over there be one of yours? I don't think I've seen it before."

The flush deepened. "Yes," Kent said. "Yes, that's mine."

"Interesting," Martha said. "Would you mind if I had a look?"

"What a question," said Hannah.

THE PIECE WAS an abstraction, about three feet high: a slender curving upright column of steel, its ascent interrupted in three places by rough-cast lumps five or six inches across. Kent had not come over with them, which was fortunate; Martha would have been hard put to formulate a comment acceptable to the artist. Generally receptive to abstract sculpture, she thought the piece should have interested her more than it did, but some failure of proportion left her unmoved. Perhaps the artist had already experienced such a reaction and had no stomach for another.

"Not?" said Hannah.

"The performance doesn't seem to come up to the concept," Martha said.

"Oh well, it never does. The physical object corrupts the purity of the concept." With that amused crinkling of the skin around her eyes, Hannah added, "That's critic-ese. In English, it means that stuff doesn't care what you want it to do. Stuff has ideas of its own. Sometimes they're better, sometimes they're worse."

"That's all very well," Martha said, "but the problem with this piece isn't the stuff, it's the eye. There's something wrong with the proportions."

"Oh, you." Hannah looked at Joe. "What do you think?"

But Joe shook his head. "I'm afraid I'm no judge. I'm new at this."

"That doesn't matter. One way or another, everybody responds." Hannah closed one hand around the slender area that Olive Quist had caressed. It was as obvious a handhold as the neck of a baseball bat. Supporting the top with her other hand, she lifted the sculpture from the base and offered it to him. "Here," she said, "forget looking at it. Sculpture is tactile. Feel it."

Joe hesitated.

"Don't be afraid of responding," Hannah said. "Let your hands feel the steeliness of it. Let your muscles support the mass."

"Won't it corrode?" Joe said. "From acids in the skin, things like that?"

"And what if it does? It's stuff. If corroding is its nature, it will corrode. Paint fades, stone crumbles, metal corrodes. Look at us; we wither and die. Have you seen the old stone saints with the toes worn away by the kisses of the faithful? That's their nature." She thrust the metal shaft toward him. "Don't be afraid."

Adversaries more experienced than Joe had been hard put to resist Hannah. He set his empty wineglass on the corner of the pedestal and took the sculpture from her, holding it as she had: his left hand gripping the slender area at the base, his right hand supporting the top. He hefted it for a moment and handed it back. "Yes, I see what you mean," he said. Martha did not detect much conviction in his voice.

Hannah thrust it toward Martha. "Your eyes don't like it. What do your muscles say?"

No more able to resist than Joe, and far more willing to go along, Martha took it. The thing was heavy, but the balance wasn't too bad. And it was a good thing that its maker had avoided coming with them, for the imp, still running the show, transported Martha five decades back in time. She moved her right hand down to grip the smooth handhold just above her left hand, planted her feet, poised the thing just above her right shoulder, leaned forward at the waist, and mimed a batter awaiting the pitcher's delivery.

"Oh, you're bad." But Hannah didn't try to hide her grin. She took Kent Reed's piece out of Martha's hands and set it back on its pedestal.

TWO

Nine-One-One

"DON'T YOU LOVE IT?" Wendy topped the pile of rice on her plate with a portion of sweet and pungent tofu from the communal dish. "Dennie's feeling the heat."

"Dennie?" Joe Gianni passed her the broccoli with garlic sauce and helped himself to a portion of General Tso's chicken.

"Dennison Simm," said Nick Warner. "The sculptor. You think so, Wendy?" Nick, dark-haired and gray-goateed, was the dealer whose gallery handled Hannah's work.

The reception was over, but, having learned that Joe was a senior partner in an established accounting firm and newly interested in contemporary art—in Hannah Gold's work in particular—Nick had urged Joe to join him and his partner, Barbara Turcotte, and Hannah, of course, in a jaunt over to Chinatown for dinner. Martha, as Hannah's friend (and possibly, it belatedly occurred to her, because Nick had pegged her as Joe's date) had been invited as well. Wendy Kahane and Kent Reed, having contributed to the construction of *Love*'s maquette, had also been invited; Wendy had hedged until she learned that Kent had declined; then she had accepted.

She said, "Explain to me why else he came out of his cave to take a look at *Love*. He's feeling the heat."

"What heat would that be?" asked Joe.

"He's entering a piece in the Minnesota competition."

"Oh," Joe said. "Yes, I see."

Hannah waved away the tofu dish and said, "You can't really think Dennie Simm could be worried about my little *chuppah*."

"Sure I do," said Wendy.

"I think Dennie was just being Dennie."

"Well, now, Hannah," said Joe, "I think she might have a point. The way he was talking, didn't you think he was trying pretty hard to downgrade your...to downgrade *Love?*"

Barbara Turcotte, who was sitting on the other side of Hannah from Martha, said, "I wouldn't be surprised." Barbara, a competent saleswoman in her own right, was a sturdy, midfortyish woman dressed in a purple pants-and-tunic outfit that was equally at home in the gallery and in the corporate boardrooms where she pitched her artists' claims to commissions. "He certainly didn't seem to be feeling on top of the world. Did you catch that little byplay just before they left? Wendy, you're a friend of Olive's. Is that marriage long for this world?"

"Dennie's feeling the heat from Hannah," said Wendy. "That's all. You know what he's like when he has an opening coming up. He wouldn't set foot out of the studio unless he was more worried about Hannah's *chuppah* than about making that one more piece that will put him up there with David Smith forever and ever, amen."

"Mark Di Suvero," said Barbara. "Not David Smith."

"If he is worried, he's right," Nick said. "The breakthrough is coming. I can smell it. Hannah Gold is an excellent bet to become the next Big Thing."

"I imagine," said Joe, "winning the competition would help."

"It certainly wouldn't hurt," Nick said, "but there are a lot of considerations besides merit involved in those decisions. It's the invitation to submit that recognizes quality, and that's already paying off." He looked at Martha.

"Those two little pieces you own? I have a collector who would go to the high four figures for either one of them, and I predict they'll go even higher by next winter." He raised his glass of Tsing Tao beer. "A canny woman, Martha Patterson."

Finding herself toasted, Martha produced a smile. In truth, she had bought the pieces, not as investments, but in recognition of the slow ripening of acquaintance into friendship. And, of course, because she liked looking at them.

"He thinks I'm Microsoft," Hannah murmured into Martha's ear.

"I wouldn't worry," said Martha.

"Your best advice, counselor? Then I won't." She slipped the paper off her chopsticks. "Advice, advice. I knew there was something. There was somebody I wanted you to meet but she didn't get there."

"You mean," said Barbara, "there was somebody in the world who didn't get there?"

"The world is wider than you know," said Hannah. "This is a neighbor of mine. She's retired and sick and having some kind of legal trouble about something medical or medical trouble about something legal. Very *very* confidential. I told her Martha Patterson was the person to see, but I guess this isn't one of her days."

"Professional consultations at parties?" said Barbara. "Shame on you, Hannah."

"Look who's talking." Hannah glanced at Nick, who was focusing on Joe.

"Don't be rude, dear," said Barbara. "It's for your own good."

"Actually," Martha said, "it needn't be a problem. One advises them to consult an attorney and stuffs one's mouth with another hors d'oeuvre. Hannah, I give you permission to give her my number."

"When I see her. I gave her a flyer for those seminars you're running. If she can travel, maybe she'll show up at one of them. Look for Florence Appleton. You'll like her. She's a retired math teacher and she still has most of her marbles."

"Speaking of math," said Barbara, "Hannah, how's the dream boy working out?"

Hannah shrugged. "It could be better, it could be worse. He's useless on the sewing machines, but I knew he would be, and it's only temporary anyway. And I guess it's a good idea for this old crone to show that she can make use of all that trendy computer nonsense."

"The internal renderings?" said Wendy. "Yes, they're nice." Her tone was that of someone resolved to be fair.

"Not that I couldn't have done them with a pencil," Hannah said, "but it was something he could do. And he's tidying my financial files onto the hard disk."

"Good," said Barbara.

"Boring," said Wendy.

"But really necessary," said Barbara.

"I like pencils," said Wendy.

"How do you run your shop without a computer?" Barbara asked.

"I've been running it just fine for years."

It was a predictable exchange. Hoping for some less tedious conversation, Martha transferred her attention to the men across the table, only to observe that Joe's attention had strayed from Nick's sales pitch to the women's computer debate. Newly interested in contemporary art he might be, but the tools of his profession were what engaged the greater part of his mind.

Nick must also have taken note, for he moved into closing mode. "You really must drop by the gallery," he said. "We have several of Hannah's pieces that I think will interest you."

"Microsoft," Hannah muttered.

SINCE NOBODY WANTED lichi or green tea ice cream, Nick proposed that they move on to a coffeehouse a few blocks from his gallery. Somehow, Martha saw, it had got to be ten-forty. Already tired from an afternoon spent in expounding imperfect solutions to intractable human problems, and only partially refreshed by her dinner, she declined. Joe, who had a train to catch, declined as well. Hannah, Wendy, Nick, and Barbara, therefore, hailed one cab to convey them into Soho while Martha shared another with Joe.

Before they had lurched a block, she was wishing she had walked. In a New York taxi fleet that, admittedly, was never capable of producing a truly luxurious ride, this vehicle was uniquely dilapidated. Broken springs pierced the upholstery, every unevenness in the pavement established that its shock absorbers were shot, and it smelled as if someone had been sick on the floor. Not only would the air have been fresher if she had walked, but her leg muscles needed stretching. It was not really *far* from Chinatown to East Eighth Street, not by Martha's standards, and the streets were still well populated; she would have been quite safe.

But the drizzle had resumed, not heavily but steadily, and she was too tired to relish creating a commotion, so she sat on the edge of the seat and breathed shallowly until the cab jerked to a stop in front of her building. Joe (quite unnecessarily from a security point of view, but that was Joe) delivered her into the care of Boris, the night doorman, and was favored with a nod, a smile, and, the ultimate accolade, a "Good evening, sir." The black Burberry, the still-sharp trouser creases, and Joe's removal, upon entering the lobby, of his black rain hat obviously met Boris's difficult standard of correctness.

Martha rather disliked Boris; therefore she took particular pains to behave toward him with the greatest possible
courtesy. She paused for a moment to exchange a few cli-
ches, entertaining herself as she did so by glancing out to
the street through the glass wall of the lobby. Thus it was
that she observed Joe heading east on foot. Evidently the
cab had been too much for him as well, for it was nowhere
in sight. Doubtless he hoped to hail another on Broadway,
or perhaps he had decided to walk the couple of short
blocks to Astor Place and take the subway to Grand Central. It was a choice Martha herself would probably have
made; the drizzle had nearly stopped and the subway might
well be faster than a cab.

She wished Boris a good night, skirted the little grove
of ficus trees that concealed the elevators, and rode up to
her apartment.

THE TELEPHONE startled her from deep sleep.

The shock of waking set her heart to hammering. Then,
as she came fully awake, apprehension joined shock. Her
son, who lived in California, was good about respecting the
three-hour time difference, but in an emergency...

The phone bleeped twice more while she fumbled in the
dark. At last she found the handset and lifted it to her ear.
"Martha Patterson speaking," she said, her voice, in spite
of her pounding heart, crisp from decades of subordinating
emotion to substance. Her free hand found her glasses on
the nightstand. She slipped them on and the clock's red
numbers came into focus.

12:37.

The phone transmitted a rustle and two muted thumps.

"Hello?" she demanded. "Who's calling?"

The hiss of a slowly drawn breath.

Irritation replaced alarm. Why on earth did one trouble
to reduce one's given name to an initial when everyone

capable of opening a telephone directory knew that the *M* of *M. J. Patterson* stood for Mary or Margaret, Michelle or Megan, Maureen, Myra, Martha...

It would be a blind call; nobody who knew that this *M* was a woman of seventy-three would select her as the stimulus for vicarious eroticism. She was on the point of hanging up when a voice quavered, "Martha?"

It sounded like... "Hannah?" she said.

"Martha?" Yes, Hannah. "What are you...I want 911." She sounded wobbly, as if she were ill.

Martha came fully awake. "You've got Martha," she said. "Where are you?"

"In...in the..." Her voice was fading. Martha heard another breath; then, "In the studio. I want 911."

"I'll call them, Hannah," said Martha, keeping her own voice brisk. "Hang up and I'll call 911 for you."

A sibilant breath.

"Hannah, do you understand? Hang up to clear my line. I'll call 911 and send them to you."

"Nine one one..."

"I'll call them. Hannah, do you understand? Hang up and I'll call 911 for you."

"Oh." It was no more than a breath. "Yes." A clatter then a click, at last the blessed emptiness of a disconnected line.

Martha depressed and released the button, heard the dial tone with a sag of relief, punched in 911 and told the responding voice that there was a serious medical emergency at the address of Hannah's studio.

NOW IT WAS a litter of police cars that choked the curb in front of Hannah's place. One roof light was still revolving, sending red flickers across the steel doors. A uniformed officer stood watchful under a street light, guarding the police-line sawhorses that blocked the sidewalk and street.

The hired car had to stop in the middle of the street forty feet away. The driver looked over his shoulder and, echoing Joe's earlier uncertainty, said, "This is right?"

Martha had used this car service for three years. Her very first destination, an apartment building in a deteriorating area of Flatbush, had elicited the same question. It translated into *Lady, do you know what you're doing?*

"Yes, thank you, this is it," she said.

"You want I wait?"

For a moment she hesitated; but having no idea what lay before her, she said, "Not this time, thanks." She handed over fare and tip and opened the door.

The policeman watched her lever herself out into the night. Leftover puddles in the potholed pavement reflected the orangish glow of the streetlights. Forty feet along, the studio's strip windows glowed.

In most New York neighborhoods, the activity would attract a crowd, but not after business hours in this dark street of warehouses. Half a block behind her, where the street crossed a busier avenue, a few passersby glanced down, but none turned aside to investigate.

"What happened?" Martha asked the policeman at the barricade. She heard an edge of agitation in her voice, drew a deeper breath, and summoned coherence. "I'm Martha Patterson. I'm the one who called 911. Is Hannah ill?"

"That's the lady who lives here?"

"Hannah Gold, yes. She called me. She sounded disoriented and I called 911. What's wrong? Is she ill?"

"Are you a relative?"

"A friend. The one who called 911. What happened? How badly—"

"Hold on a second, okay?" he said, not unkindly. He walked the forty feet to the door and spoke to someone just inside. After a moment he came back and said, "Detective'll see you in a minute."

"How badly—" Martha began again, but at that moment the door opened, releasing a shaft of light onto the sidewalk.

The man who emerged was quick-moving, a white man with a narrow, sharp-featured face, a detective in plain clothes: slacks, tweed jacket, dark shirt whose exact color was impossible to determine in the sickly glow of the streetlights. His tie was unknotted and his collar was unbuttoned.

He came over to the barrier, skirting a puddle in the gutter that held something sludgy and granular. The public vomiting of wandering drunks, Martha noted, was not limited to the island of Manhattan. The detective studied her for a moment and then said, "Well, I'll be damned. It is the same Martha Patterson."

Sharp-featured. Sharp... The mnemonic worked. "And the same Detective Sharpman," she said. "Please, what has happened?"

"That's what we're working on," he said. "How are you involved?"

Again she explained. He nodded.

"Is she injured?" she demanded.

"Gray-haired lady, about five-two, heavyset?"

"Yes. Hannah Gold. How bad is it?"

"She has a head injury. She was unconscious when the responding officer found her, but she roused a little when the medics came. EMS took her to St. Hilda's."

St. Hilda's. The nearest hospital.

The nearest, yes, but by no means near. She shouldn't have dismissed the car service. Maybe she could flag a cab on the avenue.

Sharpman read her intention. "Before you go," he said, "I need you to tell me about the setup here."

She hauled her attention back. Of course. There was no help for it. "Hannah Gold makes sculpture with fabric,"

she said. "This downstairs space is her studio. She lives
upstairs."

He was writing in a notebook. "Does she live alone?"

"Yes."

"What about that apartment at the back?"

"Oh. Her assistant is living there at the moment. It's only
a temporary arrangement."

"What's his name?"

"Kent Reed."

"Do you know him?"

"We met for the first time this evening."

"Could you describe him?"

A quiver started in her solar plexus. "Perhaps six feet,"
she said. "Slim. Light-skinned African-American. Young,
mid-twenties, I suppose."

"Do you know of any relatives?"

"His? I have no idea. Hannah has a sister in Atlanta.
Detective Sharpman, I don't want to appear obstructive, but
my friend is unconscious and alone in an emergency room.
That is not a good situation."

"She isn't alone. An officer is with her."

"Detec—"

"Please." Sharpman raised his hand like a traffic cop.
"Bear with me for just a minute or two. This officer's first
career was emergency room nurse." He smiled briefly.
"Trust me, she'll look after your friend as if she was her
mother. I know you're anxious, but I need your help."

And one way or another, he would get it; resistance
would only lead to delay. Reluctantly, she nodded.

"Thanks." He reached into the inner pocket of his jacket
and pulled out an envelope. "These aren't meant to be
evidence," he said. "They're just for my own information.
I'd appreciate it if you'd take a look. It's a little unpleasant,
but it's far from the worst I've ever seen."

The worst a NYPD detective had seen would be well

beyond what Martha cared to think about; a *little unpleasant* would be a considerable understatement. But Martha Jenkins Patterson, only child of a justice of the supreme court of the state of Nebraska, had been born into a household committed to civic responsibility. "Very well," she said.

Sharpman slipped a little stack of Polaroid prints out of the envelope, shuffled through, selected one, and held it out.

The orangeish glow of the streetlight turned the blood in the photograph to brown, but there was no doubt that it was blood that matted the hair of the man lying on the floor. He was lying on his side, his face toward the camera. One arm, bent at the elbow, was half under his rib cage, the other arm was stretched forward. One leg was straight, the other bent at the knee. He was still wearing the black jeans and turtleneck. Behind him, out of focus, was a blocky white structure that looked like the base of one of Hannah's pedestals.

"Yes," she said. "Yes, that's Kent Reed." She drew a breath. The air smelled of wet city, a hint of garbage and exhaust underlying the scent of fresh rain. "He's dead?" Her voice rose at the end, but it wasn't really a question.

"Yes." Sharpman thumbed through the photographs again and held out another. "What can you tell me about this?"

It took a moment for her brain to interpret what her eyes were transmitting. At first it looked like an abstract collage, but then the jumble fell into focus and realization exploded into shock.

It was the maquette. What was left of it. The armature was twisted and wrenched apart at the soldered joins; the fabric dangled in shreds; a litter of torn-up paper must be the remains of the blueprint and the internal renderings.

Sharpman was watching her face. "Tell me," he said.

The first time Martha had had dealings with Detective Sharpman, he had all but accused her of withholding evidence, although she had only been observing the lawyer's ethical mandate to protect a client's interest. Here there was no client. She told him everything: the party; Dennison Simm's behavior in front of the maquette; the Simm-Quist soap opera; the foolishness she had perpetrated on Kent Reed's sculpture; even the Chinese dinner.

Finally Sharpman folded his pen into his notebook and pulled another photograph out of the packet.

Brownish, drying blood caked the lumpy area at the top of Kent Reed's not-quite-right-steel column; in the crevices, some of the blood still glistened wetly.

A stroke of guilt that she knew to be irrational shook her. "Yes," she said. "Yes, that's it."

THREE

Concussion

DETECTIVE SHARPMAN had not exaggerated the efficacy of Hannah's escort. When Martha inquired at St. Hilda's emergency room, she was informed that patient Hannah Gold had already been admitted.

Advocacy skills sharpened by five decades of law practice took her through the security system and up to the neural unit on the hushed eighth floor. There, a sturdy RN answered her anxious questions with a variety of phrases that all translated into *Wait and see*. One hard fact emerged: Hannah was scheduled for a CT scan first thing in the morning.

Finally the nurse led her through an open door into a single room where Hannah, in a white hospital gown, was propped at a low angle between safety bars. Her eyes were closed; her hair, undone from its customary bun, straggled across a thick dressing that covered the right side of her head. Tubes led to her nostrils from a piece of medical paraphernalia standing beside the bed, and an IV needle was taped to the back of one hand.

A uniformed policewoman sat next to the bed, a crossword puzzle book open on her lap. She set it aside, got to her feet, and asked to see identification. It hadn't crossed Martha's mind that a guard might be posted; the realization sent a chilly trickle down her spine. While the nurse took Hannah's wrist between her fingers, Martha dug her driver's license out of her handbag. The policewoman looked it over, said, "Okay," handed it back, and resumed her seat.

Still holding Hannah's wrist, the nurse said, "Hey, there. Want to wake up and tell me your name?"

Hannah expelled a breath which, unimpeded by the tube, would have been a snort. "Told you already," she said without opening her eyes. Her voice was barely louder than a whisper. "Golda Meir. Can' you remem' anything?"

"Tch." The nurse released Hannah's wrist and shook her head. "Still confused."

But the impudent response lifted Martha's spirit. She took Hannah's hand and said, "Behave yourself."

Hannah's fingers tightened on hers. "Martha?" She opened her eyes. "Martha."

"The same."

"Got Martha." Hannah squeezed tighter and released Martha's hand. "What happened?"

"You got a bump on the head."

Hannah laid the flat of her hand on the dressing on her head. "That's how?"

"That's how. It was quite a bump, so they're asking obvious questions to see how well your mind is functioning."

"So-called mind."

"If you say so. It would help if you'd stop teasing."

"Fun."

"Just so, but you're worrying them. How about putting the fun off for an hour or two?"

"Oh." Hannah's gaze moved to the nurse. "Oh, well." Miming a good girl behaving herself, she laced her fingers together on her sheet-covered lap. "Hannah," she said. "Hannah Gold, okay?"

"Well, now, that's more like it," the nurse said. "How are we feeling?"

"We?"

"What?"

"You an' me, we. You, don' know. Me, dizh—" A pause to draw breath. "Dizzy. Got a headache." She frowned and looked at Martha. "Nine-one-one. Got you. What happen'?" She looked around, her eyes moving but her head still. "Hospital."

"Saint Hilda's," said Martha.

Pause. "Got no saints."

"Tch," said the nurse.

"Actually," Martha said, "I believe it's another of her so-called jokes. She's Jewish, and Jews don't recognize Christian saints."

"Jew'sh," Hanna confirmed. "No saints."

"Well, that's all right, hon," said the nurse. "The kitchen can do kosher."

"Don' keep kosher."

"That's fine too."

"Cheeseburger. Shrimp. Lobster."

"Well, I don't know about that."

"What time?"

"Breakfast gets up here around seven. You can order—"

"No. Now."

"Now?" The nurse consulted her watch. "It's one-fifty-eight."

Hannah's eyes turned toward the dark window. "A.M.?"

"That's right. Almost two in the morning."

"No way!"

"Sure is. Lots been happening while you been asleep."

"No way. Martha." A ghost of that crinkle around the eyes. "Party poop. Sleep at ten, up at six."

True. "Nevertheless," Martha said, "two in the morning it is and here I am." She heard a rustle behind her and glanced back. A notebook had replaced the crossword puzzle book on the policewoman's lap. She met Martha's eyes and moved the hand holding the pencil in a rolling motion: *Keep her talking.*

The police officer was more than an escort and a guard; she was also supposed to get Hannah's statement. And at the moment, Martha Patterson looked like the person most likely to elicit anything approaching a coherent narrative.

Very well, she would try. But eliciting a narrative that was both true and coherent was likely to prove tricky. Just now Hannah was probably highly suggestible; one must avoid prompting for fear of inducing false memories. One must, in the language of Martha's profession, ask no leading questions.

She took a moment to put her thoughts in order; then she asked the most open-ended question she could think of. "Hannah, what do you remember about last night?"

"What day?"

"Last night? Tuesday. May twenty-first."

The response was immediate: "Reception."

"All right."

"You brought that...Joe. Giotto? Giovanni?" Hannah frowned. "Gianni?"

"All right. Yes, I did. What else?"

"Dennie, doing his shuffle shtick."

"All right."

"About my *chuppah.*"

"Yes."

The frown dissolved into that amused crinkle around the eyes. "Corroded Kent's Brancusi."

"Brancusi?"

An impatient attempt at a snort. "Kent's bird. The bat."

Bird? Bat? Oh, of course. The basic shape of that sculpture of Kent Reed's, which Martha had impishly handled like a baseball bat, did somewhat resemble a famous abstract sculpture: Brancusi's *Bird in Flight*. No lumpy bits, however, interrupted the upward sweep of the Brancusi. "Just so," Martha said. "Anything else you remember?"

"Chinatown. Nick, selling like a stockbroker. You party-pooped."

"Yes, I did. You're doing fine. What else?"

A long pause. Hannah closed her eyes and again laid the flat of her hand on the bandage on her head. Distress creased her forehead. "Can't remember."

The nurse stepped forward. "Okay, that's enough, now," she said. "Don't worry yourself."

But Hannah ignored her and continued to scowl. "Studio," she said at last.

Martha glanced at the nurse, who hesitated for a moment. Then she nodded and drew back half a step. "You remember getting to the studio?" Martha asked.

"Not...*getting* there. Just *there*. On the floor." The frown eased into a middle-distance stare of concentration. "Had this headache. Seeing double. Couldn't get up."

"What did you do?"

All at once, Hannah's eyes widened. "Crawled!" she crowed. "I crawled! Crawled to the desk and grabbed the phone cord and pulled it down. Like a baby. *Ma-ma, Da-da,*" Hannah mocked herself, and then, "Smart?"

"Indeed."

"Aha!" Hannah pushed herself higher. "That's how! It's the next button."

"Next button?"

"On the phone. Nine-one-one is next to yours. That's how."

"You mean the memory dial? The button for my number is next to the button for 911?"

"*That's* how I got you." Hannah relaxed against the pillow. "I'm not crazy."

"Far from it." Martha glanced back at the policewoman,

who raised the hand with the pencil and again made that rolling motion.

The nurse registered resigned acquiescence.

Go on. But go on to what? *Who, what, when, where, why...*

Who. "Did you see anybody?"

"In the studio?"

"There, yes."

A frown. "You mean Kent?"

It wasn't what Martha had meant. Amazingly, she had forgotten about Kent Reed. Perhaps later she would be ashamed. Now she held her breath.

But Hannah remained undisturbed. "Didn't see him. Asleep, maybe."

Martha let her breath out. "Anybody else?"

Again Hannah's eyes widened, but this time not with triumph. She laid her hand against her bandaged head. "Somebody...hit me." She looked past Martha, for the first time acknowledging the policewoman. "Where is he?"

The cop spoke quietly: "Did you see who it was?"

"I...don't know. I don't remember. Who was it?" Hannah struggled higher. *"Where is he?"*

The nurse frowned.

"Don't worry." The policewoman's voice was still quiet. "You're okay here. He won't come here."

Hannah studied her face. "That's why you're here? To keep him out?"

"If necessary, but he isn't going to come here. And I need to find out what you remember."

"Nothing. I remember nothing."

"Maybe you do. You're saying *he.* Does that mean you remember a man?"

"I don't remember. I was on the floor. That's all."

"What about before that?"

"You don't listen." Articulating with great precision,

Hannah said, "I do not remember *anything* before I was on the floor."

The nurse frowned at the policewoman.

The policewoman smiled. "Okay, I guess we've got that straight. Try this. When you came to on the floor, where were you?"

"In—oh. By the door."

"Do you remember if the door was open or shut?"

A long silence. "Shut?" A deep frown. "I think so. No wind. Didn't feel any wind."

"Good thinking. Were any lights on?"

"Lights?" A pause. "Lights." A frown.

"Something about the lights?"

Hannah started to shake her head, grimaced, and held still. "On. I could see."

"What did you see?"

"Stuff on the floor." She expelled that gusty exhalation that in the absence of the oxygen tubes would have been a snort. "The caterer didn't sweep."

"What else?"

"Blood."

"Where?"

Hannah laid her hand against the bandage. "My head hurt. I put up my hand and...blood."

"And while you were crawling to the phone? What did you see then?"

"Desk legs. Phone cord. *Two* phone cords, seeing double." She looked at Martha and grinned. "So...got you."

"Just so," said Martha. "How are your eyes working now?"

"One Martha. That's enough." She closed her eyes and sighed. "Tired, okay?"

"Okay," said the nurse, "that is really enough."

For a moment Martha thought the policewoman would

challenge her, but then she nodded and relaxed against the
back of her chair.

Hannah opened her eyes again and said, "Don't let her
get me, okay?"

"Her?" said the policewoman, suddenly alert again.

"Whoever bash' me." Once more Hannah's eyes closed.
"Mustn' be sexist."

FOUR

Friendship

ONE PROBLEM with having an early-to-bed metabolism is that staying up really late seems, perversely, to disable the falling-asleep mechanism. When Martha at last lay in her bed, weary almost to the point of tears, she found herself stuck at the top of the slide from consciousness into sleep.

After an hour's unproductive search for a comfortable position, she gave up, clambered out of bed, pulled on her robe, and went into her office. It had once been her son's room, but as Robert had moved inexorably outward from high school to M.I.T. to Silicon Valley, from bachelorhood to marriage and fatherhood, she had bit by bit transformed it to meet her own needs. Here she carried on her freelance retirement job: legal research for small law firms that had taken on cases exceeding their in-house research capabilities. The work was just demanding enough to keep the brain from turning to Jell-O, and she could set her own hours.

She sat down before her computer screen. She was aware that the information she was after was unlikely to help her fall asleep, but having governed her life by the principle that knowledge, however distressing, is preferable to fantasy and false hope, she logged on and opened a search for information about head injuries.

A substantial blow to the head, she learned, might bruise the brain, causing the tissues to swell and producing symptoms such as unconsciousness, headache, confusion, amnesia, mental lapses, muscular weakness, and possibly paralysis. The symptoms tended to disappear over time, but in extreme cases...

If Martha had ever observed that prayer had any effect on the functioning of the universe, she would have prayed that Hannah's case should not be an extreme one.

Hannah Gold was Martha's best friend. If the schoolyard expression sounded absurd when applied to women in their sixties and seventies, so be it; one had friends, and Hannah was the best of Martha's. Not the friend whom she saw most often, but the one to whom she came closest to revealing her shielded inner self.

The friendship had its unlikely roots in a business association, albeit a considerably more intimate one than the professional ties of attorney to attorney. For a good many years now, Hannah Gold had been Martha Patterson's dressmaker.

Three and a half decades ago, Hannah, an honor graduate of the Fashion Institute of Technology, had dropped out of the frenetic world of high fashion to have a baby. Three months later, she had lost him to what is now known as SIDS. Her marriage did not survive. She reclaimed her original surname and returned to a more companionable version of the trade she knew; she became a dressmaker to well-to-do New York matrons. She never remarried.

Meanwhile, since arriving in New York City in 1949 with a brand-new law degree and an almost equally new husband, Martha had been practicing trusts-and-estates law with a conservative midtown firm. Her own income, of course, had been substantial, and when in due course Edwin Patterson's postwar air-freight business climbed out of the red, Martha, dissatisfied with the ready-to-wear apparel then available to professional women, became able to afford Hannah Gold.

Chats during fittings expanded into conversations over coffee, and then into confidences while gallery-hopping. As

Martha's discriminating but naive taste ripened into artistic acumen, Hannah began to describe her own fantasies of what she might do with fabric if freed from the limitations of the human form. She showed Martha sketches, then actual works: expertly stitched abstract forms, some stuffed, some quilted, others fitted over wooden forms or, like the maquette for *Love,* draped over metal armatures. She joined a co-op gallery and exhibited regularly, selling a few pieces at prices that barely covered her expenses and, more important, garnering a few reviews.

Watching Hannah's progress, Martha came to realize that success in the New York art world depended as much on contacts as on quality. She and Edwin purchased works of art from time to time, but not obsessively enough to be called collectors; two or three of their acquaintances, however, qualified for that designation. Martha invited them to dinner and placed her Hannah Gold pieces in hard-to-overlook locations about the apartment. One of the guests was much taken with the work. Martha saw to it that he was invited to Hannah's next opening, at which he purchased two pieces and after which he praised the work to a number of established dealers and a couple of New York's most powerful critics. A review appeared in the *Times;* Nick Warner took Hannah into his stable; and three years ago, the Minnesota Museum of Art had included three Hannah Gold pieces in an exhibition of works in unconventional media. It was the Minnesota exposure that had led to the present invitation to submit.

Hannah was able to become selective about her dressmaking clients. She continued to dress Martha for extraordinary occasions; more important, her friendship supported Martha through mandatory retirement from her law firm, through Edwin's own retirement and subsequent fatal series of heart attacks, and (largely after the fact, for Hannah had been in Minnesota at the time) through a brief stint as a pro bono attorney in a Brooklyn Legal Services office—an experience whose rewarding elements were colored but not canceled by the two violent deaths that had introduced Martha to Detective Sharpman.

Losing Hannah would be intolerable.

MARTHA MUST FINALLY have fallen asleep, for at a quarter past nine in the morning the telephone woke her. Barbara Turcotte, uncharacteristically agitated, was calling from the Nicholas Warner gallery. The police had just left. Had Martha seen Hannah? How was she?

"A little confused," said Martha, who at the moment wasn't herself all that clearheaded.

"Will she recover?"

"The appropriate phrase seems to be *time will tell*."

"Oh, my God. And Kent, how awful, his life in front of him. And the maquette. They showed me a Polaroid. It's appalling. It's got to be restored right away."

"She's in no condition to work."

"No, I talked to Wendy. She'll do it. She knows the work, she did a lot of the sewing. I had some leverage; she wants us to mount a show of her quilts. The sketches are here and I think Hannah has some extra fabric. It doesn't matter, we can buy some more."

"When is the deadline?"

"She was going to ship on Monday. There's some leeway, Wednesday will do." Barbara's voice dropped down the scale. "Martha, did anything come up about Dennie Simm?"

"I told them how he behaved at the party."

"What do you think?"

"Barbara," Martha said, "all I know about the man is that I rather liked his work the one time I saw it."

"Which doesn't prove a thing," said Barbara.

"Just so."

FIVE

*Visiting
the Sick*

WHEN MARTHA EMERGED from the shower, the answering machine was blinking. She punched Play and listened to an unfamiliar voice say, "Ms. Patterson, this is Jerry Green from the *New York Post*." He recited a number. "I've heard the report of your 911 call last night and I want to get that part of the story straight before we go to press. Would you give me a call, please?"

Having no particular interest in being quoted in the *Post*, she deleted the message and turned on her computer. Work would help ward off worry.

The next call came at eleven o'clock. She waited through four rings and her own message, heard, "Martha, it's Joe Gianni," and took the call.

Joe was more agitated than she had ever heard him. Detective Sharpman had just left his office. "Have you seen Hannah?" he demanded. "How bad is it?"

"I was at the hospital last night," Martha said. "She was conscious, but she was dazed and experiencing some amnesia. She's to have a CT scan this morning."

"Amnesia? That sounds serious. Does she have any memory at all?"

"Oh, yes. She just can't remember what happened when she arrived at the studio."

"So she doesn't know who did it?"

"Not as of last night. I understand some memory might return."

"The detective showed me photographs. The maquette—and the young man. Appalling."

"Just so."

"And that sculpture of his that we were playing around with. It made me sick just looking at it. I suppose he walked in on him, the young man, I mean, caught him in the act, whoever it was. Caught him vandalizing the maquette, and he just grabbed the first thing available and lashed out. And then Hannah must have walked in at just the wrong time." Joe's voice dropped a tone. "I told them about that black fellow. Dennison Simm? I hope that was all right."

"Told them what about him?"

"That from the way he was acting, I wondered if he might have thought the maquette was a threat to his entry in the competition. Now I wonder if I was doing him an injustice. I don't know the man. I don't have any idea what he'd be capable of."

"I described his behavior myself," said Martha.

"Oh, well, then. Good. I suppose the police can separate the grain from the chaff. Martha, I feel terrible about this."

"Indeed."

"I'm afraid it's going to be hard to concentrate this afternoon. Shall we share a cab? I could stop by for you around three-thirty."

Concentrate? This afternoon?

Oh, good heavens. She hadn't looked at her calendar this morning, and she had nearly forgotten the elder-law seminar. "Thank you," she said, "but I'll be coming from the hospital."

"Oh, of course. Please give Hannah my best, and if there's anything I can do to help…"

People always said that. He must be thanked, so she did so, and hung up and propped her elbows on the desk in front of the keyboard and rested her forehead against her laced fingers. She could think of nothing Joe Gianni could do to help, and she didn't know him well enough even to profit very much from his commiseration.

Joe, like Hannah, had originally been a business acquaintance, although of a more conventional kind. His firm had long done the accounting for both Edwin's business and their personal tax matters. The Pattersons had entertained the Giannis to dinner a couple of times, and on one occasion early in their dealings, Joe had invited Edwin to a round of golf at his country club in Westchester, where Joe had demonstrated such a strong drive off the tee that Edwin, whose game was tennis, had sworn off further such amusements. In short, since Edwin's death three years ago, Martha had seen Joe Gianni just once a year when she signed the 1040.

This April, however, Joe had surprised her by initiating a conversation about, of all things, contemporary art. Her surprise had waned somewhat when it became evident that his interest lay not in esthetics but in investments. He had heard of Hannah Gold as a rising star, he said, and had recalled that Martha owned an early piece or two. Was she, he wondered, in a position to introduce him to the artist?

"Rising star?" Hannah had exclaimed. "Investment? Bring him!"

So Martha had brought him to the reception.

But not without exacting a quid pro quo.

Some months ago Sunny Searle, a social worker of Martha's acquaintance, had asked her to conduct a series of elder-law seminars around the city, discussing legal and financial issues common to the nonaffluent elderly. Martha's expertise in trusts and estates law would be useful, said Sunny; moreover, her manner was approachable; and, if Martha didn't mind Sunny's saying so, her age would probably enhance rapport with the clients.

Martha didn't mind in the least.

But the task had its stressful aspects. The strain of talking more or less steadily for upwards of an hour and a half was one; the chance of misunderstanding a question and giving misleading advice was another. She missed the collegiality of the Legal Services office where, for reasons too irritating to be dwelt on, she was no longer serving as a volunteer. Seeking Joe's help might be rather scraping the barrel (in her opinion, he was a bit short on a couple of her qualifying characteristics) but it was worth a try. As compensation for introducing him to Hannah, therefore, she asked him to address the meetings on a few issues that were more financial than legal, and in general to back up her own presentation in case she slipped.

Somewhat to her surprise, he had agreed, on condition that his debut not take place until after tax season. That debut had occurred yesterday at a community center on the Lower East Side. Martha judged that he had performed acceptably. His matter-of-fact appearance—medium build, unremarkable face, a horseshoe of neatly barbered straight dark hair edging an unashamedly bald crown—seemed reassuring to the audience, and he was patient with questions. Today they would travel out to Sunny's agency in a blue-collar Brooklyn neighborhood.

And Joe was right: concentration might be difficult.

She rubbed her eyes, put her glasses back on, and returned her attention to the computer screen.

HER MORNING'S WORK finished, Martha acquired a pot of red tulips at a florist shop around the corner and then hailed a cab, which carried her downtown and over the Brooklyn Bridge and through a tangle of Brooklyn business streets to St. Hilda's Hospital.

The medical report was encouraging. A nurse at the station in the neural unit told her that the CT scan showed no fracture, and thus far the concussion, though severe, had produced no complications beyond the headache and that partial amnesia. And Hannah's general health was excellent. How long her physician would keep her in the hospital remained to be seen.

Hannah had been moved. A uniformed security guard checked Martha's driver's license and then escorted her to the new location, a semiprivate room just across the corridor from the nurses' station. Hannah, in a skimpy, tied-in-the back hospital gown, was alone in the room. The bed nearer the door was unoccupied and stripped to the mattress, and the policewoman had apparently not been replaced at the end of her shift.

The head of Hannah's bed had been cranked to its highest position and Hannah was sitting up with the bed table rolled across her knees, sketching with a pencil on the back of a cut-open envelope. The IV was still taped to the back of her left hand, but the oxygen apparatus had been removed and no tubes impeded her nostrils. Her hair, once more in its usual bun, had been arranged to conceal some of the bandage. A dozen red roses crowded the nightstand beside the bed.

Hannah turned her drawing, which seemed to contain a good deal of black, face down and said, "You can tiptoe through the tulips if you want to, but I know it's you."

"You're sounding like yourself." Martha looked around for a place to put the pot.

"And who else would I sound like?" Hannah pointed to the windowsill. "Over there."

The sill already held a mixed bouquet. Martha sidled around the foot of the bed and placed the tulips beside it. The card on the bouquet was visible: it said, "Best wishes for a speedy recovery from Eileen and Joe Gianni."

"That's nice," Martha said. "Who sent the roses?"

"For Microsoft? You have to ask?" Hannah's brows drew together, "Martha, do you know? Did you hear?"

"I've heard a good many things," Martha temporized.

If someone had judged Hannah to be well enough to be told about Kent Reed and the maquette, Hannah would have to say so explicitly; Martha was not going to accept the responsibility of dumping the news of that disaster on a woman recovering from a severe concussion.

"You know," said Hannah. "You're playing dumb, so I know you know." She closed her eyes. "*Love*, smashed to bits, and my beautiful young man dead."

"And you," Martha said.

"And me," Hannah agreed, and just then a rap on the door frame brought her eyes open.

The security guard peered in. "There's some people want to see you," he said. "A gentleman named Simm and a lady named Quist. I don't have them on the list."

Martha would have demurred, but Hannah tugged at the neck of her hospital gown and said, "They'll do."

The guard backed out of the way.

The first thing through the door was a flat green bowl from which sprang the green leaf blades and delicate white blooms of paperwhite narcissus. The bowl was balanced in Dennison Simm's large, square, brown hands in front of his large, solid body, above which gleamed his shaved brown scalp. Today he was wearing a locker-room gray sweatsuit. The flowers partly masked his face but did not entirely hide its expression, which was a blend of social smile and worried frown. Behind him, chic in black stirrup pants and an embroidered tunic, came Olive Quist. The powerful fragrance of the narcissi billowed around them.

"Love," said Simm.

"Peace," said Hannah. She waved toward the window-sill. "Over there."

Simm nodded at Martha as he edged past. He set the bowl of narcissi next to the tulips, leaned his shoulder against the wall beside the window, and said, "Anything to get on the tube, huh?"

"It's in the news?"

"Morning shows, the whole ball of wax. What you tell the man, anyway, get him beatin' down my door before I'm out of bed?"

"Oh, Dennie." Olive had stopped halfway between the bed and the door. "They rang the bell."

He looked across Hannah's sheeted legs at her. "And just try not answerin'."

"Police?" said Hannah. "The police were ringing your bell?"

"Wasn't me," Simm said. "Even if I had the thought—and I'm sure too busy with my own shit to have that kind of thought—I wouldn't have had the chance. I was hanging out with my lady here"—another glance at Olive—"the whole night."

Hannah said, "What are you telling me? They think it was you?"

"Why you surprised? Got a nigger in the woodpile, where else they gonna look?" His voice rose into *Amos and Andy* mode: "Man think maybe this nigger be worryin' 'bout some li'l ol' lady's li'l ol' weddin' marquee givin' him a hard time in Minneapolis..."

Olive said, "Dennie—"

"Man think maybe this nigger figurin' to bust up the competition, 'long with anything else gettin' in the way."

Hannah started to shake her head, grimaced, and held still.

"Hey." Simm's voice dropped back to its normal baritone. "Hurt you bad?"

"Yes," said Hannah.

"Wasn't me. I don't go beating up little old ladies." Again he looked across the bed at Olive. "My lady and me, we left your party together, and we hung together all night."

Olive nodded.

"So it wasn't me."

"I never said it was," said Hannah.

"Well, and I never said you said, did I? The man didn't say, far's that goes, but I read his thinking. Be a help if you happened to see who it was."

"I can't remember."

"Switched off the remembering button, did they? Well, you just remember I don't go beating up old ladies. Don't go busting up somebody's work, neither. Man showed me a Polaroid of that tent of yours, what's left of it. Not my thing. We got us a little competition here, no argument about that, but I'm gonna whup yo' butt fair and square. You got a backup piece?"

"Wendy's working on it."

"Wendy back working for you?"

"Emergency service."

"Well, that's good. Get that tent fixed up so I'll have me a little hometown competition out there in the heartland."

"And we'll see whose butt gets whupped," said Hannah.

"Now what kind of language is that for a little old lady?" Simm pushed himself away from the wall. "Well, don't want to wear you out. Just wanted to stop by and check up on the competition. You get better fast, now."

BEFORE MARTHA LEFT, she offered to pick up some clothes for Hannah. Hannah beamed and groped in the nightstand drawer for her handbag. Her police escort had found it in the studio where she had dropped it and had brought it along. She extracted a key ring. "I only have the ones to my apartment," she said. "I gave Wendy the ones to the outside door and the studio. You'll have to go when she's there so she can let you into the foyer. There's a full set in the top right drawer of the bureau. You keep those and bring these back to me. And find Kent's. They ought to be in his apartment. I don't want them hanging around loose."

"Call Wendy to let me in with the keys you loaned her; get into your apartment with these; find the ones in your bureau and keep them; find Kent's keys; and bring these back." Martha saluted.

"And clothes."

"And clothes. Where's the dress you were wearing? It must need a trip to the cleaner."

"The police took it."

Oh. For forensic examination, in case her attacker had deposited any identifiable fibers or body fluids on it. "I don't suppose you'll get it back."

"It was ruined anyway," said Hannah. "You can't clean blood out of silk."

SIX

Elder Law

WHILE MARTHA STRUGGLED to stay awake and review the outline of her presentation, the cab carried her out of the deteriorated neighborhood of St. Hilda's Hospital and down the diagonal of Flatbush Avenue to the triumphal arch at Grand Army Plaza, and turned into the quiet spring-green hills and valleys of Prospect Park. At the bottom of the park, it emerged onto Ocean Parkway, a broad divided street of meticulously tended lawns and flowering shrubs in front of tile-roofed stucco-and-brick mansions that were widely alleged to be the homes of Mafia dons. As the cab rolled south in sync with the traffic lights, well-kept brick apartment buildings supplanted the mansions. Presently it turned onto King's Highway, a wide avenue of small low-rise businesses. Down the side streets, Martha glimpsed block upon block of big old maples shading semidetached frame houses, most of them long since re-sided with asbestos or aluminum.

Just around the corner from the business street, in front of a steel-faced door centered in a buff-colored brick wall that bore traces of scrubbed-away graffiti, she paid off the cab and clambered out. A small sign on the door read

WELFARE ADVOCATES ORGANIZATION

and squeezed onto the bottom in fresher paint,

Association For The Elderly & Retired

A wedge held the door open. Inside, a well-lighted concrete stairway led up to a landing, off which a door opened into a room half the size of a gymnasium. In the middle, ranks of chairs faced a lectern; on a long table at the rear stood a couple of coffee urns and some plates covered with paper napkins.

A dozen or so members of the audience had arrived. Some of them had taken chairs; some stood around conversing. Joe Gianni was standing at the side of the room talking with Sunny Searle.

Sunny, the executive director of both WAO and AFTER, was a sturdy woman in her midthirties with a square jaw, a wide and mobile mouth, straight light-brown hair that she had recently trimmed to shoulder length, and a supply of energy which, if not inexhaustible, seemed at least infinitely renewable. Martha had met her three years ago during that brief but eventful tour of duty at West Brooklyn Legal Services, and after leaving, had continued to provide Sunny's clients with a few hours of pro bono legal advice each week.

Sunny carried Martha's coat back to her office and Joe asked, "How's Hannah?"

"Better," said Martha. Not until she heard how curtly the word came out did she realize how severely the events of the past twenty-four hours had shaken her normal composure.

But Joe seemed not to take offense. "I'm glad to hear it," he said. "Do the police have any more information?"

"I'm not in their confidence," she said. Her voice was still sharper than she liked. So be it.

MARTHA SPOKE FIRST. The topic of the day was one of her least favorite: how to pay for long-term home care in order to stay, or keep one's ailing spouse or parent, out of nursing homes. A few solutions did exist, but since most of them were hedged around by the limitations and red tape of Medicare and Medicaid, they were complex in principle and cumbersome in operation. Explaining them in a limited span of time to a variously educated group was an exacting task, which the incipient ache at the back of her eyes made no easier. She suppressed the ache by attending to her audience's body language. Most of them were women past sixty, largely Jewish, Italian, and Irish. Financially, they were three or four levels above the public assistance clients Martha had counseled at West Brooklyn Legal Services; they subsisted, by and large, on Social Security supplemented by more or less adequate pensions from former civil service or union jobs. "Going on welfare"—even supplementing the grocery money with food stamps—was a fate to be addressed in whispers accompanied by gestures designed to ward off evil.

As she scanned the audience for signs of comprehension or confusion, one neatly dressed black woman in the back row caught her attention. The neighborhood was not an integrated one, nor was it a culture that went in for nannies; Martha would have supposed her to be a disabled patient's home attendant, except for the fact that, emaciated and wearing a wig, she was unmistakably a patient herself.

Eventually Martha's presentation was finished and she was able to sit down behind the podium while Joe took over to explain the reverse mortgage, often one of the least hurtful of the options, but sometimes the hardest to understand.

AND AT LAST it was over. Questions from the audience had dwindled to a trickle and finally dried up; Sunny had thanked the speakers, led the audience in applause, announced next week's subject, and advised everyone of what they already knew: refreshments waited on the table at the rear of the room. Those who found face-to-face conversation easier than speaking up from the audience had clustered around Martha and Joe with their questions; now, at last, they were gathering their coats and shopping bags and drifting out the door. Sunny was folding the chairs and stacking them against the wall and Joe had adjourned to the restroom tucked behind a door in a far corner.

The black woman had remained seated while the others had stood and chatted, but she had turned her chair to face the refreshment table, and now she was slowly getting to her feet. Taut muscles puckered her mouth.

Martha mustered one more smile.

"Good evening, Mrs. Patterson," the woman said. Her voice was modulated and her enunciation was precise. "I am Florence Appleton."

Martha groped.

"Hannah Gold suggested that I consult you," the woman added.

Ah. The neighbor with the medical-financial-legal problem. The retired math teacher who had kept most of her marbles. "Yes, of course," Martha said. "Hannah spoke of you."

"Do you know how she is? The hospital switchboard gave me a number, but I could get no answer."

She had heard, then. "Perhaps she turned off the phone," Martha said, "She had a concussion, so using the telephone may be painful."

"It is serious?"

"Serious, but not nearly as bad as it might have been."

"I will pray for her."

"That will please her," said Martha. The response striking her as possibly inadequate, she added, "As well as helping her. I'm glad you introduced yourself. She told me you have a question I might be able to help you with."

Florence Appleton looked around. They were not talking in isolation; Sunny was coming out of her office and Joe was returning from the restroom. "I'm afraid it is getting late," she said, "and I'm afraid my story is rather long." She glanced around again. "And confidential."

Martha had planned to share a cab back to Manhattan with Joe, but he could perfectly well ride back by himself. "As a matter of fact," she improvised, "I need to go to your neighborhood to get some things for Hannah. If you would like to share my cab, we could discuss your problem on the way."

"You're very kind," Florence Appleton said, "but my niece is taking me to dinner."

Having gone to some trouble to arrange this conversation—traveling, while obviously unwell, to an alien neighborhood and sitting through a rather lengthy presentation—Florence Appleton now seemed less than eager to carry it forward. Martha suspected that the niece might be an invention.

Clients with second thoughts were nothing new. Martha rummaged in her handbag and produced her business card. "Then why don't you call me when you're free. I will be happy to hear what you have to say and to help if I can."

"Thank you." The lines around Florence Appleton's mouth relaxed a bit. She tucked Martha's card into her handbag and said, "Thank you very much. I must be going. Camilla should be downstairs soon."

MARTHA'S SUSPICION was proved false within minutes; when she and Joe reached the street, a well-dressed young woman was holding the passenger door of a small red car open for Florence Appleton to climb in.

"THIS IS DRAINING," Joe said. "Could you live that close to the edge?"

Their cab, out of sync with the Ocean Parkway lights, was stopping and starting with the rest of the rush-hour traffic, but Martha didn't think he meant the ride. A proper presentation of reverse mortgages obliged one to explain that, while this arrangement provided a steady supplementary income, it did so by depleting the mortgagees' equity in those old houses in which they had raised their families. The money must be repaid upon the death of the mortgagee or the house would be gone, foreclosed, not available to the heirs, the children who had grown up in it. This loss was difficult for one's audience to accept, and Joe had heard their dismay.

The Mother Teresa syndrome: that was what Martha's mentor at Legal Services had called the vicarious anxiety of the advocate for the poor and near-poor. He had advised her to avoid it at all costs. The ache behind her eyes was growing and she found that she was too tired to pass the advice on to Joe.

"Maybe," Joe said, "it's easier if you never had much to begin with."

Closing her eyes helped a little.

Some minutes later, Joe said, "I keep thinking about that Simm fellow."

Martha suppressed a sigh. The subject was bound to come up.

"I haven't heard anything about an arrest," Joe said. "I wonder if he's off the hook or if they just don't have enough to charge him."

"He says he and his wife were together all night."

"The police told you that?"

"He did."

"You've seen him?"

"They visited Hannah this afternoon."

"Really? Wasn't that pretty nervy of him?"

"Yes," she said, "if."

"If?"

"If he is the...culprit."

"Is there really a question?"

At first, Martha hadn't thought there was, but the sick-room visit had rather shaken that belief. "I imagine there is always a question," she said, "until the jury renders a verdict."

"Well, yes, I suppose so. I'm not sure a verdict always answers the question, either, does it?"

"And if he isn't the culprit, then the visit was simply a matter of courtesy and an expression of mutual respect."

"I didn't notice much respect from him at the reception."

"Oh, I think Hannah may have had it right: that was probably just Dennie being Dennie."

"If you say so. Does his wife back him up?"

A good question. Olive's subdued demeanor was impossible to interpret; it could have expressed grief, intimidation, or even assent. "I think so," Martha said. "For what a wife's statement is worth."

"Well, yes," said Joe. "After all, who else would want to wreck Hannah's maquette?"

In the back of her mind, Martha realized, she had been pondering that question. Now she said, "What if the maquette wasn't the primary target?"

After a moment Joe said, "You mean, you think... somebody might have been after the young man?"

Kent, she thought irritably. *Kent Reed. Stop robbing him of his name.* "He's the one who's dead," she said. "What if somebody wanted Kent out of the way and destroyed the maquette as a piece of misdirection? To cast suspicion on Dennison Simm."

Joe was silent for another moment. Then he said, "That's an interesting idea. Do you have anybody in mind?"

"I know nothing about his past life."

"Simm seems so obvious," said Joe. "It looked to me as if he could have wanted to get rid of both the young man and the maquette." A short silence fell; then he said, "But you raise an interesting point. I wonder if something Hannah said might bear on the question."

"What's that?"

"She said the young man..."

"Kent," Martha said. "Kent Reed."

"Oh. Yes, of course. Hannah said he was...Kent Reed was working with her financial records."

Martha had nearly forgotten that exchange. But of course it was the sort of thing Joe would recall.

Joe said, "What if he discovered that somebody was misappropriating funds?"

The suggestion struck Martha as far-fetched. "I don't think her art produces enough cash flow to make fiddling the books worth the effort," she said.

"Not by itself, maybe, but what if the gallery was skimming from a number of accounts? I imagine it could add up."

"Hannah's been running her own business for decades," Martha said. "She'd be hard to cheat. And Wendy would have to have been involved, and I certainly can't see that."

"You really don't think so? I thought she seemed pretty hostile to the...to Kent Reed."

"No," said Martha. "Absolutely not Wendy."

"Well, I suppose you have your reasons for saying so."

"I do. And anyway, Joe, just think about it. Would anybody kill someone just to cover up a bit of financial fiddling? *Kill* someone? It isn't as if an art dealer can be disbarred."

"No, but he could go to prison. I've seen embezzlers take some pretty desperate measures to try to cover up."

Well, yes. Five decades of law practice had introduced Martha to something of the sort herself. And how much did she really know about the Nicholas Warner Gallery's business practices? Joe was no fool; in spite of her inner resistance, which was very likely a product of her fondness for Wendy, she owed it to him to consider this idea objectively.

But she was so tired that her mind kept sliding around the concept as if trying to walk on ice. "Have you mentioned this theory to the police?" she asked.

"It didn't occur to me until just now. I suppose I should."

"It's possible that they'll think of it themselves," she said. But without knowing that Kent Reed had been working with Hannah's old financial records, would the police realize their relevance?

She was reluctant, on the basis of a theory in which she had no genuine belief, to embroil Wendy and the gallery people any more deeply in this disagreeable situation. On the other hand, her best friend having been grievously injured, Martha had a lively interest in advancing the progress of the investigation. "Joe," she said, "if you took a look at the records yourself, you'd be able to tell if anything untoward had been going on, wouldn't you?"

"Not everything. A good many discrepancies wouldn't show up in a single set of books. But if it was something obvious enough for the young...for Kent Reed to notice, yes, I'd certainly be able to spot it."

"If I could persuade Hannah to let you look, would you be willing? Then if you can't find anything, there'd be no need to set the police on a false trail. That would spare Wendy and the gallery people a good deal of disagreeableness."

"You think I'd be better at it than a police accountant?"

"Well, I should certainly hope so."

He didn't smile. "I'd have to have Hannah's permission. She might not want me prowling around in her books."

"I'll ask her. If you wouldn't mind putting in the time."

"Not at all. Actually, I think you're right. Checking it

out before setting the cat among the pigeons sounds like a good idea.''

THEY WERE halfway through the Brooklyn-Battery Tunnel and Martha was half dozing when Joe roused her by saying, "Martha, to change the subject to something more pleasant…''

"Yes?''

"Eileen and I are coming into the city Saturday to look at Hannah's things at the gallery, and we'd like it if you came with us. Maybe have lunch first?''

Well. Evidently suspicion wasn't to interfere with Joe's search for the Next Big Investment in contemporary art.

"And it would be a big help, too.'' Joe said. "You know art, and you know the players.''

True. And her presence might raise their comfort level to the point where they would actually buy one of the works. "Thank you,'' she said. "I'd like that.''

By Saturday, it might even be true.

SEVEN

Picking up the Pieces

EVEN FOR MARTHA, seven-fifteen was too early to retire.
Food would help. She had eschewed the supermarket cook-
ies on the elder-law seminar's refreshment table and now
she was hungry. She would proceed in a leisurely, thoughtful fashion to assemble a big salad, boil an egg, and toast
a slice of bread. After she had eaten and cleaned up the
kitchen, it would be late enough to get into bed and proceed
with her third rereading of *Persuasion* until her eyes closed
of their own accord.

But when she had hung up her coat and gone into the
kitchen, she discovered that the only foodstuffs in the place
were a stale bran muffin, a withered carrot, four wilted
lettuce leaves, and a half-inch of dubious milk in the bottom
of a carton. Visiting Hannah had preempted the time she
had allotted to shopping.

She could order in, but she had sated her appetite for
Chinese the evening before; pizza, even a small one, would
be too much; and none of the local deli offerings sounded
even remotely inviting. If she was to eat, she would have
to go out.

But first, tea. She never allowed herself to run out of tea.

And the tea performed its assigned task. Half an hour
later, her headache had abated and resolve had oozed back
into her muscles. She wasn't ready to go to bed after all.
She had an errand to run for Hannah, and tomorrow she
should put in a full day of uninterrupted work. It was a

quarter of an hour short of eight o'clock; why not travel out to Williamsburg right now?

But she would need Wendy to unlock the street door. Was it conceivable that Wendy might still be working on the maquette?

She picked up the phone, punched in the studio number, and waited through four ringing tones. Just as she was preparing herself to address the answering machine, the fifth ring was cut off and Wendy's voice barked, "Hello."

"Hello, Wendy," she said. "It's Martha."

"Oh." Wendy's voice softened. "Sorry if I sounded crabby. I was working." Hannah needed clothes? Good grief, yes. Wendy had seen that terrible hospital gown; why hadn't she thought of it herself? Martha should come on out; Wendy would just go on working until she got there.

THE EVENING WAS DRY and mild, ideal for walking. Tired of taxis and enjoying a sort of second wind, Martha resolved to take the subway.

In the back of a closet, she found a zippered tote bag, a giveaway from an old Channel 13 fund-raiser. She rode the elevator to the lobby, smiled at Boris, walked half a block east, descended to the subway platform, and boarded the R train. She rode uptown one stop to the Fourteenth Street station, where she negotiated an intricate connection involving stairs down and stairs up and turns to the left and turns to the right, and eventually arrived at the L platform. The eastbound L train carried her under the East River to the Bedford Avenue station, where she disembarked and climbed into the lingering evening light in Hannah's neighborhood, the area of northern Brooklyn known as Williamsburg.

For decades, working artists had moved into a succession of New York neighborhoods, had rendered them safe and fashionable, and had then been priced out of them. Greenwich Village had been the original *in* place. In the seventies, the action had moved south of Houston Street to Soho, where much of it (including the Nicholas Warner Gallery) still flourished. Still farther south, Tribeca was holding on, and northwestward, pushing against West Street and the Hudson River, Chelsea's aggregation of galleries and studios was expanding. But all these places were squeezed onto the island of Manhattan, and the cost of Manhattan real estate was, as always, rising beyond unreasonable toward exorbitant. One result was that a number of artists and dealers had recently been migrating across the East River to colonize the low-rent apartments and disused factories and warehouses of Williamsburg.

Hannah had been one of the first of these pioneers. She had expected others to take over more of the buildings on her street, but most of them had settled several blocks farther north and west, leaving the rest of the warehouses on her street to carry on their original business.

Williamsburg was a horizontal neighborhood. Only a few scattered buildings were more than one or two stories high, leaving the dome of the sky open to view nearly from horizon to horizon. Martha had felt no need to return to the great plains of Nebraska since her father's death ten years before; but each visit to Williamsburg aroused in her a faint and oddly invigorating nostalgia for the wide sky of her childhood. The four-block walk to Hannah's studio cheered her.

Hannah's street was empty of traffic and the police barriers were gone. Martha rang; presently the peephole rattled; then the door opened and Wendy, in faded jeans and an out-at-the-elbows plaid flannel shirt, her hair even wilder than usual, admitted her into the constricted little foyer.

Straight ahead, the studio door stood open; to the left, stairs led up to Hannah's apartment. Martha greeted Wendy and took half a step toward the stairs, but Wendy said, "Come on in if you've got a minute."

"I don't want to interrupt," said Martha.

"Not to worry, I'm done for the day. Come on in and give me a little human contact."

Martha went in.

For some reason, the first thing she noticed was that the rug was gone. Just inside the door, an unworn rectangle showed where the three-by-five mat had protected the painted concrete floor.

"The rug is gone," she said.

"It was gone when I got here. I think the police took it." Wendy pushed her hands through her hair. "It must have had blood on it. There were, like, spots? On the floor where it didn't cover? I guess whoever it was must have bashed Hannah right here, just when she was coming in the door. I scrubbed them up."

"Ah."

"There's more back there." Wendy gestured toward the back of the studio. "Back there the floor was a real mess. It looks like that's where Kent got his. I cleaned it up as much as I could, but some of the paint's worn off and it sort of soaked into the cement. I couldn't get it all out."

"It's brave of you to work here," said Martha.

Wendy shrugged. "Blood's harmless. It's people that do the damage." She pushed her mop of hair off her forehead with both hands. "The police were asking about Dennie and Olive."

"I suppose that's to be expected."

"Yes, I know. But..." Wendy shoved her hands into her jeans pockets. "I wish it was some stranger who broke in. You know, some lowlife the world would be better off without."

That would be Martha's preference as well. "I suppose that can't be entirely ruled out," she said.

"I wish. The problem is, nothing was stolen. The computer's still here, and the sewing machines, and all the art. And if it was nothing but vandals…" She gestured at Hannah's works, still standing where they had been placed for the reception. "Why just *Love?* Why not everything?"

"Just so."

"And the door wasn't jimmied and the alarm didn't go off."

Martha hadn't thought about the alarm. "Perhaps Kent hadn't turned it on."

"Well, maybe. Hannah says never to stay here alone without turning it on, but who knows how much attention he paid."

Or perhaps, unsuspicious, he had turned it off to admit the attacker.

Would he have admitted Dennison Simm?

Well, locks and alarms were the sort of thing the police were accustomed to taking note of; the surviving civilians had other matters to deal with. "How are you getting along with the maquette?" she asked.

Wendy shook her head as if dislodging flies. "Come and see. I'm sort of proud of myself."

Martha followed her to the working end of the studio. The caterer's cloth was gone from the cutting table. A new stuffed creature, still lacking its features, was lying on the table beside a heap of fabric. Wendy picked it up and tapped it under the chin with a finger. "This little monster was trickier than I remembered. Don't you want to take him home and feed him up?" She laid it down. "He took up so much time that I'm behind with the tent. And the cutting is taking a long time because I'm short of fabric and I'm having to piece."

Wendy, engaged in a scheme to defraud Hannah? Ridiculous.

Still, even ridiculous notions must be checked. "When is it to be shipped?" Martha asked.

"Next Monday. If the armature's okay, we should make it."

The armature, yes. Kent Reed had done the final construction of that soldered wire support. "Who's making the armature?"

"Stefan Wolinski? He's a friend of Barbara's. Maybe you saw his show last year. He's supposed to have it here by Friday. I'm going to have to start putting the tent together tomorrow, and we'll just have to hope it fits." Wendy picked up a square of white linen, which Martha recognized as the altar cloth. "I can do this embroidery at home."

"Good luck." Martha looked at her watch. "Thank you for the guided tour. And now, if I'm to get Hannah's things to her tonight, I must do what I came for."

ONCE SHE HAD negotiated the three locks on Hannah's apartment door, it didn't take long. She packed into the Channel 13 bag a couple of nightgowns, a red silk dressing gown of Hannah's creation, a pair of embroidered velvet slippers, several days' supply of underwear, and, in contemplation of Hannah's eventual discharge, a pair of khaki pants, a shirt, socks, and shoes. She found the spare set of keys in a bureau drawer, just where Hannah had said they would be. She tucked them into her handbag and went back downstairs.

Wendy was waiting. "I don't want to hold you up," Martha said, "but Hannah asked me to look for Kent Reed's keys. She thinks they might be in his apartment."

"Want me to stay with you?"

"If you wouldn't mind. I don't feel altogether easy prowling through his things, but Hannah asked."

The door to the apartment was in the middle of the rear

wall, a couple of steps from the empty pedestal that had held Kent's sculpture—more sensationally, the murder weapon. Against her better judgment, Martha glanced at the floor. Wendy's scrubbing had been effective; only a few faint brownish stains remained.

Wendy unlocked the door and they stepped straight into the apartment.

"You have this key, too?" Martha asked.

"Hannah loaned it to me so I wouldn't have to run upstairs to her bathroom. I lock it when I leave."

The apartment hadn't originally been an apartment; in fact, it hadn't originally been a room at all. Some earlier owner of the warehouse had created it by partitioning off the back of the space. It was a single big room, whose two rear corners had been further partitioned to form a closet on the right and a bathroom on the left, giving it the shape of an obese inverted T. The kitchen, ranged along the forward half of the left-hand wall, consisted of a tiny refrigerator, too small to accommodate much more than a six-pack and a half-dozen eggs; an equally tiny sink; a twelve-inch countertop upon which stood a toaster; a cabinet under the sink and another under the countertop; and a two-burner stove whose oven was barely large enough to heat a TV dinner.

A desk constructed of a door supported by a pair of filing cabinets stood against the opposite wall. On it were a computer and printer, a box of diskettes, and a pile of paper. Next to the desk was a small bookcase full of computer texts and, on the bottom shelf, an eclectic array of paperbacks. In the rear of the apartment, under the only three windows in the place, the space between the closet and the bathroom was occupied by a futon and a trunk.

The computer, the trunk, probably the books, and possibly the futon were the only objects of obvious value in the apartment. The rest of the furniture consisted of a battered chrome-and-Formica dinette table, three mismatched straight chairs, a sagging sofa whose ruined upholstery was concealed by a machine-brocaded bedspread, a bureau with chipped veneer and a clouded mirror, and a collection of wobbly lamps. All of them were shabby enough to have been scavenged from the street. When Hannah had bought the building, she had made an effort to civilize the place by sanding the floor and painting the Sheetrock walls white, but that was the extent of her efforts. She had intended the apartment for emergency use only.

"I'll take the kitchen and the desk," Wendy suggested, "and you can paw through the underwear and socks back there."

There was no reason to divide the work otherwise, but it was with a bit of reluctance that Martha set about examining the personal effects of the dead young man. *(Kent Reed; don't rob him of his name.)* But Hannah had asked.

She began with a gray sweatsuit that lay where it had been tossed on top of the futon. The pockets held only a wad of used tissues. He had not stashed any keys in the pair of Nikes that lay on their sides beside the futon. On top of the bureau were two pencil stubs and a half-empty pocket pack of Kleenex; in the drawers were the expected clothes: socks, jockey shorts, T-shirts, a couple of turtlenecks, a heavy Scandinavian wool sweater, two dress shirts still in their laundry wrapping. Hanging in the closet were two pairs of black jeans, a fleece-lined warm-up jacket, a tweed sport jacket, and a pair of dress slacks. Martha felt in all the pockets and found no keys. She moved on to the bathroom; in the medicine chest she found the obvious: a razor, a tube of shaving cream, a bottle of aftershave, a stick of deodorant, a bottle of Advil. The hamper held a few socks, some underwear, three black T-shirts, and a pair of jeans with empty pockets.

She returned to the front. Wendy had finished her search and was sitting at the table.

"I give up," said Martha.

"He must have had them on him," said Wendy.

"Then the mortuary must have them. Or the police. And that's a matter for another day." Martha looked at her watch. If she could flag a cab somewhere, she could still get to the hospital before the evening visiting hours ended. The burst of energy that had brought her here had spent itself and she was once more ready to drop with weariness, but she had promised Hannah, and tomorrow she really had to work.

EIGHT

Fraud?

HANNAH HAD ACQUIRED a roommate, a young woman with a leg in traction, who was watching television and barely nodded as Martha edged past the foot of her bed. Hannah was sitting in a chair beside her bed, her back turned to the TV, sketching on a pad that someone had brought her. Her head, she said, felt better; her temper had certainly improved. She carried the Channel 13 bag to the bathroom and returned resplendent; then, walking rather more slowly than usual, she led Martha down the hall to a visitor's lounge. Another television was jabbering to the empty room. Hannah turned it off and they took seats in a pair of faded chintz easy chairs, and then Martha propounded Joe's theory.

"Fraud?" Hannah started to laugh. "Go away."

"You'd vouch for Nick's rectitude?" Martha said. "And Barbara's?"

"Rectitude, schmectitude. I vouch for my business sense."

"They couldn't have been working a scam on you?"

"Aren't you thinking? Wendy'd have to be in on it." Hannah looked past Martha toward the door and said, "Hello. I think I'm supposed to know you."

Martha looked around. Detective Sharpman, in blazer and slacks and shirt and tie, was entering the room. "Phil Sharpman," he said. "We met last night. Hello, Ms. Patterson."

Martha nodded.

"The detective," said Hannah.

"Good. I wasn't sure I was registering." He sat down in the middle of a sofa. "How are you feeling?"

"Don't ask."

"It's my job to ask."

"What a job."

"It isn't for everybody. How are you feeling? It isn't just for the job. I'd like to know for my own sake."

"I feel like somebody who got hit on the head."

"I can't say I'm surprised. Have you remembered any more about what happened last night?"

Hannah closed her eyes. "No, I don't remember any more about what happened last night. Don't keep asking, I *hate* not remembering."

"I'll bet you do."

"So don't keep asking."

"Believe it or not, I didn't come here to upset you."

"Then don't."

"How about we make a deal? If you promise to tell me when you do remember more, I'll promise to stop asking."

"If you mean that," Hannah said, "we've got a deal."

"Deal," said Sharpman. "The other reason I'm here is because Kent Reed's father is coming from St. Louis to claim the body tomorrow."

"Father," said Hannah. "Body. You think *that* doesn't upset me?"

"I know. It isn't my favorite part of the job, either."

"Human, are you?"

"Off and on. Anyway, he wants to know if he can collect his son's belongings from that apartment behind your workroom."

"Oh, that poor man."

"Yes."

"You're going to say you need somebody to let him in."

"That's about it. I need your permission for him to enter,

and I need somebody to let him in and hang around to help him tell the difference between your property and his.''

Hannah looked at Martha. Then Sharpman looked at Martha.

She really must put in a day's work tomorrow. "What time?" she asked.

"He's flying in sometime in the afternoon," Sharpman said, "and he has to make arrangements at the mortuary and talk to us. Figure about seven p.m.?"

The working day was secure. "Very well," she said. "And while you're here, we haven't been able to find Kent Reed's keys. Were they on his...did he have them with him?"

"Keys," said Sharpman. "I don't remember any keys in the medical examiner's inventory. I can check the report and let you know. Why don't you call the precinct tomorrow?"

"I'LL HAVE TO KEEP the keys that were in the bureau," Martha said when Sharpman had left. "I'll need them to let the father in. And I'll need the alarm code."

Hannah glanced at the door, picked up the pencil she'd been sketching with, and scribbled on the corner of the paper she'd been sketching on. She tore the corner off and handed it to Martha.

Martha read 888, folded the scrap, and tucked it into her handbag. "All right," she said, "let's get back to it. Joe Gianni is willing to take a look at those financial records Kent was computerizing. I think it would be a good idea, instead of his haring off to the authorities with nothing more than an unsupported theory."

"You're nagging."

"I believe I am."

"What's the point?"

"To clear the air."

"It isn't foggy."

"Hannah, don't be unnecessarily obstructive. Your beautiful young man was violently done to death, you were beaten senseless, your maquette was wrecked, and the police don't seem to have made much progress in finding out who did it. A hypothesis has occurred to Joe, but I'd like him to test it before he casts public doubt on anybody. Now, if Joe examines your records, either he'll find irregularities or he won't."

"He won't."

"Then he will have cleared the air. If, however, he should find something wrong…"

"He won't."

Martha closed her mouth.

For some little time, neither of them spoke. Presently Hannah said, "Is he still thinking about Hannah Gold's work as a hot investment?"

"He's visiting the gallery Saturday."

Hannah's eyebrows rose.

"With his wife."

"So. All right, let him play."

WHEN MARTHA let herself into her apartment, carrying a loaf of bread, a quarter of a pound of prosciutto, a packet of Roquefort, a little jar of mayonnaise, a Ziploc bag of arugula, and three Israeli tomatoes alleged to be vine-ripe, her answering machine was blinking. She stowed the groceries in the kitchen, came back to the chaise in the living room, and activated the playback.

The slow, precisely enunciated voice of Florence Appleton dictated her telephone number, then said she would like Ms. Patterson to call her at Ms. Patterson's convenience, then recited her number again.

Convenience?

The events of the past twenty-four hours having been

notably deficient in any consideration of Martha Patterson's convenience, the word proved irresistibly seductive. Martha paused for only the briefest of moments to consider whether a quarter to ten might be too late to call a woman in Ms. Appleton's fragile state of health. Never mind; Martha was licensed to proceed at her convenience and the present hour suited her convenience. If it was too late for Florence Appleton, let Florence Appleton say so.

It was not too late; Ms. Appleton's *Hello?* held no hint of drowsiness.

She would like to discuss her confidential question, but not over the telephone. What she wished was a face-to-face consultation.

"I am at my best in the afternoon," she said. "What I would like, if it suits your schedule, would be to entertain you to tea at my home." Her voice dropped to an apologetic murmur, which in no way impaired the distinctness of her articulation. "I am not allowed coffee, so to avoid temptation, I do not keep it available."

Tea? When it suited her schedule? Good heavens. "I'd enjoy that," Martha said, and considered the immediate future. Tomorrow, a working day, would not suit her schedule; Saturday she was accompanying Joe and his wife on their gallery visit to view Hannah's work. "If Sunday afternoon would suit you," she said, "it would suit me."

Sunday afternoon would suit Florence Appleton very well. She lived just around the corner from Hannah's street; she recited street and number and apartment number. Martha should ring the bell and be buzzed in.

Martha hung up and consulted her Rolodex. Surely five minutes to ten was not too late for Joe Gianni.

It wasn't.

"Hannah's willing," said Martha. "I have to let Kent Reed's father into the studio tomorrow evening to collect his son's belongings. Are you free to come along and take a look at what's on the computer?''

Joe didn't answer immediately.

"It will save me a trip," she added. "I've been doing a lot of extraneous running around this week."

"Yes, I'm sure you have," said Joe. "I wonder—maybe you could just print out the records and I could go over them at leisure."

"I wouldn't know what to look for," said Martha. "If you're too busy, we could let this go. Hannah is positive there's nothing out of line."

"No, no, I think you're right; this should be investigated before we go public. How are the working conditions? Is the place a mess?"

"It's pretty much back to normal. Wendy scrubbed up before she started working."

"Well, then, let's get it done. I'll come by for you— when would be a good time?"

"Let's say six-fifteen. The father is supposed to be at the studio at around seven."

NINE

Henry Reed

FOR THE SECOND TIME in three days, Martha and Joe Gianni climbed out of a taxi in front of Hannah's studio. An old black van was parked in front of the door, and light from inside the studio brightened the strip windows.

The set of keys Martha had retrieved from Hannah's bureau was complete, but not wanting to surprise Wendy, she had called ahead. She had, of course, not explained why Joe was coming with her. Let Wendy think, if she liked, that Martha felt the need for a bodyguard.

She rang the bell rather than using the key. The peephole clicked open and shut. Wendy opened the door, said, "Hi, come on in," and stood back while Martha preceded Joe through the foyer and into the studio. "Olive's here."

The announcement, or, as it might be, the warning, was unnecessary; as soon as Martha entered, she recognized the smooth milk-chocolate skin and froth of black hair of Dennison Simm's wife.

Her social discipline survived her surprise. "Olive Quist," she said blandly, "how nice to see you. Have you met my friend, Joe Gianni?"

With a smile of equal blandness, Joe said, "Ms. Quist, a pleasure. I believe I met your husband at Hannah's reception. Dennison Simm, the sculptor?"

"Oh, hey, listen to that," said Wendy. "*The* sculptor. Remember to tell him, Livy. Dennison Simm, the sculptor. He'll love it."

Olive's lips moved in a tentative smile.

"I hope we're not interrupting your work," Martha said.

"Done for the day," said Wendy. "We're on our way out to dinner and a movie. Girls on the town while Dennie prowls in his cave."

Joe said, "I understand he's preparing a show?" Joe, Martha noted, was getting the hang of this milieu.

"Opening Saturday," said Wendy. "At the Friedland-Carabelli Gallery. Give it a try; he's into some new stuff."

"I'd be interested," Joe said. "Is his, ah, his studio here in Williamsburg?"

Olive found her voice. "Jersey," she said. "He rents industrial space in Jersey City." Doubtless she had sensed a nascent collector.

"Interesting," said Joe. "I wouldn't have thought of New Jersey as artists' territory."

"Oh, Hoboken was hot for a while," Wendy said. "I'm still there, but a lot of the crowd moved on when they started jacking up the rents. Dennie needs a lot of space, so he and Olive just kept going south."

"I see," said Joe. "Martha tells me you're restoring Hannah's maquette. Is it all right to ask how it's going?"

"Sure." Wendy stepped to the wall and flicked a switch, and light flooded the working end of the studio. She had moved the pedestal next to the cutting table and the sewing machines, and on it stood a recognizable approximation of *Love*.

"My goodness," said Martha.

"Stefan finished the armature ahead of schedule." Wendy rearranged a bit of drapery. "He got the angles just that little bit different, so the fitting was a pain. God, you wouldn't believe. Ripping and recutting, after all that piecing I had to do already."

"I'm sure," said Joe.

"I'll finish up the bear thing and the altar cloth at home over the weekend, and then I've got to redo a bunch of seams Monday morning, and then off it goes." She ran her fingers through her mop of hair. "Never again. Do you know the alarm code?" she asked Martha.

"Hannah gave it to me."

"Then I'll set it. When . . . when he comes, use the peephole and don't disable the alarm until you know who it is at the door."

"Yes, Mother," said Martha.

"DID YOU TELL Wendy why I came?" asked Joe.

"No," said Martha. "Of course not. Why?"

"Didn't you think she seemed nervous?"

"Actually she seemed fairly normal," Martha said. "Wendy is high-strung at the best of times, and she's been working on a tight deadline."

"Well, yes, I suppose this place makes us all a little high-strung. Under the circumstances, isn't it a little out of line for her to be entertaining that woman here?"

"I believe they've been friends for some time. But I admit I was a bit surprised to see Olive."

"I suppose she could just have been glad to have company. It just seems a little...peculiar."

HANNAH'S COMPUTER stood on a desk not far from the sewing machines and the cutting table. Joe pulled out the chair, sat down, and flicked the switch. The monitor flickered into life. He ran the mouse around and rattled the keyboard, and presently said, "Oh, yes. Good program."

Leaving him to it, Martha went back to try the door to Kent Reed's apartment.

She couldn't stop herself from looking down. If she hadn't known that the bloodstains were there, where they had permeated the worn areas of the floor, she would probably not have noticed them; knowing they were there, she was unable to avoid seeing them. Kent Reed's father was going to have to cross his son's blood to get into the apartment. She hoped he wouldn't notice.

Wendy had locked the apartment door. While Martha was unlocking it, the doorbell buzzed. It made her jump, and she rotated her head to loosen the tightened muscles in her neck; then she squared her shoulders and started for the front.

"Wait a minute," said Joe. She slowed her pace, and by the time her hand was on the knob, he had joined her. In the foyer, she flipped up the peephole cover.

A middle-aged black man wearing a black suit, a white shirt, and a black bow tie, and carrying a plastic supermarket bag, was waiting on the sidewalk. Martha reached up to the alarm box and punched in three 8s, turned the lock, and opened the door.

"Miz Patterson?" said the man. "I'm Henry Reed."

There was little doubt that this was Kent Reed's father. Henry Reed's color was walnut where the son's had been sepia, and middle age had frosted his hair and added a small, neat paunch, but the underlying slender build was the same, and the features, though lined with down-drawn furrows so deep that they surely predated his present grief, stirred Martha's memory of that dead *young man.*

"I'm glad to meet you," she said. "Please come in. This is my friend, Joe Gianni."

"Mr. Reed," Joe acknowledged.

"Pleased to meet you." Henry Reed stepped into the foyer and Joe retreated to the computer.

"I'm sorry for your loss," Martha said. "I only met your son once, but my friend Hannah valued him highly."

"I thank you for those kind words," Henry Reed said. "He was out on his own a good many years now, but we're missing him like he was still in the cradle."

Martha's thoughts turned to Robert, forty-four now, and a father twice over, but still, though she would never dare say it aloud, her baby boy. "Yes," she said. "Yes, I know."

CONDUCTING HENRY REED back to the apartment, Martha consciously avoided looking at the bloodstains, and to her relief, he did not look down.

He stopped just inside the door and scanned the room. His shoulders sagged. "Well," he said after a moment, "that old trunk back there belongs to the family. And I guess all the computer stuff is his. That's what he was going to do, computer work. I don't know about this furniture."

"I believe the futon was his," said Martha. "The rest came with the apartment."

"That sleeping pad? Well, then, I don't need to worry about that." He squared his shoulders. "Well, you don't get done unless you get started." He set the supermarket bag on the table and took out a box of heavy-duty trash bags. "His mama said to bring his clothes home. They won't fit any of us, but our church will have a use for them. I can pack them up in these and if the lady doesn't mind holding them and the trunk and the computer a little while longer, my son-in-law could drive back and pick it all up over Memorial Day."

"That will be fine," Martha said.

"I don't know about those books."

"Some of them are computer texts. Whoever takes the computer can probably use them."

"Guess so. I don't know about the others. I guess they'd go okay in a rummage sale. My son-in-law can pack them up and bring them, save you the trouble."

HE STARTED WITH the trunk. Martha had planned to keep her distance from the process, but he asked her to stay with him in case anything of Hannah's might have found its way

among Kent's. Accordingly, she lowered herself on com-
plaining knees to crouch on the edge of the futon while
Henry Reed knelt, with an imperfectly muffled grunt, in
front of the trunk.

It was only about a quarter full. The top layer consisted
of five shoeboxes full of artists' tools: pens, pencils, char-
coal pencils, pastel crayons, tubes of watercolors and oils.

"I suppose there's somebody could use all this," he said.

"Perhaps a school art program," Martha suggested.

"Well, now, that's a fine idea." He lifted them out and
set them on the floor. Under them were a couple of blank
sketch pads with half their sheets torn out. He added them
to the pile of shoeboxes.

Next was an unsealed manila envelope full of papers. As
he leafed through them, Martha caught glimpses of diplo-
mas, certificates, two or three photographs, a sheaf of news-
paper clippings. He slid them back into the envelope, re-
fastened the clasp, and laid it on the edge of the futon
beside Martha. "I'll take this home with me."

At the bottom of the trunk was an artist's portfolio, the
kind with a zipper around three sides and a carrying handle.
Henry Reed unzipped it and Martha moved crab-wise to
the end of the futon to let him lay it out flat.

It held a collection of works on paper. The first few were
landscapes in watercolor, initialed KR in the lower right
corner. Probably student work; they were conventionally
composed and competently executed, but not, to Martha's
eye, notably inspired.

"His mama'll want to get these framed," Henry Reed
said, and laid them on top of the envelope of documents.

The last things in the portfolio were several sheets torn
from sketchpads. They were lying facedown. Henry Reed
turned the top one over, exclaimed, "Oh, dear me," and
turned it facedown once more.

But not before Martha had caught a glimpse. It was a

pencil sketch of a standing female nude. She would like to have seen it better; it seemed to be a livelier work than the watercolors. But Henry Reed's face had turned from light walnut to dark mahogany, and his embarrassment touched her.

"It's just an exercise," she said. "Learning to draw nudes is part of an artist's education. And from the little look I got, I think it's rather good."

It took several seconds for the heat to leave his face, but at last he was able to meet her eyes. "I guess you're saying it's art, and that makes it all right."

His reticence deserved respect. "Mr. Reed," she said, "if it bothers you, it's none of my business."

"That's kind of you, ma'am." The lines in his face were deep and infinitely sad. He laid the drawings, still face-down, in a separate pile on the futon and pushed himself to his feet. "Well, that's the trunk. Guess it's time to tackle the closet and that chester draws."

Martha levered herself upright. "And I've already seen what's there, so if it's all right with you, while you bag up the clothing, I'm going to go sit in a chair before my knees get so stiff I can't get up at all."

"Yes, ma'am," Henry Reed said. "You get to my age, you know about knees."

SEATED AT the kitchen table, Martha propped her elbows on the table, leaned her forehead on her cupped hands, and let her mind go blank, until at last Henry Reed came forward. He was carrying the portfolio in one hand and in the other, a stiff flat package wrapped in one of the trash bags. She looked toward the back and saw that he had rolled and tied the futon and stood three filled trash bags next to the wall behind it.

He gestured with the flat package. "I don't really know what to do with these pictures," he said. "I can't bring myself to throw out anything he made, but I know his mama won't give them house room. To her, they'd just be naked girls. Dirty pictures."

"I understand."

"So I was wondering, do you know any friends he had, art people who wouldn't be bothered and might want these pictures? Maybe to remember him by?"

"That's a fine thought. Hannah is sure to know someone who will appreciate them. That's his employer, Hannah Gold. She may even want them herself."

"If you wouldn't mind asking her?"

"I'd be honored." Martha took the package, pushed herself to her feet, and accompanied him through the door into the studio. Joe looked up briefly before returning his attention to the computer.

"He did like the young ladies," Henry Reed said. "And they did like him."

"He was a handsome young man," Martha said.

"Oh, yes. Even his daddy could see that. Don't know how many times we had to remind him, handsome is as handsome does. Well, ma'am, I do appreciate you giving me your time this evening."

"It's the least one can do." Somewhat reluctantly, Martha added, "Mr. Reed, I'm sorry to bother you with this, but we haven't been able to find your son's keys. Did the mortuary give you any of his personal effects?"

"What he had in his pockets? It was the police had that. They gave me his wallet and some small change, but they didn't say anything about keys."

AND AFTER ALL, he looked at the floor. Martha hoped that he would miss the faint stains, or attribute them to an innocuous spillage—paint, perhaps, or strong coffee—but it was a vain hope. "This where it happened?" he asked.

"Yes," she said.

"Seems like nobody knows who it was."

"The police had nothing to tell you?"

"No." He sighed. "Well, I don't know that it'd help much, anyhow. Knowing, I mean. The good Lord says forgive, and I'm afraid if I knew who it was, I'd have a hard time with that."

TEN

Anomalies

MARTHA DIDN'T BOTHER resetting the alarm after Henry Reed left. She crossed the studio to where Joe was staring at the computer screen and asked, "Are you finding anything?"

"Um?" He was in another universe. "Oh." He returned. "Well, I've turned up some anomalies, but I don't know if they're significant."

"What kind of anomalies?"

"It looks as if the gallery may have sold some things that she hasn't received payment for. I'd need to compare the entries with inventory. And there are a few other peculiarities, but they may just be functions of her individual system. Are you ready to go?"

"When you've finished."

"Well, that could take quite a while." He looked at his watch. "You don't want to wait around. Why don't I just copy these files to disk and work on them at home?" He began pulling out drawers. "She must have some disks...ah, here we are."

AT HOME, Martha dug Detective Sharpman's card out of her bag and dialed his number. He was not in, but after a few minutes of explanation and several more of hold, she was connected with someone who claimed familiarity with the case.

Sharpman's memory had been accurate: the inventory of

Kent Reed's personal effects showed no keys of any description.

That night she kept drifting in and out of a dream in which someone of shadowy identity but unchallenged authority kept demanding that she explain how an artist had achieved the effect of a golden key floating with no visible support in a substance that was gaseous like air but black like ink. She kept failing at the task.

HANNAH TELEPHONED while Martha was dressing to meet Joe Gianni and his wife for lunch before their gallery visit. "They're going to let me out," she said.

"Wonderful."

"But I have to have a keeper."

"They want someone to stay with you?"

"Who could stand that? My place doesn't have anywhere to hide."

"I suppose that apartment downstairs wouldn't..."

"No, it wouldn't."

Someone, then, for Hannah to stay with.

Martha quelled an impulse; two independent old women knocking into each other in her space? No, no, no.

But then Guilt began to whisper: *What kind of friend are you, anyway? It would only be temporary. You could move the computer...*

"You remember Nell Willard," said Hannah.

Hauled back from good-girl fantasies, Martha did not at the moment remember Nell Willard.

"Paul's wife," Hannah prompted. "Paul Willard, the sculptor. You saw his show. He works with tree branches, and Nell's a needlewoman."

Oh, yes. "They live upstate somewhere, don't they?"

"Not that far, and they have all kinds of room. When Paul's work started to sell, he built himself a studio out in the woods."

"Wouldn't you be lonely all the way up there?"

"Martha, it is not *all the way* anywhere, it's one county north of Westchester. And Nell has a decent sewing machine so I'll be working anyway."

"I stand corrected."

"Yes, you do."

"And I hope you have a good time."

"Well, it isn't set yet. I just left a message, so first they have to call me back and say yes. But they will. Nell's been after me for years to come up. Could you stand to make one more trip to my place? I'll need country clothes and sketch pads and the big box of pencils in the desk. And you'll have to give me back my keys. Did you find Kent's?"

"They haven't turned up."

"You looked?"

"All over his apartment, and the police say they don't have them, and they weren't among his effects that the mortuary gave his father. What a nice man the father is. I wish you could have met him."

"I did."

"He came to see you?"

"We cried. So, no keys. I don't like that."

"Nor I. You should have the locks changed."

"Do it."

"Consider it done. Hannah, I've got a question for you. Kent's father came across some drawings, some nudes, among Kent's things. He said his wife wouldn't give them house room. I gather she's somewhat straitlaced. He hopes someone who knew Kent will want them."

"Where are they?"

"I have them."

"Keep them. I'll take care of them when I get home. Oh, I nearly forgot. Damn this head. Did your accountant friend look at my money files?"

"Yes, he did. He said he may have found some anomalies."

"What anomalies?"

"He thinks you might not have got paid for some things the gallery sold."

"That's an anomaly?"

"You know about it?"

"What do you think, I don't know what happens to my babies? Nick solves his cash-flow problems by not paying his artists. They all do. The art business is feast or famine, and it's a long time between feasts."

"HANNAH ALREADY KNEW about your financial anomalies," said Martha. She and Joe and Joe's wife, Eileen, a well-tended country-club blonde, were lunching at a coffeehouse in Soho before moving on to the gallery. "I told you, Joe; Hannah has been a businesswoman all her life. She isn't easily taken advantage of, and certainly not without her knowledge and consent. She says slow payment is endemic in the business and nothing to kill for."

"Kill?" said Eileen. "I thought it was that other sculptor who did it. The one she was competing with. You know, breaking up that maquette thing and getting caught. What do financial anomalies have to do with it?"

"Joe had a theory that Hannah's dealers might have been cheating her," said Martha, "and killed her new assistant to cover up."

"Why him?"

"Because he was computerizing all her records and might have noticed the anomalies."

Eileen looked at Joe. "You didn't tell me about that bright idea. What are you trying to do, turn yourself into what's-his-face, that Frenchman with the little gray cells?"

"Hercule Poirot," said Martha, who detested the expression *what's-his-face*. "He's Belgian."

"Whatever. Joe, I'm not following this line of thought, if that's what it is. Why would Hannah's dealers wreck the whatcha-call-it, the maquette? Isn't that what they make their money off of?"

Joe shrugged.

"The theory," said Martha, "is that they wanted to cast suspicion on Dennison Simm."

"That other sculptor."

"Just so. And while I don't believe for one minute that Nick or Barbara could possibly have had anything to do with it, one may note that they were instrumental in getting the maquette restored after it was vandalized. They persuaded Wendy to drop everything and set to work restoring it, and if she is to be believed, she'll have it finished in time to get it to Minneapolis by the deadline."

"Oh, that's neat," cried Eileen. "They knocked off the assistant to hide their embezzlement, then they broke up the whatcha-call-it, the maquette, to incriminate the other sculptor but they knew they could get it fixed, and they bashed what's-her...Hannah because she came home before they expected her?"

"Eileen." Joe took a bread stick from a basket on the table and broke it in half.

Martha said, "The suggestion that Hannah's arrival was unexpected is why this particular fantasy doesn't stand up to scrutiny. Hannah was with them that night until she left to go home, so they would have known she was on the way, if in fact she wasn't already there."

"Well, then, what if it was Hannah they were really after?"

"Eileen," said Joe again.

"No, think about it. They make money selling her stuff, and you've been telling me that the price of art depends on a lot of things besides artistic quality or whatever. Reputation, and publicity, and what about supply and demand?"

She leaned back to let the waiter set her plate in front of her. "What I'm saying, as long as Hannah Gold is alive and well, she keeps turning out the art and the inventory keeps getting bigger. Why not knock her in the head before she's a glut on the market?"

It was a joke to this silly woman.

It was not a joke to Henry Reed.

But this woman and her husband, perhaps on the verge of buying a Hannah Gold work, ought not to be offended, if offense could be avoided. Martha directed her attention to the problem of picking up her sandwich. A complex arrangement of oily eggplant, smoked mozzarella, and a great many big green leaves flopping over the edges of a wedge of focaccia, it was bound to fall apart if picked up. She picked up her knife and fork instead, and finally trusted herself to say, "I don't think it works quite like that."

She had succeeded in avoiding offense: Eileen laughed and said, "You mean you can never have too many Rembrandts?"

Perhaps she was not entirely silly. Martha cut off a manageable chunk of sandwich and said, "In a manner of speaking."

"Well, then," Eileen said, "maybe they did it for the publicity."

"Eileen," said Joe. "It isn't really a joke."

ELEVEN

The Body of the Work

BY THE TIME they entered the Nicholas Warner Gallery, Martha had changed her mind about staying with Joe and Eileen while they viewed Hannah's work. The fact that she was not eager to spend a great deal more time with Eileen might have had some influence on her decision, but a more serious consideration was the fear that her presence might discourage the free flow of the selling process. So while Nick escorted Joe and Eileen back to a private room, Martha remained out front to view the gallery's current exhibitions.

The gallery had two exhibition spaces. The larger one opened off the street; the other, smaller, was reached through an archway in the rear wall of the front room.

This month the front room was given over to a video installation. It was set up to resemble a department store's living-room display, grafted onto a demented version of a television sales floor. A curved sectional couch large enough to accommodate seven or eight viewers occupied one corner; the walls forming the opposite corner were covered floor to ceiling with television sets. They were of various sizes and models and of differing qualities. Some of the images were sharp, some blurred; some pictures were steady, others flickered; two or three were black-and-white; the colors on the color screens did not quite match from one to another. On all of them, the same tape, endlessly recycled in slow motion, showed a brick falling from the top course of a high wall such as might enclose an English

country garden. No two sets showed the same part of the
fall at the same time; at any given moment, on one screen
the brick might be detaching itself and beginning its fall
while others would be showing different portions of the
fall. Presently Martha noticed that even the rate of slow
motion varied from picture to picture. The effect was hypnotic and, ultimately, vertiginous.

Two people were sitting, apparently transfixed, at one
end of the sectional. Martha sat down at the other end, at
right angles to them, and closed her eyes until her head
ceased to spin. Then she opened her eyes and, curious to
see what it was that dislodged the brick from the top of the
wall, tried to follow just one of the pictures until it recycled
to the beginning of the loop. Concentration was hard to
maintain, for the adjacent moving images assaulted her pe-
ripheral vision. She began to suspect that if she didn't get
out of there, her equilibrium might be gone for the day.
Seasickness, in fact, wasn't altogether to be ruled out. But
then she discovered that by making a tunnel of her hands,
she could block out the interference and stay with the single
screen; she managed this focused vision long enough to
perceive that no moving force was shown. The brick edged
out apparently of its own accord, until it overbalanced and
fell.

Presumably the installation was intended to convey some
message, but what it might be, Martha couldn't even guess.

She hoisted herself out of the soft depths of the couch
and, keeping her eyes fixed on the floor, passed through
the archway into the back gallery.

This exhibition had at least the virtue of motionlessness.
It consisted of three large white amoeba-shaped panels,
each centered on a different wall, each about ten feet high
by twelve feet across, each painted with an abstract monochromatic pattern, one yellow, one a dull reddish brown,
one a thick, rich brown. All were studded with wire brack-

ets that supported an assortment of small transparent containers.

The work on the wall that faced the entrance was the yellow one. The pattern consisted of spatters that swept in an arc, like the trail of a skyrocket or a comet's tail, from upper left to lower right. In the spaces above and below the arc, tiny stoppered glass bottles full of yellow liquid stuck out from the surface of the work.

The reddish brown one was on the wall to the right of the yellow one. It too was spattered, but all over rather than in a discernible pattern, and ten or a dozen handprints were randomly superimposed on the spatters. This one was not entirely monochromatic; the attached containers, small corked test tubes, contained a bright red liquid.

The third panel, across the room from the reddish-brown one, was the dark brown one; it looked like a fingerpainting done in a substance that might have been a child's modeling clay. The containers on this one were set in a rigid diagonal line slanting down from upper right to lower left. They were larger than the little bottles and test tubes; they were transparent four-by-five boxes with snap-down lids like those provided at a self-service salad bar. They contained cigar-shaped lumps of the plasticine which was the medium of the fingerpainting.

Martha stepped to the middle of the room and turned to look at the fourth wall.

The Body of the Work
Is
The Work of the Body

appeared in foot-high black lettering above the arch through which she had entered.

She contemplated this legend for a moment, and then moved closer to the fingerpainted work.

As she had begun to suspect, the "fingerpaint" was not paint; it was the substance that an unsupervised toddler might discover in its diaper and apply to the nursery wall. And the lumps in the salad containers were, or perhaps had been made to resemble, what she had never quite learned to call turds.

And the yellow...

and the reddish brown...

The Work of the Body.

The room, however, had no particular smell. Looking more closely, she observed that the surfaces were heavily coated with something on the order of varnish or polyurethane, and that transparent tape sealed the lids of the containers.

Heels clattered on the hardwood floor behind her. She detached her attention from *The Work of the Body* and turned to find Barbara Turcotte coming through the arch.

"Oh, Martha," Barbara said. "Nick said you were here and I had to come and say hello."

"And hello to you." Martha glanced at the work once more. "Are they real or simulated?"

Barbara smiled. "Real."

"I suppose it would diminish the impact if they weren't the real thing."

"It would. Not to worry, they're sealed, and his tests are negative."

"I see. How does he keep the blood liquid?"

"An anticoagulant. Martha, was it you who got the Giannis interested in Hannah's work?"

"Is there a problem?"

"Not a bit, we're very happy with them. I just wondered, because they don't seem to have retained a consultant, and Nick and I are wondering who's giving them such nice advice."

"I don't know. Joe said somebody told him that Hannah

Gold was a growth stock, and he'd seen my pieces, so he asked me for an introduction. Why don't you ask him?''

"We did. He doesn't remember who it was he talked to.''

Again heels clicked beyond the arch and Eileen Gianni's voice called, "Martha?''

"We're in here," said Barbara.

Eileen came through the archway. "Oh, thank God, this is holding still," she said. "Those damn TVs were making me seasick." She glanced around. "God, they're big. Where would you put them?''

Barbara smiled.

Male voices sounded in the other room. Evidently the sales conference was over. "In here, Joe," Eileen called. She moved closer to examine the one with the reddish brown handprints.

Footsteps approached the arch.

Eileen said, "Wouldn't it look better without all those little…oh. Oh, my *God!*" She wheeled toward the arch. *"Stop!"* she exclaimed.

But Nick was already through the arch, and Joe was at his elbow.

Eileen advanced toward them with her palms out. "Joe, don't…''

But the words were as futile as the gesture; Joe was already looking at the brownish-red painting.

Martha watched the color drain from his face as if a plug had been pulled. His lips tightened into a thin line and he turned away abruptly.

Nick was perhaps not altogether unprepared. He gripped Joe's arm, said, "This way," and steered him rapidly out through the arch.

"Oh, God," said Eileen, "I hope he makes it in time."

"Damn it," said Barbara, "I *told* Nick we should put up a warning."

"HE'S ALWAYS BEEN like that," said Eileen. She and Martha had gone back to the coffeehouse where they'd had lunch, leaving Barbara to tell Joe where to find them.

"This is a typical reaction, then?" asked Martha.

"Oh, God, yes. The boys, the teeniest little scrape, if there's any blood, it's Mommy who has to put on the Band-Aid. He'll only use an electric razor so he shouldn't nick himself. That woman—Barbara?—she's right, they should put up a warning. I mean, come on, that's supposed to be art? Shit and piss and blood?"

Martha had picked up a flyer at the gallery's front counter. She extracted it from her handbag and unfolded it. "'This installation by Jay Jasper,'" she read, "'confronts the ever-present contradictions of secrecy and outwardness, revulsion and attraction, terror and—quite literally—guts.'"

"What the hell is that?" asked Eileen.

"A review of the show." Martha returned to the flyer. "'In using products of his own body as the medium for these visually seductive abstractions, Jasper challenges—'"

"Visually *what?*"

"Seductive."

"You're making it up."

Martha shook her head. "I couldn't if I tried."

"My God."

"'Jasper challenges us to journey beyond the arbitrary boundaries that our priggish society has erected between the acceptable and the disgraceful, into a fresh universe of freedom and ecstasy.'"

"Freedom and *what?*"

Martha refolded the flyer and returned it to her handbag. "Ecstasy."

"Is this guy serious? There'll be some kind of ecstasy if Joe pukes all over the floor."

"I imagine the ecstasy will be the artist's," said Martha.

"Not many works induce that strong a reaction. Tell me, did you see any of Hannah's work that you liked?"

"I really don't know," Eileen said. "It takes a while to start thinking of cloth as art, I guess."

Martha was not particularly surprised. A bit disappointed, yes, but not surprised.

Eileen giggled. "I'll say this for it. It didn't make Joe throw up."

"Who was it told Joe about Hannah?"

"One of his clients. If he ever told me the name, I must have been too surprised to pay attention. He never took any particular interest in art before."

"Art," said Martha, "or investment?"

"Yes, well, it is Joe, isn't it? But it's more than that. Lucy was into art before she—before she died."

"Lucy?"

"His daughter."

His daughter. Eileen was Joe's second wife. Martha had never met the first, but now, her memory jogged, she did recall hearing something about a daughter. "I'm sorry," she said. "I didn't know she had died."

"Well, you know Joe. He doesn't exactly wear his heart on his sleeve."

"Was it recent?"

"Last summer." Eileen began rummaging in her handbag. "It was really pretty awful. She left two little girls and Joe just never sees them. He doesn't really know his own granddaughters." She pulled out her billfold and opened it. "This is from before she was married. The last several years we didn't see her at all. He kept inviting her back, but she just stopped coming. He didn't say a lot, but it really bugged him."

"The young have many interests."

"That's what I kept telling him, but he wouldn't believe it. He kept blaming Frances." Frances must be the first wife. "That's baloney, but you know men. Lucy was Daddy's little darling, and if she didn't come see Daddy every time he crooked his finger, it wasn't because she wasn't interested, it was because she wasn't allowed. Somebody else's fault."

Martha took the billfold. A snapshot showed a slender girl in her late teens with dark curls tumbling to her shoulders, a pretty girl who would have been prettier if her lips had curved upward in a smile instead of downward in a pout. She was sitting beside a pool with her arms around her drawn-up knees. Two little boys were sitting with her, one on each side. Lucy's children? No, Eileen had just said Lucy's were girls. In any case, in this photograph, she was obviously only a girl herself, much too young to be these boys' mother. The photograph must be an old one.

There was, Martha now noticed, something familiar about the girl's features. Then she realized that what she was seeing were Joe's cheekbones and chin. Lines and planes that were commonplace in Joe were transformed by some alchemy of girlishness into near-beauty in his daughter. Hannah would know just where the magic lay.

"I can tell you, I was just as glad," said Eileen. "She was bored out of her skull when she was here—well, can't you tell that from the picture—and it wasn't a pretty sight. Joe had all this tennis and golf lined up, but she was into artsy stuff, music and painting and all that. She was taking courses at some art school in Philadelphia when she died, and that was when Joe all of a sudden took up this art thing. Like trying to get her back, you know? Now that it's too late?"

Martha closed the billfold and handed it back. "Sad," she said.

"Oh, yes." Eileen tucked the billfold away. "But I'm not carrying that around in memory of my stepdaughter. It just happens to be the best picture I have of our boys when they were that age.''

Our boys. Joe's and Eileen's. Martha had met those children. "I'm ashamed to say I've lost track of the years," she said. "How old are they now?''

"Eight and ten. I'm turning into a soccer mom.''

TWELVE

Hugger Mugger

PRESENTLY Joe joined them. *The Work of the Body* had obviously, although Martha hoped only temporarily, dampened his interest in contemporary art; in spite of her assurance that Dennison Simm's work was nonorganic, consisting largely of I-beams and rivets, Joe was done for the day. They finished their cappuccino, the Giannis headed for Grand Central, and Martha proceeded to Simm's opening on her own.

The Friedland-Carabelli Gallery was four blocks north and five blocks east of the coffeehouse, in the northeastern corner of Soho where galleries were still withstanding the invasion of boutiques. Martha made her way along the crowded, uneven sidewalks past the much-admired cast-iron facades of the former factory district. Although her intellect had long ago accepted that arbiters of taste found architectural charm in the Soho street scene, her midwestern-bred eyes, in spite of her best efforts, continued to register it as shabby and cluttered. But the day was a proper blue-sky-and-white-clouds May day and walking was pleasant. She was rather sorry to be going indoors and almost envious of Hannah's proposed flight to the country.

She did not need the arrows painted on the fourth-floor wall to direct her to the gallery; the babble emanating from the far end of the hall announced its location. Inside, the density of the crowd at first prevented her from spotting Dennison Simm, but she finally located his bulky form and gleaming brown head in the middle of the room where, laughing uproariously, he was holding court.

Surely no one of normal sensibilities could be so ebullient only a few days after wrecking a competitor's work and battering a man, who might have been his wife's lover, to death.

Query: Was Dennison Simm innocent, or was he psychopathic?

Answer: Martha had no idea.

Be that as it may, one must speak to the artist. First, however, one must view the new work and formulate appropriate remarks. Martha possessed herself of a glass of wine and began a circuit of the gallery.

Commentators had occasionally compared Dennison Simm's previous work to the abstract structural work of Mark Di Suvero. The kinder of these critics employed the word *influence,* the fiercer, *derivative.* The works in this show, however, had taken a new, and what must probably be termed an anthropomorphic, turn. They did, to be sure, employ Simm's usual structural materials, but the way in which they were joined now suggested bodies rather than buildings—bodies standing, bodies sitting, bodies recumbent; bodies possessed of protruding steel bars and bolts that suggested legs and feet, arms and hands, heads, female breasts and male genitals. If Simm had located these protuberances where they commonly appeared on real bodies, he surely would have been accused of constructing tediously obvious unmechanized robots. But he hadn't, and it was probably just as well that the Giannis had retreated to Westchester. On the first piece that Martha examined, one armlike structure, complete with fingers, emerged, not from the shoulder, but from a location that on a human being would be the mouth, while the other protruded from the crotch. Across the room, an angular steel buttock sprouted three long bolts soldered into a pyramid resembling a nose.

On another work, a leg grew from the chest and three rods that perhaps represented penises sprouted from the top of the head. (*Rebars,* that was the name of those rods; they were used to reinforce concrete.)

The effect was both absurd and chilling. Martha's mind tossed out *Love Canal* and *Chernobyl* and *Three Mile Island.*

Mutant robots.

She was ready to approach the artist.

As she did so, Simm saw her coming. "Good to see you," he boomed. "How's Hannah doing?"

Martha discerned that he recognized her by context but not by name. "Martha Patterson," she said and held out her hand to be seized and compressed. "Hannah is progressing satisfactorily, thank you." She retrieved her hand and gestured around the room. "A new departure, isn't it? Do I detect a comment on the law of unintended consequences?"

Simm shook his head. "Sounds good, but you'll have to cut it up into little pieces for me." The booming laugh. "I'm just a welder."

He was asking to be contradicted. She obliged with, "Much more than that," and was about to deliver a learned observation (or possibly a spate of utter twaddle) about genetic damage as an unintended consequence of technological advance when she noted that Simm's attention had shifted to one side of her. She turned and found Olive Quist at her elbow. As if trying to camouflage her arresting figure and avoid attention that properly belonged to the artist, the artist's wife was wearing a neutral-colored jumpsuit. The attempt, if that's what it was, did not meet with notable success.

Martha left the observation/twaddle undelivered, and said, "Hello, Olive."

"Do you have a minute?" Olive's voice was a mere

murmur. "I need to ask you something." Before Martha could say, "Yes, of course," Olive began edging sideways; Martha would have to abandon Simm if she was to avoid seeming to snub his wife.

She glanced back. In that brief moment of inattention, she had lost Simm to a fierce-eyed woman in draperies and bangles. She edged away after Olive.

When they had moved out of earshot, Olive said, still in a murmur but with a discrepantly brilliant smile that might have been designed to impress onlookers with the vacuity of the conversation, "Wendy says you're in charge of getting Kent's things sorted out."

That was not quite how Martha would have defined her role, but it was not wholly inaccurate. "Is there something you're interested in?" she asked.

"I loaned him a book and I really need to have it back."

"I haven't looked through his books."

Again Olive looked over her shoulder. When her attention returned, she dropped her voice even further. "It's by Maya Angelou. *I Shall Not Be Moved.*"

Martha would be picking up Hannah's clothes tomorrow. "I suppose I could take a look," she said.

"Oh, could you? And bring it home and call me so I can pick it up from you?"

Martha dug in her handbag for notepad and pen. "What's your number?"

Olive took the pen and pad from her, scribbled, and handed them back. "If it isn't me answering," she murmured, "don't say what it's about."

Maya Angelou. That would be poetry: the heightened language of heightened emotion. This exercise was not about a simple recovery of borrowed property.

Did one really want to involve oneself in this marital hugger-mugger? "If I'm pressed for a message, what am I supposed to say?'' Martha asked. She wasn't sure if she had kept her distaste out of her voice.

"Oh, heavens, just say you called." Olive glanced past Martha, straightened from the conspiratorial heads-together posture into which she had drifted, and said in a conversational tone, "Have you seen Dennie's newest piece? I'll bet you haven't. Over here." She put a hand on Martha's arm, her grip just firm enough that resistance would create a discernible scene, and maneuvered her toward the end of the room. "He was working on it all night. We couldn't move it over here until noon, but he was determined to get it here. It's something new, newer than the big ones, even. Dennie told Barney—you know Barney Friedland, don't you, the Friedland half of the gallery?—Dennie told him it was coming and to leave room for it, but you see what a squeeze it is."

The piece toward which she was guiding Martha stood against the wall, looking indeed a bit wedged in, and indeed not like anything else in the show. Nor did it resemble any of Simm's earlier work. It was uncharacteristically small, no more than three feet in any dimension, and uncharacteristically delicate. The medium was wire and the form was a combination of interlocking geometric shapes.

It would look good in her apartment, Martha realized; it would, in fact, probably play well off one of her Hannah Gold pieces. "I like it," she said. "Is it a maquette, or is that its final form?"

"That's it. The very first piece of his miniature period. Martha, excuse me, please. There are some people I have to talk to."

GOOD SALESMANSHIP; show the customer the object, then leave her alone to develop her fantasies. Martha had possessed herself of a copy of the handlist. The entry, squeezed in at the bottom, listed the piece as untitled and the price, in the low four figures, as one she could afford. There was no red sticker on the pedestal; it had not yet been sold.

Yes, it would look quite interesting next to *Confused Euclid,* an early Hannah Gold piece that consisted of vividly printed fabrics stretched over wood frames to form a sphere, a tetrahedron, and a cube. The frameworks were rigidly accurate geometric forms, but the way in which the elements were grouped on a reflective stainless-steel surface caused the fabric patterns to form complex designs that shifted as the viewer moved. Martha never tired of looking at it.

It enhanced a tabletop in a corner of the living room. At present, a side chair stood next to the table. If she were to move the chair into her study and acquire a longer table…

No.

Of course not.

What was she thinking of? She was certainly not in the market for anything created by a man who might have assaulted her closest friend and destroyed that friend's work.

But…

But in case, just in case, the investigation should absolve Dennison Simm…

She stepped back to see it from a new angle and her foot landed on someone's toe. She turned to apologize and, in spite of the fact that he had apparently attempted to disguise himself in the current artist's uniform of black jeans and a black turtleneck, she recognized her victim. Detective Sharpman had come to Dennison Simm's opening.

He was clutching his own glass of red wine and his demeanor as much as his costume indicated that he was, in a mild sort of way, under cover.

"Well," she said, "fancy meeting you here."

He gestured restrainedly around the gallery. "I couldn't miss this fresh facet of Dennison Simm's already monumental accomplishment."

After a startled moment, Martha realized that he must be quoting from the gallery's press release. "Good heavens," she said, "you've memorized it."

"I have to be ready to say something. Maybe you can give me a little help."

"What sort of help did you have in mind?"

"Well, I'm a little beyond the stag at eve on black velvet, but I'm still your basic ignoramus. Sailboats on the sea, cows in a pond, that's my kind of thing. This stuff leaves me way behind. Help me out. If somebody wants to strike up a conversation, I don't want to sound like the real Phil Sharpman, if you see what I mean, so maybe you could tell me what I should really be saying."

"To fit in."

"Right.

"Well, that depends on what your goal is."

"If I say I'm damned if I know what my goal is, you'll think I'm lying."

"The police are baffled?"

"The investigation is continuing. Come on, what should I say if one of these people latches on to me? You know you're required to assist the police in the performance of their duties."

"Just so. Well, first, tell me what you really think."

He studied the nearest work for perhaps five seconds. "To tell you the truth, it looks to me like a deformed robot without an engine."

"I think that will do very well. You might want to substitute 'mutant' for 'deformed.' Or perhaps 'genetically altered.' It isn't necessary to sound approving, but if you did, you could tack on 'extending his vision.' That would probably entitle you to all the Brie you can hold."

"Too bad I don't like Brie. What were you and Ms. Quist conspiring about?"

Some part of Martha's mind must have been expecting

something of the sort, for she felt no surprise. She didn't pretend not to understand, nor did she feel obliged to dissemble. "She says she loaned Kent Reed a book of Maya Angelou's poems and she wants me to get it back for her."

"Did you agree?"

"I believe I implied that I'd look for it, and if I found it, I'd give it back to her."

"Where is it?"

"She supposes it to be in his apartment. If it exists at all, it probably is; his father left his books to be picked up later."

"I want to see it."

"Will it help?"

"How about now? Can you get in?"

"Yes."

"And can you leave this affair soon without looking bad?"

"I've discharged my minimal obligation."

"Okay. I'll leave now. Wait at least ten minutes before you go, and then meet me by the fountain in Washington Square."

He was, she noticed, assuming her cooperation.

"Washington Square?" she said. It was about five blocks uptown.

"I didn't think parking right outside a subject's party would send the right kind of message. Is that too far?"

"Not at all, as long as you aren't planning to set me up for drug dealing."

"It isn't my beat, but keep your nose clean."

THIRTEEN

Déjà Vu

WHEN MARTHA GOT TO Washington Square, she found Sharpman perched on the rim of the fountain, his gaze wandering, to all appearances idly, over the skateboarders around him, the chess players at the tables on the west edge of the park, and the dog walkers everywhere.

He had parked in a No Standing zone across from the north side of the park. The car was unmarked, but the observant and experienced could have inferred its ownership and purpose from the elaborate antenna.

Inside, isolated from possible eavesdroppers, Martha said, "Is Dennison Simm a suspect?" She asked only out of mischief; she did not expect an answer.

Maneuvering around a double-parked truck, Sharpman said, "Anybody who was at that cursed reception *could* be a suspect." He had probably meant to evade the question, but the emphasis on *could* made it more of an answer than she had expected.

She said, "My fingerprints must be on the—on the weapon."

Sharpman braked to avoid a lane-changing cab. "As far as I can tell," he said, "you're pretty well vouched for."

"You checked me out."

"No stone unturned."

Of course. And Joe would have vouched for her whereabouts as far as the lobby of her building, and it wouldn't be the first time the NYPD had asked Boris to confirm her "movements" after she had arrived home. Although disapproving of both the questioner and the occasion for the question, Boris would have answered: No, Ms. Patterson hadn't gone out again after the gentleman had escorted her in.

After a silence, Martha said, "They told Hannah they were together all night."

He glanced sideways. "Simm and Quist?"

"Yes."

"Husband and wife." His tone dismissed the uncorroborated joint alibi of husband and wife. "I wouldn't say no to a witness."

His frustration must be considerable, she thought, if he was volunteering that kind of remark.

The ensuing silence lasted long enough to bring them to the approach ramp to the Williamsburg Bridge. Then Martha said, "There's something I've been wondering about." She hadn't, in fact, been wondering for more than perhaps ten minutes, but failing to think was the particular fault she was at all times most reluctant to confess to. "Three years ago, you were investigating a homicide on Court Street. Now you're in Williamsburg. Does the precinct cover that big an area of Brooklyn?"

"I was transferred," he said. His tone did not invite further inquiry.

THE DAY being a Saturday, the street was of course empty. Sharpman parked directly in front of Hannah's place. Martha manipulated locks and alarm and stepped into the studio, Sharpman all but treading on her heels. As soon as she flicked the light switches, she knew something was wrong. She couldn't have said why her first glance had been to the right end of the studio rather than to Kent Reed's apartment door at the rear, but it had, and this time she had no trouble comprehending what she was seeing. A black hollow seemed to open in the middle of her chest. Once more the intricately stitched fabric of the maquette lay in shreds around the wrenched-apart armature.

"I was going—" Her voice caught. "I was going to change the locks Monday."

THEY WAITED FOR the crime-scene unit outside in the car with all the antennas. Sharpman asked questions and Martha answered them.

The maquette had been whole the evening before, Friday, when she and Joe had left. That had been at around half past eight. It was now a little after five-thirty on Saturday. So there had been a span of twenty-one hours (Sharpman actually used the phrase *window of opportunity*) during which the damage was done.

"Who had keys?" he asked.

Martha and Wendy, and whoever, if anyone, had Kent Reed's.

Who knew the alarm code?

Martha and Wendy, and whomever else Hannah—or Kent—might have told it to.

What if Kent Reed had given Olive the key and the alarm code, and Olive had passed them on to her husband?

If Wendy and Olive really had spent the evening together at dinner and a movie, Dennison Simm would have been alone in his studio in New Jersey for several hours—time to get to Williamsburg and back by any mode of transportation faster than walking. A car, a taxi, even the PATH train under the Hudson plus the subway across Manhattan and under the East River to Williamsburg, could not take much more than an hour. And the work of destruction would not have taken long. When had he started that new little work he claimed he had been working on all night, that little cat's cradle tangle of wire Martha had liked so much? Could he have made the round trip, destroyed Hannah's maquette, and still finished the piece in the time that remained?

While they waited, Martha and Sharpman discussed all this.

"Is that Minnesota business that important?" Sharpman asked.

Receiving the commission, Martha assured him, would be a giant career step.

THE CRIME-SCENE UNIT arrived in less than half an hour. Martha waited in Sharpman's car while he went back in with the technicians. Before long he reappeared and took her back into what had been Kent Reed's apartment. It was Sharpman who did the searching while Martha watched. He found the Maya Angelou book quite quickly: a slim little volume with a purple streak down the spine of the dust jacket, tucked incongruously between two computer manuals. He pulled it out by hooking a fingernail over the top edge of the spine, opened the front cover by its edges, and looked at the flyleaf for a moment. Martha craned her neck and was just able to make out, in purple ink that matched the streak on the dust jacket, a curly but legible inscription: *"K—Page 11."*

Sharpman leafed through, touching the pages by their edges. He stopped at what must be page eleven, paused long enough to read it, and carefully closed the book. "Wait here," he said. He took it out into the studio and returned without it.

Martha said, "I told Olive I'd look for it. Shall I tell her you have it?"

"I'd rather you didn't," said Sharpman. "Maybe you can tell her you couldn't find it."

"That will not be a problem," she said. "I didn't find it. You did."

"That's right," said Sharpman, "you're a lawyer."

EVENTUALLY Martha was allowed, under escort, to go out to the foyer, mount the stairs, undo the locks on Hannah's apartment door, and collect a suitcase full of clothes suitable for a week in the country. She was allowed to use the telephone up there to call the gallery. Barbara Turcotte answered, swore, then began to plan. After a moment of thinking aloud, she broke off. "Please," she said, "would you be the one to tell Hannah?"

"WHO?" HANNAH EXPLODED. "Who's *doing* this?"

Martha had found her once more sketching at the card table in the visitor's lounge. "Apparently someone with a key," she said. "I feel perfectly terrible. I was going to get the locks changed Monday."

"Don't."

"Oh, I think I'd better. You'll be coming back—"

"No, no, no, I mean, don't do the guilt thing. It wasn't you that butchered the baby. What's today, Saturday? There's still time to fix it."

"Barbara's getting hold of Wendy."

"Forget Wendy." Hannah scooped up sketch pad and pencil, pushed back her chair, got to her feet, headed for the door. "Forget Monday. I'm calling Nell. I'm getting out of here right now."

Martha followed her out of the lounge and stopped at the nurse's station while Hannah went into her room.

The nurse on duty turned a disapproving glare on Martha and said, "What's going on?"

"She's had some disturbing news," said Martha. "Would you please tell me the procedure for checking oneself out?"

"She wants to check herself out?"

"She was scheduled to go Monday, anyway."

Well, yes, but…the doctor…medical advice…they really couldn't…

"Actually, you can," said Martha. "She's well over twenty-one and this isn't a jail. If her friends are free to take her in today, I really think she'll be better off with them. What's the procedure, please?"

The looks they exchanged, while not exactly glares, were undeniably intense gazes. After a moment, Martha observed a softening; the normally immovable object had recognized the irresistible force. The nurse picked up the phone and summoned the resident. The resident arrived in less than a minute. He listened to the story and paged Hannah's doctor. While he waited for the response, Martha went to Hannah's room.

Hannah was on the phone. Hearing only one end of the conversation, Martha was still able to discern that Nell Willard, the friend who lived sixty miles up the Hudson Valley and had agreed to take Hannah in, was perfectly willing to advance the arrival time. Furthermore, Martha gathered, fabric outlets with extensive stocks were available within easy driving distance and open seven days a week. Nell and Paul would start driving within the hour. Give or take a traffic tie-up or two, they should arrive in a couple of hours.

While Hannah packed, Martha went back out to the nurses' station. Hannah's physician had responded to the page. If Hannah's blood pressure was all right, she could safely be discharged, provided there was a neurologist within easy call of (the nurse moved the phone from her mouth) where was it again? Phillips Landing? Where was that?

"Western Putnam County," said Martha.

"Western Putnam County," said the nurse into the phone.

After a longish wait while the physician presumably looked through a list of some sort, the nurse began to scribble on a note pad. She hung up, tore off the sheet, and

handed it to Martha. It had the names of two neurologists
within reasonable reach of western Putnam County.

Martha went back to Hannah's room. Hannah was on the
phone again, issuing orders to Barbara Turcotte. Stefan, or
somebody just as good, was to get the armature done and
shipped to Phillips Landing no later than Tuesday night.
UPS, Fed Ex, special messenger, Brinks Armored Cars,
whatever it took. Price no object. If necessary, Barbara
should drive it up the river herself. They'd planned to ship
the maquette on Monday, but if they sent it via air freight,
Wednesday would be soon enough. And right now, Barbara
was to send the sketches and patterns to the hospital. Right
now, this minute, immediately. If not a messenger, Barbara
herself...

Barbara was finally able to wedge in the good news:
Wendy had the starveling creature and the altar cloth at her
place; they were almost finished and would be shipped to
Phillips Landing with the armature.

By EIGHT-THIRTY Hannah was sprung. Paul Willard, a
bearded, oversized teddy bear of a man, had laid a narrow
mattress, thick enough to absorb any jolt their country roads
might deliver, in the rear of his Jeep, in case Hannah
needed to lie down before they got her to a real bed. Nell,
a motherly match for her husband, had brought a picnic
hamper. Martha stayed until the Jeep was loaded, waved
them on their way, and took a cab home.

Once more she dreamed of the gold key suspended in
inky air, and of the demand that she explain how the effect
was achieved. She awoke still without a clue, and now with
a sense of unsatisfied curiosity about another subject altogether.

What was on page eleven of that Maya Angelou book?

She dressed and went out for breakfast and the Sunday
Times. She had finished the Week in Review and the Book

Review and was diverting herself with the crossword when Hannah called to report a pleasant drive, a safe arrival, the best night's sleep she'd had in a year, and a pending raid on fabric outlets.

Martha expressed gratification and returned to the crossword, but her concentration was frayed.

What *was* on page eleven of that Maya Angelou book?

The branch library was closed on Sundays, of course, but not the chain bookstore a few blocks west of Martha's building. And there was plenty of time before her appointment with Florence Appleton.

The poetry section had two copies of *I Shall Not Be Moved*. Martha took one from the shelf and turned to page eleven.

The poem was entitled "Love Letter." It sang of lips and hands, of urgencies, of leaping and floating. But seven words from the end, a single phrase—almost a single word, such was the poet's mastery—turned the song at a right angle. "Oh, but then…" began the seventeenth, and penultimate, line.

Then.

Just so.

FOURTEEN

Tea

FLORENCE APPLETON'S apartment building faced on Bedford Avenue, at the corner where it crossed Hannah's Sunday-quiet street of warehouses. Brick-faced and four stories high, it was bulky in comparison with the surrounding low buildings. Its steel-clad outer door had recently been painted navy blue.

Florence Appleton's name was neatly hand-printed on a sliver of card next to bell-push number 21. Martha pressed the button. The speaker crackled and a voice said "Yes" so promptly that she wondered if her hostess had been waiting beside the bell. She identified herself, and the precise voice of Florence Appleton said, "Yes, do come in. I am in the second floor front." The buzzer buzzed, the latch clicked, and Martha pushed through.

The hallway was adequately lighted and unexpectedly clean. The walls, painted a white that was barely tinged with blue, were scarcely marked; the floorboards had resisted scuffing; and the air smelled of furniture polish. Martha's throat muscles relaxed; she realized that she had been braced against less agreeable odors.

The building was a walk-up. At the top of the first flight, Martha found Florence Appleton, a flowered shirtwaist dress snugly belted around her narrow waist, waiting in the doorway of the front apartment. "Do come in," she said. "What a lovely day." The dress hung loose above and below the belt, but the bones of her face seemed a little less sharp than they had last Wednesday. The wig was the same.

The living room was not large as living rooms go—perhaps ten by fifteen feet—but tall windows and the small scale of the sofa and easy chairs, slipcovered in a light flowered fabric, made it feel spacious. A Windsor chair, its seat padded with a thin cushion of crocheted granny squares, was drawn up facing the windows; an oval braided rug covered the floor; two white-painted chairs and a gate-leg table divided the living room from the cubicle that constituted the kitchen. Beyond, a narrow hall led back to what Martha surmised was the bedroom.

One leaf of the table was folded down flush with the wall and the other one was extended. The table was set for two with cups, saucers, and small plates decorated with a floral design, set out on embroidered placemats. Martha was invited to take a seat at the tea table while Florence Appleton ("*Miss,* please," she requested when Martha addressed her as "Ms.") busied herself with teakettle and pot.

GETTING TO the point of this odd occasion, partly tea party and partly consultation, took a while. Pouring the tea—English, served from a teapot and accompanied by Peek Frean biscuits—Florence Appleton opened the conversation with an inquiry about Hannah. Martha told of her discharge into the care of friends and then, in a maneuver that forestalled further questions, segued into additional praise for the delightfulness of the day. This innocuous subject led to a thorough review of the weather patterns of the past several weeks. Presently the conversation became modestly personal, and Martha learned that Florence Appleton's friendship with the art teacher in the school where she had taught had led her to choose Williamsburg as the setting for her retirement. Her reasons were much the same as those for which the artists had chosen it: adequate space, good light, and reasonable rent.

Something over half an hour passed in this harmless fashion. Then the hostess got up, not without a bit of difficulty, removed the dishes to the kitchen sink, sat back down, and said, "You've been very patient, but now I must get to the point."

Martha rearranged her posture to express professionalism.

"This will be confidential?" asked Florence Appleton.

"If you wish it to be, yes."

"I do. And the fee?"

Martha had given this matter some thought. On a retired teacher's pension, Florence Appleton could probably not afford the hourly rate Martha charged for her research, but obvious charity would probably be received as an affront. "For the initial consultation," she said, "ten dollars. If more is required than a few words of advice, and if I am competent to handle the problem, we can discuss terms that will not destroy your budget."

"I'm afraid my problem is more complicated than ten dollars will cover," said Florence Appleton.

"I will be the judge of that. Are those terms acceptable?"

"Yes, thank you. If you will excuse me..." The client pushed back her chair and went down the hall. Martha busied herself by filling out the simplest possible retainer form, which she had brought with her, and presently Miss Appleton returned with a ten-dollar bill in her hand. She sat down and handed it across the table to Martha, who tucked it away in her handbag and slid the retainer across to the client for signature.

This transaction completed, Florence Appleton said, "Yes. Well, to begin. It is obvious, of course, that I have cancer." She touched the wig with her fingertips. "I have had a radical mastectomy and I am undergoing chemotherapy.''

A health problem. Maybe a Medicare issue. Martha was competent to deal with that sort of thing, although, health coverage being what it is, no answer was likely to be particularly satisfactory. She nodded.

''The chemotherapy was very trying,'' said Florence Appleton.

Martha nodded again.

''The nausea was intolerable and the prescribed medications had no effect. I was tempted to say the treatment was worse than the disease. I considered discontinuing treatment and dying in peace, but death from cancer is not peaceful.''

A silence fell. It was not altogether clear where this consultation was headed, and the client seemed to be having trouble knowing how to proceed.

Martha considered what she had heard so far. ''You have been speaking in the past tense,'' she said, ''which leads me to suppose that the situation has changed.''

Miss Appleton looked down at her folded hands.

''May I ask what is making the difference?'' Martha prodded.

Florence Appleton stirred. She glanced toward the windows, turned back, leaned across the table, and dropped her voice nearly to a whisper. ''Marijuana.''

''Ah.'' Martha had guessed right.

Uttering the forbidden word had loosened the constraint. The client leaned back and spoke in her normal tone. ''When I complained of the chemotherapy's effects, my doctor prescribed Marinol. I don't know if you're familiar with the pharmacopoeia. It is the active ingredient of cannabis, extracted from the plant and made into a medication that can be legally prescribed.''

"I've heard of it," Martha said. "I didn't know its trade name."

"It didn't help. It must be swallowed, and since my problem was intense nausea, I simply couldn't keep it down. And the one time I did manage not to throw it up, the effect was terrible." Miss Appleton leaned forward. "Have you ever experienced a panic attack?"

"I have experienced fear, but I don't believe that's what you mean."

"No, it is not. I am talking about being overwhelmed with anxiety, without any outward cause. I complained and the doctor changed the prescription, but nothing helped. Then one day the nurse told me quietly, in the middle of a wide empty hall where nobody could overhear"—again she glanced toward the windows—"that smoking was different. To make Marinol, the pharmaceutical company extracts only one ingredient from the plant. She said there are other ingredients in the smoke that prevent the anxiety. And, of course, smoking does not require swallowing."

"Just so."

"I resisted at first. I have been a churchwoman all my life. I don't drink alcohol and I have never smoked. But the nurse gave me articles to read, and I prayed for guidance, and in the end, I asked if she could get me a...joint?" The word might have been in a language she had only begun to learn. "She said she couldn't risk it. So I—" Again that glance at the windows. "I asked my niece for help."

"The young woman who picked you up after the seminar?"

"Camilla, yes. She knows how to get such things, and she says if I simply keep quiet, there's no risk to either of us. But I worry. She has a responsible position with a broker's firm. An arrest would destroy her."

"I understand."

"I would simply take her advice and keep quiet," Florence Appleton said, "but something has come up. The night—" She broke off. "Let me start at the beginning. The day of Hannah's reception, I tried my first dose of..." speaking the word *marijuana* still gave her trouble.

"The new medication," Martha suggested.

"Yes. Thank you. As a trial, Camilla had given me just the one—the one dose. She had to teach me how to smoke it. I hadn't known that smoking it effectively requires practice."

"So I have heard."

"It was a strange experience, breathing smoke into my lungs."

"Just so." In her college days, Martha had twice tried smoking—tobacco, of course; that had been in the 1940s—and had found the experience so unpleasant that thenceforth she had ignored her sorority sisters' accusations of self-righteousness and remained a nonsmoker. Now she was grateful for her youthful obstinacy.

Miss Appleton said, "I smoked it here, and then she drove me to the clinic for the treatment. I could scarcely believe the difference. I felt no nausea and no anxiety, and when it was over, I was exhilarated. For the first time in many months, life seemed worth living. I was hungry. I wanted to live. I asked Camilla if she could bring me a supply before my next treatment and she said she would. But that evening she called to tell me that she had the—medication—but an emergency had come up at work and she'd be late. She suggested waiting until the next day, but I insisted that the risk should be mine, not hers. I told her she shouldn't keep it in her possession, but should bring it to me that night."

"When was this?"

"Last Wednesday."

The night of Hannah's reception.

"I was watching for Camilla. And it was while I was watching for her that I saw something strange. At the time, it seemed to be no more than a curious event, but later, when I learned what happened at Hannah's studio that night, I remembered." She stood up from the table and gestured at the Windsor chair next to the windows. "If you will sit here and look down…"

Martha obeyed. The window was on the Bedford Avenue side of the building and provided a bird's-eye view of the intersection. Leaning close to the window, she could even see most of the front sidewalk in front of the apartment building.

Miss Appleton sat down in one of the easy chairs. "A woman was lurking down there at the corner," she said.

Lurking? It was a judgmental word. "What exactly was she doing?" asked Martha.

"She kept looking down the street in the direction of Hannah's studio. Now and then she took a few steps down Hannah's street, around the corner where I couldn't see her, but then she would step back again."

Martha thought the behavior sounded more like dithering than lurking.

"I was worrying about Camilla," said Miss Appleton. "I wondered if the woman might be a narcotics agent. But then Camilla came along, and the woman didn't pay any attention. She just went on staring down Hannah's street. I lost sight of her when I went to the door to let Camilla in, and I never saw her again. I looked out the window when Camilla left and she wasn't there."

"What time did Camilla arrive?"

"It was past eleven-thirty."

"Do you know whether she saw the woman?"

"I asked. Camilla said she hadn't noticed."

"Have you told the police about seeing this woman?"

Florence folded her arms and seemed to shrink into herself. "That is what I need to consult you about."

Martha waited.

"I knew nothing about what happened at Hannah's that night. My bedroom is at the rear and the window is on an air shaft. I had gone to bed and I must have slept through the commotion. It wasn't until I was looking out the window the next morning that I saw a police car."

The position of the Windsor chair indicated that Florence Appleton looked out the windows a good deal. Daytime television being what it is, the street scene doubtless offered better entertainment. There was no television set in the room; perhaps she didn't even have one.

"I saw an officer get out of the car and come up to the front door of this building," said Miss Appleton. "My bell rang, and I didn't answer. I was afraid the woman had been a narcotics agent after all, and had reported Camilla's visit."

"You had some of the medication here in the apartment?"

"Several doses. Later I heard someone come upstairs and knock on my door. Again I didn't answer, and after a while whoever it was went away. I didn't learn what had happened at Hannah's studio until later."

"How did you learn?"

Miss Appleton nodded toward the back of the apartment. "It was on the news."

The TV must be in the bedroom.

"When I saw the report," said Miss Appleton, "I realized that what I saw might be helpful, but I knew I must have legal advice. I had already told Hannah I needed to consult an attorney when I began to think about using the...new medication, although I didn't tell her I was considering an illegal action. She gave me your name and the flyer for that seminar out on Kings Highway. I felt well enough that day to attend. I wanted to see what you were like and decide if I felt comfortable consulting you.''

And evidently she had felt comfortable. Martha, on the other hand, did not. This consultation had the potential to be a knotty one, and criminal law was not her field.

But what, after all, did this statement of Florence Appleton's amount to? A sick and possibly stoned elderly woman's oblique view of an unidentified dithering stranger on a dark, rainy street corner. No one could fault her if she said nothing at all. On the other hand, Martha was not inclined to ignore any evidentiary detail, however tiny and inconclusive, that would help nail Hannah's assailant.

And perhaps some gaps could be filled in that would render this little story more definitely evidentiary. "How clearly did you see this woman?" Martha asked.

"Fairly clearly. The corner is quite well lighted.''

"Was it raining?''

"Not just then.''

"What kind of description can you give? Was she tall, short, medium? Fat, thin?''

"Not outstandingly tall or short. Medium, I suppose I would have to say. She was wearing a loose-fitting coat, so it's hard to say much about her build. She was certainly not fat. And when she turned, the coat flapped open to show a short skirt. Men, I'm sure, would say she had good legs.''

Martha stifled an unprofessional eagerness. "Could you see what color the skirt was?'' she asked.

"It's hard to say. The streetlights are deceptive. It might have been red.''

"The coat?''

"Light-colored.''

"Was she wearing anything on her head?''

"No, I could see her hair. It was black and teased out around her head.''

Martha had to struggle to keep her voice even. "Could you tell anything about her age?"

"I think she was young."

"Can you say what gave you that impression?"

"I suppose…" Miss Appleton raised her folded hands and tapped her lips. "It could have been the miniskirt. I'm not sure. It could have been the way she moved."

It had to be asked: "Her race?"

"She was a young woman of color."

Belatedly, it occurred to Martha that she should have waited with that last question; the next question she was about to ask would come awkwardly after that answer. She interpolated a different one: "Was she alone?"

"I didn't see anybody with her."

Well, she'd better get it asked. "Could she have been a prostitute?"

Florence gave no indication that she took offense. "I thought of that, but I don't believe so. I don't believe a lady of the night would look for customers down that deserted little street. And her posture was wrong. She didn't seem to be trying to draw attention to herself. It was more as if she was trying to make up her mind about something." She tapped her lips with her folded hands again. "I must tell the police, mustn't I?"

Martha didn't answer at once.

Miss Appleton took her silence for agreement. "But if I tell them, they will need to know more, won't they? They will want to know why I was looking out the window that late at night and why Camilla was here."

And there was the problem. If someone were ever charged, and Florence Appleton were called to testify at the trial, the prosecutor trying the case would need to know the answers to those questions, because the defense attorney would have explored the questions and would jump at any hint of illegal activity to impeach this witness's credibility.

"If it were only myself," Florence Appleton said, "I don't think I would hesitate. Nothing could be worse than what I've been through already. But I can't involve Camilla. She was only helping me."

"I understand," said Martha.

Florence folded her hands and raised her laced fingers to her lips. "What can I do?"

FIFTEEN

Improvisation

MARTHA DID NOT ANSWER at once. She had not made a close professional study of the Fifth Amendment minefield and the ins and outs of immunity from prosecution. In short, Martha Patterson was not competent to handle this mess. This much, however, she did know: the rules of her profession bound her to give only advice that was in her client's interest, and other things being equal, Florence Appleton's interest would best be served by staying as far from the police as possible.

On the other hand, Martha had a notion that withholding evidence pertinent to a police investigation was itself a criminal offense. If this vague recollection of the New York Penal Law was accurate, was Miss Appleton's sighting of the lurking woman actually evidence pertinent to the investigation? And assuming it might be so construed, just what degree of reticence would constitute a criminal withholding?

The answer would surely depend on just who that lurking woman was. Miss Appleton's description had led Martha to assume that she was Olive Quist; but what if she were someone else, someone altogether unconnected with the violence in Hannah's studio? In that case, Martha was as certain as is possible in an uncertain world that her client would not be committing any offense by simply keeping quiet...

But none of this havering took into account the complicating factor of Martha's personal interest in bringing Hannah's assailant before the bar of justice...

When confused, gather more facts.

Martha knew immediately that the plan forming in her mind was not ideal. First of all, it would entail some shading of the truth, possibly some outright lying. Under the circumstances, this prospect did not trouble her unduly; she had already consented to something of the sort in her conversation with Sharpman about the Maya Angelou book. A more serious risk was the possibility of tainting a witness's testimony. And if Sharpman had already confronted Olive Quist with the Maya Angelou book, the plan would be sunk before it was launched.

One could not conduct one's life entirely without risk. She said, "I'd like to suggest an experiment."

Florence Appleton's face became alert. Such, thought Martha, might have been the expression with which the math teacher had awaited a bright student's recitation.

Martha said, "If someone were to appear in the same place while you were looking out the same window, do you think you would know if it was the same woman?"

Miss Appleton's gaze did not waver. "Do you know who she is?"

"I don't *know*," said Martha, "but I know someone who, at least superficially, meets the description."

Miss Appleton tapped her lips with her folded hands. "I could try," she said.

"That's all one can ask."

"And if she is the same woman, I will have to tell the police."

"Probably. But you would be in a position to provide them with something they want."

"Yes, I see."

"And you would not be left to deal with them on your own."

"You would go with me?"

"I would rather refer you to someone with more experience in such dealings. If this experiment indicates that your information will help the investigation, I will call a lawyer I know who specializes in these matters." She looked at her watch. It was five-thirty. "If you're willing, I'd like to try this experiment as soon as possible. Possibly this evening, if I can persuade the person I have in mind to show up."

Florence Appleton's lips tightened; now she might have been contemplating how to discipline a difficult student. But after a moment she nodded and said, "Yes, I'll try." The difficult student, Martha surmised, had been Florence Appleton herself.

THE CONSULTATION OVER, Martha descended the stairs and pushed out through the navy-blue steel door to the street. As long as she was in Williamsburg, there was something else she should be doing.

Oh, yes, the locksmith. The horse was out of the barn, of course, but Kent Reed's keys were still missing, and plenty of damage could still be done.

She reconnoitered a bit and found an open shop about a quarter of a block past Florence Appleton's building. Layers of flyers and posters were taped to its windows, nearly obliterating the view of the interior; they sought or offered all manner of necessities: apartments, studio space, roommates, in-line skates, baby-sitters, copy services, dog walkers, bicycles, expert photography of art objects…

Here, she thought, she should be able to obtain reliable advice.

She went in.

The place was a salad bar, almost elaborate enough to be called a vegetarian deli. Six small round tables and a collection of bentwood chairs crowded the front; a refrigerated glass case held bins of salad and puddings; a vertical cooler held bottles of juices and waters. A heavy, half-bald man was sitting slumped on a stool behind the cash register, conversing with four customers at one of the tables.

The chatter broke off when Martha entered. The counterman adjusted his posture and said, "Help you?"

Martha requested a bottle of cranberry juice and asked about locksmiths.

"Scottie's Hardware," said the counterman. "Across the street and two blocks up." He slid off his stool, took a bottle from the cooler, and set it on the counter next to a pile of eight-by-ten flyers announcing, in large multicolored type on black card stock, something called Color.

Martha took out her pocket notebook and wrote down *Scottie's Hardware*. "I don't suppose they'd be open now," she said.

"He's closed Sundays, but he opens up around eight in the morning. You new in the area?"

"I'm helping a friend. Perhaps you know Hannah Gold?"

"Oh, Hannah, sure. Awful thing. How's she doing?"

"Improving."

"Good, glad to hear it. When I heard what happened, I couldn't believe it. The cops were in here the day after, asking if I saw anything unusual. Whatever that means. I mean, you know, in this neighborhood a drive-by shooting would be unusual, but face it, artists? The unusual is usual, if you know what I mean. I close at nine, so I couldn't help them. Did they find out anything yet?"

"I'm afraid I'm not in their confidence."

"Where is she?" asked one of the customers. He was a man of about forty with ponytailed hair that must have been carroty when he was younger. Martha remembered seeing him at the reception. He was with the same short, chunky Asian woman. "I talked to her at the hospital a couple of days ago," he said, "but when I called today her number didn't answer. Did they move her or something?"

His concern seemed genuine, but all Martha was prepared to say was, "She has been discharged into the care of friends."

"She's out? Great. Do you have a number?"

"It isn't being given out."

His eyebrows rose. "You mean somebody's after *Hannah?*"

"Well, she was attacked."

"I thought that was just because she walked in on the dirty work."

"I don't think it's altogether clear what went on," said Martha.

"Death and destruction," he said. "Vandals, Goths and Visigoths. Disgusting."

"Wendy was in the other day," said the counterman. "Wendy Kahane, used to work for Hannah? She said she's restoring the piece."

Martha said, "I believe that's right." Evasion was beginning to come naturally.

"Is Hannah going to be home by Tuesday?" the Asian woman asked.

"I don't know," Martha said. "Is there something she should be doing?"

"She was going to come to Ian's new film." *Eye-an,* she pronounced it, with a long *I*.

The man with the ponytail said, "Hey, listen, why don't you come too? Even if she can't." He must be Ian. *Eye-an.* "Todd, give her a flyer."

The counterman, who must be Todd, took one of the black posters from the pile and handed it to Martha.

COLOR
A New Ian Rosenbaum Film

Premiere Showing
ALSO preview of work in progress
8:00 p.m., Tuesday, May 25, Wong Gallery

"Thank you," Martha said. "I'll try to attend." Thinking that she might even mean it, she added the flyer to the burden in her handbag and picked up the bottle of juice.

"If you talk to her," Ian said, "tell her Ian was asking."

"Amy, too," said the woman with him. "Tell her all of us."

THE ANSWERING MACHINE was blinking. Martha ignored it. She put the bottle of juice in the refrigerator, went into the bedroom, and before second thoughts could assail her, punched in the number Olive Quist had scribbled on her notepad.

Olive answered. Martha identified herself. Olive said, "Yes, okay."

Martha said, "I have had second thoughts about that matter we were discussing."

"The book? It's okay, we can talk. He's over at the gallery. What's the problem?"

"I have realized that since the book isn't my property, it would be inappropriate for me to remove it. However—"

"Oh, *please*."

"*However...*" Martha repeated, and succeeded in quieting Olive.

"However," Martha said more peaceably, "I am willing to accompany you to the premises and let you look for it yourself."

She hoped Olive would not examine too closely the basic illogic of this position.

"Oh." Evidently Olive was not in an analytic frame of mind, for all she said was, "Yes. Yes, okay."

"And it would be wise to do this as promptly as possible. Could you meet me there this evening?"

Another pause. "Okay. Give me about—oh, an hour? The tunnel may be bad."

Tunnel, to anyone living in New Jersey, meant one or the other of those perpetual bottlenecks, the Lincoln or the Holland.

Olive would be driving.

Martha had long ago concluded that if the deity in charge of the metropolitan Northeast had intended for Martha Jenkins Patterson to negotiate gridlock at the wheel of a motor vehicle, He, She, or It would not have created subways and taxis. Feasible rail connections ran under the Hudson between New Jersey and the city of New York; Martha had not even considered the possibility that Olive would be driving.

So be it. "An hour it is," she said. "There is a salad bar around the corner from the studio. We could meet there."

Olive said, "Oh, let's just meet at the studio."

The studio, of course, was out of Florence Appleton's line of sight. "That little street will be deserted," Martha improvised. "If I'm delayed, you shouldn't have to wait out there."

"No problem. If it doesn't look okay, I'll lock myself in the car."

"And if I get there first?"

Olive's impatience returned. "You're the one with the keys. Just go on in and I'll ring the bell."

The improvisation was becoming more elaborate than Martha had anticipated. She sighed as audibly as she could and forced a note of unease into her voice. "I'm sorry," she said. "The fact is, with everything that has happened, the studio gives me the creeps. I'd—I'd just rather not be there alone." That whining *just* was hard to manage.

But it served its purpose. "Oh, all right," said Olive. "Tell me where the salad bar is."

FLORENCE APPLETON answered the first ring.

"Assuming all goes according to plan," Martha said, "the woman I spoke of should be passing by at some time after seven-fifteen. I'm sorry I can't be more precise about the time."

"I understand. I will be watching."

LIGHT STILL LINGERED in the wide-open sky when Martha ascended yet again into the low-rise environment of northern Williamsburg. The situation was probably not ideal for identifying someone previously seen by streetlight. It would have to do.

As she was passing Florence Appleton's building on the way to the salad bar, she heard a honk from some distance up the street. The same sound in Manhattan would not have entered her consciousness, but here in Williamsburg on a quiet Sunday evening, it attracted her attention.

Olive was beckoning from the driver's window of an old black van parked across the street and several doors up. Martha let two northbound cars and a southbound van pass, then crossed.

"Get in," Olive said. "I'll drive you over."

There was no way Florence Appleton could see Olive inside the van from that distance. Martha said, "Why don't we walk? You don't want to give up your parking place."

"There'll be plenty of room on Hannah's street."

"But it's one-way. You'd have to drive four blocks, and it's only half a block on foot. We'll do better walking. And," Martha added in mild desperation, "it's such a nice evening." She stepped back as if in no doubt that Olive would comply.

Whether it was Martha's determination that prevailed, or

merely some early acculturation involving respect for advanced age, Olive complied. She said, "Oh, well," climbed out, and locked the van.

Having achieved that much, however, Martha was for some reason unable to maneuver Olive to the outside of the sidewalk. Side by side they walked back toward the intersection with Hannah's street, on the opposite side of Bedford Avenue from Florence Appleton's building, with Martha on the street side, unwillingly shielding Olive from those second-floor windows in the front of Florence Appleton's apartment. Martha maintained a babble about the delightfulness of the May weather while she considered further maneuvers. Simulating an interest in a window display was not feasible: the storefronts they were passing were dark and locked, and even if open, would have presented nothing of even remotely plausible interest; they ran to useful, dull enterprises such as a dry cleaner, a coin laundry, and a realtor-cum-law-office. The salad bar across the street was open and alight, but nothing was to be gained by enticing a reluctant Olive to that side of the street.

They were within about fifty feet of the intersection, just opposite Miss Appleton's building, when Martha came up with a plausible ruse. She halted, muttered, "Oh, bother, I seem to have stepped in something," and pawed at the sidewalk with her left foot.

Rather than walk on without her, Olive stopped.

Martha stepped over to the curb, leaving Olive open to the view from across the street, and began vigorously scraping her shoe sole on the edge of the curb. After enacting this charade for several seconds, she took a step or two; then, with full awareness of the double entendre, said, "That should do it," and proceeded with Olive to the corner, where they turned, crossed Bedford Avenue, and walked down the deserted street to Hannah's place.

THE MAQUETTE'S pedestal stood empty; the police had removed the ruins. Olive must have been questioned about the second destruction, but neither of them mentioned it, and the absence of comment loomed like the proverbial elephant in the room. Martha avoided looking at the traces of blood on the floor outside Kent Reed's apartment. She unlocked the door, found the light switch, and flicked it on.

"Do you know where he might have kept the book?" she asked.

"I've never been in here," said Olive. The fact obviously aggrieved her.

"His books are by the computer," said Martha.

SHE WAITED QUIETLY in one of the kitchen chairs while Olive searched. Since the book had been removed to an NYPD evidence room, Olive did not, of course, find it. Failing to discover it among the computer manuals and assorted paperbacks, she went on to rummage through drawers; she undid the twisties on Henry Reed's plastic bags and pawed through the clothes; she came back to the front and searched the kitchen cupboards. She even opened the refrigerator. It smelled faintly of mildew. Perhaps Martha should arrange to have the place cleaned before Hannah returned.

Olive slammed the refrigerator shut and said, "Shit."

Martha said, "His father may have taken it. I can get you his address if you like."

"Oh," said Olive. "No, don't bother. If it's his father, that's cool. Come on, I'll drive you home."

THE WILLIAMSBURG BRIDGE was congested. The subway would have been faster and Martha would rather have been spared any more of Olive's company; but she was tired of combat and merely asked Olive to drop her off at her neighborhood Chinese takeout.

Up in her apartment, the fragrance of lemon chicken penetrating the carrying bag, she found the answering machine still blinking; a second message had joined the first. She set her dinner on the counter, filled the teakettle and set it on the stove, went back to the living room and punched Play.

The first message was from Wendy; three words: "Martha, call me!"

The second message was from Florence Appleton; she said, "Mrs. Patterson, I'm sorry I can't be of help. I cannot say that I recognized the young woman who was with you this evening."

SIXTEEN

To Do

CLIENTS LIED. Some, Martha's father had been given to remarking, lied smart and some lied stupid, but by and large, at one time or another, almost all of them lied.

Was this one lying? She said she had prayed for guidance. Had the celestial counselor assigned to the Florence Appleton case favored self-preservation over truthfulness?

Martha considered her wording of the message. ''I cannot say I recognized...'' Which could mean *she was not the one I saw that night,* but could equally be construed as *I couldn't tell whether she was,* or even *I'm not going to tell you.* Not an outright lie; an equivocation.

In any case, Martha's immediate reaction was relief. The client's lie, or equivocation, or whatever it was, made it unnecessary to continue balancing her professional obligation against her personal outrage. She should not have allowed herself to be drawn into that ambiguous encounter, part tea party, part consultation; fortunately, the client's own statement had rescued her from the consequences of that ambiguity.

Annoyance didn't strike until she was transferring her dinner from the takeout containers to a plate. If Miss Appleton didn't mean to carry through, why had she gone to the trouble of consulting Martha in the first place? Why couldn't she have kept her observations to herself from the start, and spared Martha the effort of enacting that farce with Olive Quist?

The fragrance of lemon chicken calmed her. Perhaps, she

thought, the delay wasn't altogether the client's fault. The celestial traffic in prayers was doubtless heavy; perhaps the reply to Florence Appleton's had simply been slow to come through. And a careful review of the events of the day reassured her that, no matter how her personal interest might conflict with her client's, she had given that client no harmful advice.

She hit the Delete button on her answering machine and concentrated her attention on her dinner. It wasn't until she had turned out her bedside lamp and pulled up the covers that it occurred to her that perhaps Florence Appleton had *not* equivocated. Perhaps the dithering woman had not been Olive Quist.

MARTHA AWOKE Monday morning with a to-do list dominating her consciousness. Her current research project was pushing against a deadline; and she must call the locksmith; and she still owed Florence Appleton a nonlegal service, quite unconnected to the equivocally unidentified dithering woman.

She finished breakfast, rinsed her plate and juice glass and propped them in the dish rack in the sink, carried her half-empty teacup into her study, and turned on her computer. She had completed the research and the introductory paragraphs of her memorandum; what remained was the rest of the writing, printing the draft, proofreading, entering the corrections, making a backup disk, and e-mailing the product and her bill to the law firm.

By ten-thirty she had finished. She went to the kitchen to reward herself with a fresh cup of tea, carried it to the telephone, and made her first call.

Dr. Klaiman was out on his rounds. She added her name and number to the answering service's list.

Whenever she thought about it, which was as a rule only once a year when she underwent her annual physical examination, she realized that she didn't particularly like Herman Klaiman, M.D. But Dr. Klaiman had treated her, and Edwin before his death, with what seemed to be decent medical competence, and the amount of investigation entailed in comfortably establishing herself with some other M.D. had never seemed to be quite worth the effort.

She put in her next call.

Physicians had morning rounds; criminal-defense attorneys had trials. Brian Irish's secretary took Martha's name and number, but made no promises as to when he'd be free.

Directory assistance for Brooklyn provided the number for Scottie's Hardware. The locksmith was in. What kind of locks did she have now, he asked, and did she want the same kind or something else?

"An excellent question," she said. How stupid of her not to have thought of it. "I'll call you back."

No problem, said Scottie's locksmith.

Up in Putnam County, Hannah's hosts' answering machine picked up. Martha recited her name and number and hung up. The ball was now in everyone else's court. She carried what was left of her tea back to her computer and explored the Net.

By lunchtime she had accumulated a good deal of anecdotal material on the medical efficacy and harmlessness of smoked marijuana, not only for chemotherapy patients whose nausea resisted prescription drugs, but for a range of other severe maladies as well. It corroborated Florence Appleton's experience but didn't help with the problem of advising her.

The first return call came through while she was printing the most convincing of the entries. It was Dr. Klaiman, exuding bedside manner.

No, she assured him, she didn't need treatment; she needed information. Not for herself, for professional counseling. She was interested in the use of marijuana for treating chemotherapy induced nausea.

"Mm," said Dr. Klaiman.

"You're familiar with its use?"

"I've heard of some success with the extract, yes. I don't have the details at my fingertips; I'm not an oncologist. Marinol, I think it's called. If you'd like, I could look up the literature."

"I'm interested in smoked marijuana."

"So are a lot of people, but I wouldn't have expected you to be one of them."

"For medical use."

"So-called."

"You aren't convinced?"

"What I'm convinced of is that a bunch of overaged hippies are still trying to resurrect the sixties."

"Hasn't the American Medical Association gone on record in favor of legalizing its medical use?"

"The AMA isn't infallible. There's been no clinical testing to speak of, and with smoking, there's no way of calibrating the dosage. Self-medication is risky at the best of times. You really shouldn't even take aspirin without medical advice. A hallucinogenic drug . . . not on your life."

Hanging up, Martha moved the item *look for a new physician* up several places on her long-term to-do list.

Her eyes ached and her brain was fuzzy. Too much computer, too much frustration, too much indoors altogether. Let *them* wait for *her* for a change.

THE OUTDOORS was muggier than was ideal in late May, but this was New York, where ideal weather is in a class with Man Bites Dog. More briskly than she at first felt, Martha walked a couple of blocks across town to University Place and another couple of blocks down to the corner of Washington Square Park, where established trees and

fenced-off grass provided the illusion of coolness. For half
an hour she strode the paths among skaters and skateboarders and dog walkers, past chess players and bench loung-
ers, some of whom, for all she knew, might be drug dealers.
She paused to listen to a trumpet player blaring "When the
Saints Come Marching In." The hat on the ground in front
of him held a handful of quarters and a few dollar bills;
she added her own dollar and received a nod and an un-
scored riff. She bought a hot dog at a Sabrett wagon and
ate it sitting on the edge of the fountain. Finally she returned home. There were no messages on the answering
machine.

Chilled by the air-conditioning, she stripped and showered, and while she was dressing in fresh clothing, realized
that a social worker might serve her present purpose better
than an M.D. She went back to the phone and punched in
the number of the Welfare Advocates Organization.

The part-time administrative assistant was in; Sunny
Searle was at an all-day meeting in New York. (Meaning
Manhattan; in spite of a century of incorporation, Brooklyn,
to Brooklynites, is not New York. New York is that per-
ilous land beyond the East River.)

Again Martha left her name and number.

She had no sooner hung up than the phone rang. It was
Hannah. "Sorry," she said, sounding anything but, "we
were all working. Martha, bubbala, how are you?"

"As usual," Martha said. "How is it going?"

"Wonderful, wonderful. New ideas, new forms. The fabric we got is a different print so the piece adapts itself. I've
got a new armature. Paul knows a welder, so Stefan can go
back to whatever he was doing. Barbara's bringing the
cloth and the bear tomorrow. Oh, Martha, I wish you could
see it now. It's better, it sings a serenade, and those interior
renderings, those slicky, icky up-to-date computerized
things that look like plans for Disney World? They don't

match anymore. I'm rid of them and I'm drawing new ones. Everybody should have a piece broken up.''

"Assuming one is still able to meet the deadline.''

"Did *you* ever not meet a deadline?''

"I never got knocked in the head, and nobody ever destroyed my product.''

"Nobody's destroying this one. The product spends the day in my hands and the night in Paul and Nell's room. You saw Paul.''

"Just so. Hannah, I'm about to get the locks changed on your studio, and I need to know what kind you want.''

"The kind nobody else has keys to.''

"That's any kind, if you don't give out the keys. Do you want to replicate what you have or go to something new?''

"Questions, questions.''

"Should I take the locksmith's advice?''

"Who is it, Scottie's?''

"He was recommended by the man who runs the salad bar around the corner.''

"That's Todd. Yes, go to Scottie's and do what they say.''

"It shall be done. By the way, Ian and Amy and their friends send best wishes.''

"They were in Todd's?'' A sigh gusted down the phone line. "If I dared to stop working, I'd be so homesick I couldn't breathe. I was supposed to go to Ian's showing.''

"He invited me.''

"So go. Tell him I'm sorry.''

It had crossed Martha's mind, though not very seriously, to accept the invitation. "Will I like it?''

"Like? Who knows? Go find out.''

"He wanted a phone number for you. I told him it wasn't being given out.''

"Ian's all right.''

"But who knows whom he'd tell. It would be like giving out a key to the studio."

"Not if you told him—" Hannah broke off.

After a moment of silence, Martha said, "Hannah?"

"Hush. I'm remembering something."

Martha hushed.

"I've got it. I know where Kent's keys went."

"Where?"

"It was those stupid computer renderings. One of them got torn while he was putting it up—this was that morning, he was setting things up for the party—and he took the disk out to get a new print. My printer isn't big enough. So he went out to the copy shop, and when he came back he had the keys in his hand and he put them down on the computer desk while he was putting the disk away. The caterer found them, but he'd gone out again for something, and I said just drop them in the drawer for now, out of sight. I was going to get them out and give them to him, but I forgot all about them."

THE LOCKSMITH agreed to meet Martha at the studio at around five that afternoon, when he would install a system guaranteed to withstand anything short of a battering ram. For that kind of security, she'd need a steelworker.

Another trip to Williamsburg. Fine, she would look in the desk drawer for Kent Reed's keys. Changing the locks would remove the danger of leaving them at large, but finding them would remove a splinter from the mind.

And while she was at it, why not take Kent Reed's nude drawings, of which Hannah had agreed to assume custody, back to Hannah's apartment?

She got them out of the back of her closet. Henry Reed had wrapped them in one of his plastic trash bags. Curious to see how well her initial assessment held up, she unwrapped the bundle and laid the drawings on the dining table.

This was her first close look at them. There were five of them, meticulously detailed, almost photographic portraits of young female nudes of a variety of races and ethnicities. The one on top, of which she had already caught a glimpse, was a frontal view of a standing, full-bodied, dark-haired woman, so classically Mediterranean that she might have illustrated an olive-oil commercial. The next was of a small-breasted Asian, probably Chinese, sitting straight-backed on a wooden kitchen chair with her hands folded on top of her thin thighs. Next, a standard-issue pretty girl with tumbling hair, delicate lips, and wistful eyes, reclining on tangled sheets with one arm crooked under her head; after her, a thirtyish woman with a snub nose in a freckled Irish face, sitting on the edge of what was probably the same bed, staring defiantly into the face of the viewer. Last, a full-breasted, full-hipped black woman...

Olive.

Kent Reed had executed a nude drawing of Olive Quist.

Well, what did that prove? Martha had already assumed that Olive Quist and Kent Reed had been lovers. This nude drawing neither confirmed nor refuted that assumption: everyone with any knowledge of the art world knew that the artist-model relationship was often but not always a purely professional transaction, the model's body no more provocative than a vase in a still life.

Was there any point in showing this drawing to Sharp-man? Would failing to show it to him amount to withhold-ing evidence or obstructing justice or whatever it was for-mally called?

Martha shook her head. Actually shook it, with an abrupt back-and-forth motion that caused a little twinge behind her eyes. Her mind was waffling.

She knew the workings of her mind rather well. This

fussing was a surface disturbance, akin to the tsunami caused by a volcanic eruption on the ocean floor. Somewhere below the level of her consciousness, some unwelcome realization was struggling to rise to the surface.

She also knew that any conscious attempt to bring this perception up into the light of consciousness would simply drive it deeper into concealment. It would come out on its own or not at all.

Back to the question: should she show this drawing to Sharpman?

Even the answer to that essentially rational question eluded her. She rewrapped the drawings and stowed them back in the closet.

SEVENTEEN

The Wrong One

"IT'S THE WRONG ONE!"

The cry woke her, her own cry, wrenched from her own throat so fiercely that her throat ached with the effort.

Slivers of daylight were slicing through the venetian blinds. She found her glasses and slipped them on. Her bedside clock said 6:00 a.m. As sleep slid away, she clutched at the fading memory of the dream.

It had started like the one she'd had the other night, the one about the demand to explain a key suspended in inky air, but this time she had rebelled, insisting in an uncharacteristic shout that it was *the wrong one!*

It was curious, this sense of *wrongness*. It echoed something she had felt yesterday afternoon on the way to Hannah's studio to admit the locksmith. Turning into Hannah's street on her walk from the subway, she had, of course, passed the side of Florence Appleton's building. And as she had glanced across the intersection toward the spot where, on Sunday evening, she had stopped and pretended to remove nonexistent chewing gum from her shoe sole, she had been fleetingly aware of that sense of *wrongness* which had now resurfaced in her dream. The sensation had been distinct enough to make her wonder if she had chosen the wrong spot for her performance—to wonder if that location would not, in fact, give Florence Appleton a clear view of Olive.

But of course, there was nothing wrong with the location; the place where she had stopped, and caused Olive Quist to stop, was squarely in the line of sight from Florence Appleton's windows.

So what *was* wrong?

And where were Kent Reed's keys?

THE LOCKSMITH had proved to be an affable, middle-aged man with "Lennie" stitched on the pocket of his khaki shirt. Martha had accepted all his suggestions and left him to his drilling and clattering while she searched the drawers of the computer desk.

She had found no keys.

She had expanded her search to the drawers in the sewing machine stands, where she had found pins, thimbles, needles, spools of thread, packets of elastic and bindings and trimmings, a box of loose buttons—but no keys. In a wide drawer under the top of the cutting table she had found shears, dress patterns, and more pins, but no keys. She had prowled the studio looking for other drawers, found none, and at last had pulled out the chair in front of the computer and sat down to wait.

Presently tools had clattered up front and the locksmith had called "Okay." She had dropped the new keys he gave her into her handbag and headed for home.

But she had not taken the usual route back to the Bedford Avenue station on the L line. She couldn't have said exactly why; perhaps annoyance at Florence Appleton had made her reluctant to walk past the client's apartment building yet again; or maybe it had something to do with that obscure sense of *wrongness* that had assailed her on the way to Hannah's place, or maybe it was both or neither. Whatever the reason, after setting the alarm and locking the new locks, she had not headed back up Hannah's street to Bedford Avenue, but had instead gone down to the other end of the block and proceeded along a street that ran parallel

to the avenue, turning into the street with the subway entrance from the east instead of the west.

All that this inexplicable choice of route had achieved
was to lengthen her walk by about three-quarters of a block,
and demonstrate that the street intersecting Hannah's at the
bottom of the block was extraordinarily dull, lined almost
entirely by the brick-faced sides of the warehouses that
faced on Hannah's street and those that ran parallel to it.

FULLY AWAKE NOW, she wondered if Hannah might have
been experiencing a false memory.

One could pursue that notion later. Right now, she would
assume *arguendo* (a Latinate legalism insisted on by the
senior partner of her old firm, in spite of the fact that *for
the purpose of argument* was both idiomatic and unambig-
uous…)

Waffling again. She hauled her mind back.

For the purpose of argument, assume that the keys had
been put in the desk drawer as Hannah remembered. Then
what? It was possible, of course, that Kent Reed had retrieved them from the drawer at some time during the evening; but if he had, what had he done with them? They
hadn't been found on his body and Martha was prepared
to take her oath that they weren't in his apartment. Could
he have loaned them to his current lover?

Might one of those nude drawings be a portrait of the
current lover? *Was* there a current lover?

Again Martha dragged her mind back.

She must tell Sharpman about the keys in—actually, *not*
in—the drawer. No, that was Hannah's memory. It was
Hannah who must tell Sharpman. She, Martha, must tell
Hannah to tell Sharpman…

Too much was going on. If she wasn't careful, she was
going to forget something of importance, and she no longer
had a secretary to remind her. Hadn't had a secretary for

years and still missed the service. She went into her study and checked her calendar.

She had forgotten something: the elder-law seminar at five o'clock, the last, thank goodness, until next fall. This one was in Astoria, a neighborhood of the borough of Queens that, also thank goodness, presented many of the same issues as last week's in southern Brooklyn. Just now, getting up a new presentation would be an unwelcome challenge to her power of concentration.

She went back into the bedroom and in order not to forget again, set the alarm for 4:00 p.m.

IN THE MIDDLE OF the morning Sunny Searle returned Martha's call. It took a moment to disentangle her mind from the thickets of the parol evidence rule (a contracts issue that had nothing to do with early release from incarceration). What had she wanted from Sunny?

Oh, yes.

"What, if anything, do you know about the medical use of marijuana?" she asked.

"You aren't on a car phone, are you?" asked Sunny.

"No, I'm at home. Is the connection that bad?"

"No, it's fine. I just don't want to be overheard. Actually, I was joking. Mostly. What I know about medical marijuana is that the law sucks."

"Let me refine my question. Do you know of any legal way to obtain the substance for medical use? I have a client with a need."

"What's the medical problem?"

"Chemotherapy."

"Oh, God, yes. Hold on a minute."

Martha held on. Over the phone she heard a quiet click that might have been the sound of a door closing, and then the muted rustle of the phone being picked up again.

"There's a buyers' club," Sunny said.

"Is it legal?" asked Martha.

"Almost. It sure beats the street."

"Are you free to tell me about it?"

"Some. There's a system of cutouts. What I do is give the client the phone number of a service agency. If the client sounds legit, they give out another phone number, and so on, and after enough of that, eventually the client learns where to go and when to go there to make a purchase. The times and places move around."

"For obvious reasons. Still, I should think law enforcement could find its way through the system."

"I think it's Don't ask, don't tell. For now, anyway. The patient has to bring a doctor's letter verifying medical need, and they only sell a week's supply at a time. Nobody gets enough to bring in their friends and party."

"And if the physician is averse to writing the M word?"

"Switch doctors."

"That may not be easy."

"Tell me about it. It isn't necessary to specify the medication. Just describing the medical condition is enough. Trust me, those people know chemotherapy. Have your client call me. I'll give her—him? Don't answer that—I'll give your client the first phone number in the chain, and if the doctor's a problem, I can provide some referrals. Tell the client to mention your name so I'll know it's the one."

"Thank you very much, Sunny."

"Glad to help as long as I can. D.A.s are elected, so there's always the risk it could come undone after the next election."

FLORENCE APPLETON thanked Martha for the buyers' club information in such a reserved tone that Martha wondered if she would actually go through the process.

Neither of them mentioned the lurking woman.

Perhaps, after all, Florence Appleton hadn't lied or

equivocated. Perhaps Olive Quist hadn't been the lurking woman. Perhaps it was Olive who was *the wrong one*. Or perhaps Miss Appleton really couldn't tell.

IN MIDAFTERNOON, Brian Irish returned her call, trumpeting "Martha Patterson! A voice out of the past," in the commanding tenor she had not heard for upwards of three years. "How've you been? Are you mixed up in criminal activity again?"

She laughed. "Do you have time for a hypothetical or must you rush back to court?"

"We closed this morning and the judge's instructions won't go to the jury until tomorrow. Let's hear your hypothetical."

"Suppose that a cancer patient undergoing chemotherapy suffers debilitating nausea which does not respond to the standard medications, including that marijuana extract that has been approved by the FDA."

"Please don't tell me the NYPD has busted somebody for using medical grass."

"No, but she's worried. Someone close to her has been obtaining the item for her."

"Where is this taking place?"

"Brooklyn, and probably Manhattan."

"Any priors?"

"For the patient, I'd say no. For the other person, I don't know. Probably not. I'm told she works for a brokerage firm."

"The patient giving any of it away or selling it?"

"Not to my knowledge."

"The odds against any trouble are about equal to hitting a twelve-million-buck lottery."

"But if she just happened to be holding the winning ticket?"

"If lightning strikes? For the patient, we're talking violation, maximum penalty a hundred-dollar fine, most likely suspended. For the one procuring it for her, we're talking misdemeanor, what class depending on the amount. Possibly suspended, too, but less probable. Why doesn't she try a buyers' club? There's one operating in the city.''

''She has a number.''

''Tell her to use it. And Martha—if they bust her, send her to me. I owe the bar association some pro bono time.''

''Actually,'' Martha said, ''there's more to it than that.''

Brian Irish laughed. ''Thought so.''

''The patient may have witnessed something that may bear on a criminal investigation.''

''A lot of *mays* in that. What kind of investigation? Narcotics?''

''Homicide.''

''Oh ho.''

''Just so. She wants to be a good citizen, but she's afraid that if she goes to the police with the information…''

''Say no more. Was she smoking the stuff at the time, or had she recently been smoking it?''

''She'd smoked one joint that afternoon, just prior to receiving chemotherapy. The event she witnessed was a good deal later, around eleven-thirty at night. She was looking out her window watching for the person who was bringing her an additional supply.''

''You're advising her?''

''I'm trying to.''

''It's too bad she hasn't forgotten she saw anything.''

Martha took a moment to untangle that. When she understood what he was not quite advising, she said, ''You're a defense attorney, of course.''

''A prosecutor would hate it, too. Think of the credibility problems. Sick and stoned? The defense would eat her alive on cross.''

''Only if they found out about the medication.''

"You think they wouldn't? A homicide witness? Any defense attorney that didn't dig out that shit would be committing malpractice."

So, SHE THOUGHT as she hung up, Florence Appleton's celestial counselor was advising her to make the safe choice. If it was a choice and not the truth.

In the bedroom, the alarm buzzed.

What on earth…oh. It was time to go.

EIGHTEEN

Work in Progress

NOW THAT tax season was over, Joe had evidently increased his workout time. His face seemed more defined and the family resemblance to that photograph of his daughter—the daughter, now dead, whose interest in art, according to Eileen, had triggered Joe's—was more evident.

She wondered whether his interest in art was holding up after Saturday, or if he had linked Hannah's fabric fantasies with the visceral assault of *The Body of the Work* and was now experiencing revulsion by association?

Well, at least the artist would be gratified.

She quelled her inclination to snicker. "Last Friday when we were at Hannah's studio," she asked as their shared taxi carried them toward the Fifty-ninth Street Bridge, "did you happen to notice a set of keys in the desk where you were working?"

"Keys?" Joe rubbed his nose. "I don't remember seeing any. Not on top, I'm sure. I don't think I opened any drawers."

"When you were looking for a disk?"

"Oh, you're right. I did open a couple of drawers, didn't I? I don't recall seeing any keys, but that doesn't mean they weren't there. Keys can slip under things. Is it important?"

Apparently he hadn't heard. "Someone got into the studio and destroyed the maquette again."

"Good God! How is Hannah taking that?"

"Furiously."

"I should think so. Will there be time to reconstruct it?"

"She thinks so. The reason I asked if you'd seen the keys is that the doors hadn't been forced, and Hannah has remembered seeing someone put Kent Reed's keys into a drawer of that desk just before the reception."

"Oh. Yes, I see." A silence. "I wish I could help." Another silence. "His wife was at the studio that afternoon, wasn't she?"

There was no need to ask whose wife he meant.

BY HALF PAST SIX, the groups at the refreshment table had dispersed. Martha was glad to be done.

She would, in fact, like to be done with everything that had been occupying her for the past week. She hadn't had a proper weekend; she wanted entertainment. Jane Austen was all very well, as was the song recital she would be attending with friends next Sunday; but these pleasures were predictable and the recital was some days in the future. Like a three-year-old, Martha wanted to be entertained *right now;* unlike the three-year-old, she wanted to be entertained by something unpredictable...

She groped in her handbag for the black poster she had acquired in Todd's vegetarian deli.

Color, Ian Rosenbaum's new film, would be shown at 8:00 p.m. on Tuesday, May 26. Today was Tuesday, May 26.

Color?

Yet another documentary exploring Race in America?

Perhaps the predictability of *Persuasion* was to be preferred after all.

But the poster also mentioned work in progress. Work in progress, by definition, is unpredictable.

She declined Joe's offer to share a taxi back to Manhattan, found a restaurant down the street, dined on Greek salad and hummus and falafel with a glass of retsina as capacious as a water tumbler, and flagged a cab of her own.

THE WONG GALLERY was a narrow storefront up five steep concrete steps from the street. Just inside the open door, on a chest-high parapet that divided the business area of the gallery to the left from the exhibition space on the right, stood a stack of plastic wineglasses, a somewhat depleted bowl of Pepperidge Farm Goldfish, a barely tapped liter of white grape juice, and three half-empty bottles of wine: red, rosé, and white. Ranks of folding chairs in the center of the room faced a projection screen on the back wall. Twenty or so people in the room clustered around the edges, largely concealing a display of large, unframed, rather crudely executed oil paintings. Martha identified Ian's mahogany ponytail about halfway back.

As she was pouring herself a glass of grape juice, the short, chunky Asian woman she had previously seen with Ian detached herself from the nearest group. "Welcome," she said. "I'm Amy Wong. I know you're Hannah's friend, but I've lost your name…"

"I'm Martha—" Martha was beginning when a dumpy, wild-haired figure elbowed her way forward crying, "Martha!" Wendy Kahane had come to Ian Rosenbaum's show.

There was no reason to be surprised; during her years of working for Hannah, Wendy had come to know a good portion of the Williamsburg art colony.

"Listen, you." She planted her fists on her hips and demanded, "Where the hell is Hannah and what's happening with *Love?*"

Oh, dear. This was what came of failing to return phone calls. Amy nodded to Martha and moved off, and Martha said, "I'm sorry. Didn't Barbara Turcotte call you?"

"Barbara." If the soft syllables of the word had permitted it to sound like a snort, that's what it would have

sounded like. "Yes, *Barbara* called me. *Barbara* said somebody busted up *Love* again and I'd have to start all over, and then *Barbara* called back and said never mind, all she needed was the animal and the altar cloth. The end, period. Not one word more. What the hell is going on? And don't tell me to ask *Barbara.*"

"Hannah decided to do it herself."

That checked the flow. "Oh." Wendy closed her mouth, opened it, closed it, and finally said, "Oh," again.

"She means nothing personal," Martha said.

"Yes. No, that's Hannah. She's feeling that good?"

"She would rather work than not."

"That's Hannah. Where is she?"

"She's been discharged."

"Oh, come on, the hospital told me that much. Where is she? Her phone isn't answering at home."

"Nobody knows."

"Come on. Not even you?"

Martha looked deliberately around the room and back at Wendy. "It's a matter of security," she said quietly.

"Oh." Wendy drew in a breath and let out a gust. "Well, is she okay?"

"Her doctor agreed to her discharge."

"Well, that's a relief. I wouldn't put it past Hannah to just go off on her own. But *where?* She's got to be *some-where.*"

"Wendy," said Martha.

"You know," Wendy said. "You know and you're not telling."

Silence.

Wendy sighed. "Oh, well. Yeah, all right, I guess I'll go on speaking to you. Just so she's okay."

BY THE TIME Ian announced loudly that the show was about to begin and would they all please sit down, Wendy had introduced Martha to nearly everyone in the room. Several minutes of shuffling and scraping ensued. Presently everyone was seated, Ian took his place at a projector behind the chairs, and Amy Wong drew blackout curtains across the storefront windows and switched off the lights.

COLOR'S SUBJECT WAS evidently *color* in its primary dictionary sense, and its intention seemed be to ravish the eye. It opened silently with a brilliant image of a rainbow that filled the screen. Presently the letters *C, O, L, O, R* appeared in white, one at a time, within the arc. The rainbow dissolved into an unbroken field of blue, which held for about ten seconds; then the screen abruptly went black. After about two seconds it filled once more with color: a series of blurrily mottled pastels—pink, lime green, pale yellow, robin's-egg blue, peach, lavender—each dissolving into the next, all of them shimmering with an effect rather like that of a windswept wheat field. Then they separated into bands of different colors, which shifted from horizontal to diagonal to vertical, and then re-formed into shifting colored blobs.

The experience was as engrossing as watching fireworks, as hypnotic as gazing at reflections on rippled water.

And as the images shifted and flickered, the sound began. At first it was no more than a rustle at the threshold of hearing. As the colors shifted, it became the sound of rain falling, softly and then gradually more insistent. As the sound strengthened, the colors intensified to the pure hues of oil paint squeezed directly from tubes: fire-engine red, strong yellow, blazing orange, royal blue, deep purple. Then the purple grew dull and duller still, until it was a field of gray, plain at first, then mottled with black. As it changed, the sound grew into lashing wind and driving rain.

Then the camera drew back until the gray-and-black field was revealed to be a towering thunderhead in a stormy sky.

That image held for a few seconds; then, with a crack so loud that the room seemed to shake, a fork of lightning split the cloud and dissolved it into grainy gray blur that recoalesced slowly into an image, blurry at first but gradually sharpening until it was identifiable as a black-and-white photograph of a street scene at night: a cluster of uniformed police gathered, with nightsticks raised, around a recumbent figure at their feet.

A still from the Rodney King video.

Race in America after all.

The screen went dark, the lights came up, and the room came alive with the susurration of many exhalations. Voices murmured things like *awesome* and *serious, man.* Martha's arms prickled with the goosebumps raised by effective theater.

Was it, though, perhaps a bit obvious? If the question occurred to anyone else, it was not voiced in Martha's hearing. And did it matter? Good theater is not achieved every day.

IAN FIDDLED with the projector; people milled around; Martha stood and stretched cramped muscles; Wendy went for more wine. Presently everyone sat down again and the room was darkened and Ian, having warned them that the work he was about to show them existed only in the roughest of cuts, was back at the projector.

This one had been filmed in black and white, out of doors in a deserted street on a rainy night, illuminated, apparently, only by streetlights. It had been shot from a stationary camera; the angle of view was wide enough to take in both sides of the street, from a high chain-link fence on the left to the brick side wall of a building on the right.

There was no sound; in a running commentary from beside the projector, Ian said he hadn't yet decided exactly what sound to dub in, or even if he wanted sound at all.

There was an actor, however: Ian himself. He first appeared far away down the deserted street, a tiny figure dressed in jeans and a sweatshirt, dancing, his feet in white running shoes moving in and out of the reflections on the wet pavement. Far away though he was, the intensity of his movements dominated the screen, twirling, leaping, bowing forward till his hair, free of the ponytail, spread on the wet pavement, then arching backward, flinging his arms out and up. A jerkiness in the projection gave his movements an almost surreal quality.

An abrupt cut chopped off the dance in mid-leap and yanked Ian's far-off dancing figure forward into the middle distance. The sweatshirt had vanished; a T-shirt exposed muscular arms. Another sudden cut and he was closer, the T-shirt gone, his chest bare. Cut: closer yet, no clothing but jockey shorts. Deep in the background, a black figure, barely visible, walked along the sidewalk that bordered the brick wall. Cut: sidewalk empty, frontally nude dancer filling the screen...

Black-out.

NINETEEN

Coffee Talk

MOST OF the audience stayed to finish the wine and argue about the camera work, lighting, deeper significance, and future direction of the work in progress. In one corner of the gallery, Martha heard Freud invoked, dismissed, rehabilitated, and revilified; in another, Ian was describing an electronic device that enabled him to be both cameraman and actor. Someone mentioned *Ego*. Ian laughed. The discussion turned to frames-per-second. Martha gathered that his choice was unusual and had something to do with his ability to light the film by streetlight, as well as with the jerkiness of the projection, which Martha discovered was intentional.

After about twenty minutes of this, she was ready to leave technique and Deeper Meanings to the young and didactic. She complimented Ian on the theatrical power of his work and headed for the subway.

Wendy caught up before she had gone fifty yards. "Okay, now," she demanded, "where's Hannah?"

Martha hesitated.

"Come on," Wendy urged, "nobody's listening."

True, but irrelevant. "Hannah is in a safe house," Martha said.

"A *safe house?* Where?"

"If one told, it wouldn't be safe, would it?"

"Martha, come on, I want to help. She can't redo the whole thing by herself. Where is she? I'll cancel my students—"

"Wendy, no. I'm sorry, but no."

"Are you saying she doesn't trust me? Who does she think I'd tell?"

"Intentionally? Nobody, of course. But things slip out in conversation."

Silence. Then, "You mean Olive."

Olive. Again. Unavoidable.

A conversation with Wendy was in order. But not on the street, and not without something to counteract Martha's sense that her brain was filled with feathers. That retsina glass had been very large. "Is there anything like a coffee-house around here?" she asked.

Of course there was. It was less than a block away, a storefront about the size of Todd's salad bar up the street from Florence Appleton's building. It was more of a bakery than a coffeehouse, but it was equipped with an espresso machine, four little round tables, a scattering of chairs, and rather loud ambient music.

The rearmost table was taken, but the couple occupying it were so absorbed in each other—hands clasped on top of the table, foreheads nearly touching—that even without the music, nothing Martha and Wendy might say was likely to penetrate their trance. All the same, when they had picked up their steaming cups at the counter, Martha steered Wendy to the table just inside the door, farthest from the absorbed couple, and kept her voice low when she asked, "I'll be blunt. Were Olive and Kent having..." Then she stumbled; perhaps *affair* was an outdated expression for an outdated concept. But she knew no other, and after that stumble, she finished as she had intended: "...having an affair?"

Wendy seemed to have no trouble with word or concept, nor did the invitation to gossip seem to give her trouble. "You have to ask?" she said.

"I like to check the accuracy of my conjectures. Was it generally known?"

"Well, she didn't exactly go on talk shows, but anybody with eyes and ears could tell."

"Did Hannah know?"

"What do you think? Hannah has eyes and ears."

"How did she come to hire Kent?"

"That's a good question. When I quit—" Wendy broke off, sighed, picked up the long spoon, and stirred her cappuccino. She laid the spoon on the table and picked up the tall cup, tasted the contents, put down the cup, and finally said, "It's stupid to feel guilty. I couldn't know what would happen. What it was, I got this teaching offer, right around the corner in Hoboken. It didn't pay any worse than Hannah, and it left more time for my own work…"

Hannah had already told Martha all that.

"The really tricky part of the maquette was finished, so I wouldn't be really leaving her in the lurch or anything."

Hannah had assured Martha of that as well.

"So I gave notice, and it turned out Kent was leaving Dennie, he *said* to go into computer work, and he came around to Hannah and said he'd heard I was leaving and could she use him temporarily until an offer came through—"

Martha held up her hand, palm out. "Wait a minute."

Wendy stopped.

"Leaving Dennie?"

"He was Dennie's assistant. You didn't know?"

"I didn't. I see."

"Yeah, that's how it started. Kent can't—couldn't keep his hands off an attached woman. I mean, did you see how he was hitting on Amy at *Love*'s reception?"

"She didn't appear to be responsive," said Martha.

"I think that just made it more of a challenge."

"Did Ian mind?"

"Who knows. I don't think so, but who knows. Anyway, there Olive was, right on the premises and—well, Dennie isn't always the easiest person in the world to live with."

Martha recalled the twist he had given Olive's wrist while jerking her hand from that fatal sculpture. "Is he physically abusive?"

"She says not. But, you know, it doesn't take a beating to make you hurt. He's got that ego."

"So he found out about the affair and fired Kent."

Wendy shook her head. "No way. If Dennie'd fired him, he'd have been admitting something was going on."

"Kent just left?"

"Olive..." Wendy fiddled at length with spoon and cup. Martha waited.

Wendy sighed. "I guess you'd better hear it straight from me before you hear it wrong from somebody else. Olive told Kent she wanted to leave Dennie and move in with him, and he ran like a rabbit."

"To Hannah?"

"I could have killed—" Wendy slapped a hand over her mouth. "Oh, God," she said between her fingers, "you say stuff like that and you never think. Hannah took him on, but I'm a hundred percent sure she didn't know the real reason he was looking for a job. I mean, you know Hannah; do you think she'd have given him house room if she'd known?"

"What reason do you think he gave?"

"She said he said something about a personality conflict. That wouldn't be hard to believe, with Dennie. I think Kent pulled a lost-puppy act and she fell for it. I know she wasn't thrilled after she'd done it. She kept talking about how it was just temporary, and how she really, you know, could make use of his computer skills..."

"Just so." Martha sipped her own cappuccino. "I imagine Olive was angry with him."

"More like bewildered. It was so sudden. She couldn't believe it was over, just like that."

"But not vindictive?"

Wendy sighed, picked up her spoon, and put it down again. "You think it was Olive who did all that—damage?"

"Wendy, I don't know what to think. Someone believes..." Martha caught herself on the verge of one of those inadvertent conversational slips. She was obliged to keep Florence Appleton out of it; saying *she* would eliminate the male half of the population. She took refuge in the passive voice: "Olive is believed to have been seen at the corner of Hannah's street late that night."

The clumsiness of the construction didn't interfere with Wendy's comprehension. "The night it all happened? Who says they saw her?"

"I'm not free to say."

"God, Martha!" Wendy doubled her fist and thumped the table. The cups clinked. "First safe houses, now secret sources. You sound like the CIA."

"I find the situation unbelievable myself," said Martha.

Wendy engaged in more business with spoon and cup. "That night—she says she was with Dennie all night."

"So I've heard. How about Friday afternoon? How long was she with you before Joe and I got there?"

"The cop asked me that. Not long. Maybe half an hour."

"Did she go back into Kent's apartment?"

"No, she didn't. Why?"

"Do you happen to know whether Kent had given her keys to the studio?"

"Keys? No way. That's why he moved to Hannah's, to get away from her. That's what this third degree is about? Keys?"

"There was no sign of forced entry either time, and Kent Reed's keys seem to have disappeared. They weren't found on his body and as you know, they haven't turned up in the apartment.''

"Oh. Well, I gave mine back to Hannah when I quit, and I haven't let go of them since she loaned them back to me.''

"It would never occur to me to think about you.''

"Even though you won't tell me where Hannah is?''

"Wendy, please let that go. Hannah thinks Kent's keys were in a drawer of the computer desk in the studio just before the reception, but they aren't there now. When Olive was there Friday, did she go near that desk?''

"Oh, God, I don't know. I wasn't watching her, I was working.''

"Could she have?''

"I guess so. I was working at that end of the studio and...oh, rats. Yes, she did. Part of the time she was sitting in the desk chair talking to me.''

"Did she open the drawers?''

"I don't know. Maybe. I needed a ruler and she was helping me look for one, so she could have.'' Wendy drained her cup, pulled a napkin from the dispenser on the table, and wiped the foam from her upper lip. "I don't like this,'' she said, and it wasn't the cappuccino she meant.

"I don't suppose you do,'' said Martha. "What I don't like is someone's assaulting my best friend and destroying her work and battering a young man to death.''

Wendy closed her eyes for a moment. "No. You're right. It's just—Olive's my friend.'' She opened her eyes. "I guess.''

"Let's think about something else. Did Olive have a successor? Someone new whom Kent might have loaned his keys to?''

"Not that I heard of.'' Wendy cast a glance at the couple in the back, who still seemed oblivious to all but themselves, and dropped her voice nearly to a whisper. "You think Olive pinched the keys out of the desk and came back and busted up the maquette?''

"The thought has crossed my mind."

"Did your unnamed source see her *that* night?"

"Not that I'm aware of. How late were you with her?"

"Oh, God. Until about eleven, I guess. Or maybe you're thinking she gave the keys to Dennie and he did the dirty deed."

"That thought also crossed my mind, but his dealer maintains that he constructed one of the new works the night before the opening. That night, Friday."

"I don't have any problem believing that. Dennie always has said deadlines inspire him."

"And in any case, if Olive was ready to leave him, why would she bother to destroy—or help him destroy—Hannah's maquette? Why would she care about his competition?"

"Oh, that's easy," said Wendy. "Kent's dead and Don nie's alive. And he's a lot easier to live with when his work sells."

HANNAH HAD LEFT a message. It was so peremptory a demand to call that, late as it was, Martha called.

Hannah was still up—in more ways than one. They had been celebrating. The maquette was finished and would be shipped tomorrow, not by the art mover with whom Hannah had originally negotiated, but by the mover who handled Paul Willard's tree-limb sculptures. Only Hannah, Nell, Paul, and the mover knew with whom and by what route it was to travel. Barbara had driven up that afternoon to deliver the completed stuffed animal and altar cloth, and had agreed that the maquette was better than ever.

"Hannah," Martha said when Hannah stopped for breath, "you must tell Detective Sharpman about the keys in the drawer."

"What keys?"

"Kent's keys. They aren't in the drawer."

"So he took them out."

"You must tell the police about them."

"When I get home. Martha, I wish you could see it. It's gorgeous. It's *alive*. I should get knocked on the head more often."

"I wouldn't," said Martha, and went to bed.

TWENTY

Bones

TO BED, but not to sleep.

The cappuccino had replaced the feathers in Martha's brain with a jangle of images and voices and notions that refused, absolutely *refused,* to let her brain switch over to sleep mode.

Since it might be days before Hannah got around to telling Sharpman about seeing the caterer put Kent Reed's missing keys in the studio desk drawer, it was, after all, up to Martha to tell him. She must also pass along Wendy's observation that Olive had been sitting at that desk on Friday afternoon.

Olive.

While she was at it, she should probably show him Kent Reed's nude drawing of Olive. For what it was worth. It didn't seem like much: gossip had already alerted Sharpman to the affair and the Maya Angelou poem would have gone a long way toward confirming the hearsay. But it wasn't up to Martha Patterson to judge the value, or lack thereof, of any piece of possible evidence, only to hand it over. She would call Sharpman tomorrow and arrange to deliver the drawing to him.

This resolution to act ought to have persuaded her body and her brain to stop jittering, but resolution alone was not enough to neutralize the cappuccino. She lay on her right side; she lay on her left side; she lay on her back. She bunched the pillow away from her nose and lay on her front.

She lay awake.

At last she gave up and climbed out of bed. She put on the hot-pink velour sweatsuit, still cherished in spite of fading at the seams and matting at the friction points, that Edwin had given her many Christmases ago, and spent half an hour with the ancient Jane Fonda workout tape that he had tucked into the box with the sweatsuit. Then she showered for the second time that night and climbed back into bed with *Persuasion*. She had read less than a page when a further twitch of unease distracted her.

Was that drawing really a portrait of Olive Quist, or had her preoccupation with the woman led her to imagine the individual in what was no more than a study of a type?

Once more she climbed out of bed. She took the package of drawings from the back of the closet, slipped them out of Henry Reed's plastic bag, laid them on the end of the bed, and shuffled through them to the portrait of the black woman.

Yes, it was Olive Quist.

Almost certainly it was Olive Quist.

Probably it was Olive Quist.

It was near enough, anyway, to be worthy of police attention.

She rewrapped the drawings, laid the package on top of the bureau, and resumed *Persuasion*. Half an hour later, her eyes began to close.

AGAIN THE AIR was black like ink, but breathable, not liquid, and transparent in spite of its blackness: through it, she could see a gold key suspended just beyond her outstretched fingers. And that same authority figure whom she could not identify—perhaps the obstinate, white-bearded Jehovah of the Old Testament—was demanding, in a booming, echo-chamber kind of voice, that she explain this unexplainable phenomenon. The unspoken threat was that failure would lead to disbarment.

No, said a voice in her own mind, that was wrong. Old Jove *still* had it wrong. But this time she didn't waste her energy shouting. This time she knew she was dreaming, and there were ways out of dreams. Instead of shouting, she set her mind to shoving against the dream. It was a tough one; Jehovah, Jove, whatever that relentless, wrong-headed old judge was called, was no wimp. But still she shoved, and after an exhausting effort, the fabric began to shred. She shoved with renewed might, and felt it soften; and finally no more effort was needed, for nothing was left but nebulous fragments that faded and drifted like fog dispersing...

Horizontal strips of gray, barely lighter than black, marked the spaces between the venetian blind slats. A car alarm, scarcely muted by seventeen floors of elevation, bleeped and yodeled and blatted down in the street. Somewhere a male voice shouted unintelligible words. Faint and far away across town, a siren wailed.

New York, New York.

She turned her head and squinted until the bedside clock's red digits came into focus.

3:28 a.m.

It was nowhere near time for even early risers to start the day, but it would be better not to try to fall asleep again at once; the dream, still close to the surface, might decide to reemerge.

Tea.

She sat up and eased her feet to the carpet, turned on the bedside lamp, and found her glasses. She put them on and pushed herself to her feet and went into the kitchen, switching on lights as she went. She took down a mug and the canister of tea bags, filled the kettle, and set it on the stove, her physical movements automatic while her mind edged into full wakefulness.

The wrong one.

She had got something wrong.

She had no reason to doubt the message; no intellect, how ever disciplined, got everything right the first time. She would rather not undergo another reminder, so she had better work out what the *wrongness* was and what sort of *rightness* should take its place.

Dream codes were apt to be enigmatic, but if Freud was to be believed—not an article of absolute faith with Martha—the dream itself should hold the key.

The *key?*

The gold key suspended in the black air? Was that the key to the keys? The missing keys?

Key. Key, key, key…

The word, repeated, became a meaningless noise.

Leave it for now. What about the blackness in which the key was suspended?

Dennison Simm and Olive Quist were, in the cultural sense, black. Was it they who were wrong? *Wrong* in what way? *Wrong* as in *villainous?* Or the reverse: was it wrong to think the black people were wrong?

Nothing clicked; the dream was keeping its secrets.

Very well, try moving outside the dream. What had she been doing before she fell asleep?

Reading *Persuasion.* Before that, showering; before *that,* dancing to the Jane Fonda tape.

Jane? Jane Fonda; Jane Austen. Another coincidence, but no inner light flashed.

Dancing.

Ian's work-in-progress: Ian had been dancing. A strip-tease in a street. A night street. The *blackness* of a night street.

The coincidences were interesting but no burst of insight

accompanied them. Instead, the kettle whistled. She turned off the burner and poured the boiling water over the tea bag.

Table the dancing; table the Janes. Before the workout, she had been—

Aha.

She had been looking at Kent Reed's nude drawings.

She set the timer and went back to the bedroom and took the package from the top of the bureau and unwrapped it. Olive's portrait was on top.

If *black* was wrong, what was right?

She straightened the bedding and laid out the drawings: the black woman who was Olive; the Italian; the Asian; the Swede; the wistful girl-woman; the Irishwoman—

Whoa.

The wistful one. Hadn't she seen that face before?

She picked up the drawing and studied it.

Out in the kitchen, the timer beeped. She laid the drawing on the bed and fetched her tea.

Where had she seen that face?

A blank.

Leave it. If it mattered, it might come back to her. She packed the drawings away and drank her tea and climbed back into bed, where she fell instantly and dreamlessly asleep, although, of course, she didn't realize she had been asleep until she woke to broad daylight.

THE MORNING ROUTINE—dressing and breakfasting, switching on her computer, setting to work—forestalled speculation. It didn't take her long to finish. The law of contracts had changed hardly at all since her first year of law school; it would not have favored the party represented by her client firm then, and it did not favor him now. Doubtless he would be advised to try to settle, for litigation, even when successful, was costly in money, time, and irritation; to avoid a trial, his adversary, even with a winning case, was likely to accept less than he was seeking.

Not that any of that concerned her, but old habits did persist.

She sent the completed memo and her bill through cyber space, and considered lunch.

The cupboard was bare again.

She went out to a coffee shop over on Sixth Avenue. It had changed hands recently. The food was still pretty much up to its old standard, but the new owner had installed a sound system which played an eclectic hodgepodge ranging from Gershwin and Cole Porter to what must be the latest release of rap. On country-and-western days, Martha ate elsewhere, but today the era of choice coincided with Robert's high-school years: "Eleanor Rigby" was playing as she walked in the door. It stirred a ripple of nostalgia; of all the high-volume music emanating from her son's room, she had liked the Beatles best.

It wasn't until "Lucy in the Sky with Diamonds" came on, halfway through her BLT on whole-wheat toast, that Martha remembered that she had liked some of the Beatles' songs a good deal better than others. This one she had not liked at all. The melody was whiny, and when Robert had explained that Lucy in the Sky with Diamonds was an invocation of LSD ("No, Mom, I haven't tried acid and I don't plan to, come *on*, Mom, give me a *break*"), she had made no effort to broaden her appreciation.

"Lucy in the sky-y..."

Lucy!

Mayonnaise leaked onto her fingers as she stared blindly through the plate glass onto Sixth Avenue.

The photograph.

The photograph in Eileen's wallet: the pouting girl with Joe's cheekbones and jaw line, Joe's bones fined down in his daughter to feminine delicacy.

Martha had seen them again last night in Kent Reed's drawing, the portrait of that wistful girl lying on the bed.

Lucy. Joe's daughter by his first marriage, who had been studying art and who had died; the daughter to whom Eileen had attributed Joe's sudden interest in art.

Joe Gianni's daughter had known Kent Reed well enough to pose nude for that drawing.

Good heavens.

CERTAINTY did not last.

Martha decided against dessert and paid her check. She returned to her apartment and took out the drawings yet again, and it was then that doubt began to niggle. The drawing of the wistful girl on the bed certainly coincided with her memory of the photograph, but she had seen the photograph only once, probably for less than a minute. Distracted by the fear that Joe might have been too put off by *The Body of the Work* to proceed with his plan to purchase a Hannah Gold work, she hadn't given it close attention.

And, of course, drawings were not photographs; artistic purpose or inadequate skill could modify a model's features.

In fact, this wistful girl in Kent Reed's drawing could be anybody.

Couldn't she?

Well—

Where had Lucy studied art? Where had Kent Reed earned his degree? Why hadn't she paid closer attention to those documents Henry Reed had found in the trunk?

There was a way to answer one of the questions.

She picked up the phone and called Putnam County. Nell Willard's voice asked her to leave her message at the beep. Martha asked Hannah to call her back and then, fleeing unanswered questions, went back down to the street, walked down and across town to Soho, and rode the elevator up to the Friedland-Carabelli Gallery. Dennison Simm wasn't there. The big mutant robots had new labels. Now they were captioned *Unintended Consequences I, II, III*...and one of them had been sold; there was a red dot on the label of the one with the rebars sprouting from its head.

The small work Simm had reputedly made on the night before the opening still hadn't been sold. She still liked it.

The fact, oddly, helped settle her mind.

HANNAH CALLED BACK at a quarter to ten that night. "It's on the way!" she cried.

"Excellent. Hannah, I have a question for you. Where did Kent Reed go to art school?"

"Kent? Let me think. He started at some school out where he grew up, someplace with *State* in the name. Mississippi?"

"Probably Missouri. His father lives in St. Louis."

"If you say so. Then he did some work in Philadelphia."

"Where in Philadelphia?"

"A little nothing place called Liberty Art Institute, something like that. What's this about?"

"Something odd has come up. When was he there?"

"Not that long ago. A couple of years, maybe. I think Dennie was his first New York job, and that only lasted a year and a half or so. Then he came to work for me. Is this about finding out who bashed our heads in?"

"I don't know. It's just a vague idea that came to me in the middle of something else. How is your head?"

"It only hurts when I jump up and down. Martha, be careful, don't go messing around with people who bash old ladies' heads in."

OBTAINING THE telephone number of the Liberty Institute of Art from Directory Assistance could surely not be construed as "messing around." She wrote it down, went to bed, and slept dreamlessly until six in the morning.

This was just as well, since if she had not been well rested, her exchange with the woman who answered the phone in the registrar's office of the Liberty Institute of Art would have tried her patience beyond endurance. This person declined to give out any information about former students over the phone, even to the point of refusing to confirm whether or not a person of known name had been a student at that institution.

Martha hung up and looked up another number.

Eventually someone answered Amtrak's 800 number and provided the information that trains bound for Philadelphia departed at roughly hourly intervals all day. The trip took a little over an hour. No reservations were available on tomorrow's 11:00 a.m. and noon Metroliners, but an unreserved train left Penn Station at twelve-fifteen. She called her travel agent and reserved a hotel room near the Philadelphia Museum of Art; if face-to-face negotiations at the Liberty Institute produced no more results than the phone call, she could at least seek solace among deathless works of the ages.

Then she turned on her computer and worked with well-rested concentration until nightfall. In the morning, she packed a carry-on bag with nightgown and slippers, a change of clothes, the packet of drawings, and *Persuasion*, and summoned her car service.

TWENTY-ONE

Liberty Institute

NEITHER THE SNACK CAR, the view out the train window of industrial sites and wrong-side-of-the-tracks houses, intermittently relieved by spring green on scrubby woods, nor questions about why she was on this train, distracted Martha from her book. She reached the penultimate chapter of *Persuasion* five minutes before arriving at Philadelphia's Thirtieth Street station.

The taxi ride was intricate but short. She checked in and went up to her room. There, she took Lucy Gianni's portrait from her briefcase-sized handbag, concealed the nude body by folding a couple of sheets of hotel stationery over it, and put the drawing back into her bag. The Greater Philadelphia telephone directory provided the address of the Liberty Institute of Art.

The desk clerk directed her to a copy shop near a community college not more than four blocks away and provided a Visitors' Guide to the Museum Area, which showed that the Liberty Institute of Art was in the same neighborhood, just three blocks off the route to the copy shop. It was a very nice neighborhood, the desk clerk assured her, perfectly safe for walking.

AT THE COPY SHOP, Martha obtained three photocopies of the bowdlerized version of the portrait, and then went in search of the Liberty Institute of Art. Her route took her through a quiet neighborhood of old, uneven sidewalks, clean streets, and well-kept three-story brick row houses, some divided into apartments, others intact with carriage lamps beside the front doors and security-system signs in the windows.

On one corner, a free-standing Victorian mansion broke the pattern. It was huge, not so much in height—it was the same three stories as the row houses—as in bulk and complexity; a porch was wrapped around two of its sides, and added-on projections extended the rear almost to the lot line. A small black-and-white sign on the wrought-iron fence that surrounded it said Liberty Institute of Art.

Martha passed through the gate and mounted the porch steps. In case any doubt persisted, another sign beside the paneled front door also read Liberty Institute of Art. She tried the knob and found the door unlocked. She entered and passed through a foyer into a roomy entrance hall. Some distance in front of her, a wide staircase led upward along the right-hand wall. Beside the stairs, a wide passageway led to the back of the house; its walls were lined with paintings, most of them landscapes in oil and watercolor, exhibiting varying degrees of skill. Nobody was about in the hall, but voices emerged through an open door to her immediate right beneath a small sign that said Registrar.

Inside the room, someone barked, "Have a nice day," in a tone that expressed no wish of the sort. A tall, stooped man with shaggy gray sideburns emerged abruptly and nearly bumped into Martha. "Oh, I'm sorry!" he exclaimed.

"No harm done," she said.

"You're kind. Rage makes me careless. Why do the pious keep assuring me that God loves me when He saw fit to create schedules and bureaucrats? *Late getting the grades in.* What difference does a week make? Don't try to answer that, it doesn't have an answer. It's impossible to grade the creative spirit, anyway. Have a nice day."

Martha waited until the front door had shut behind him; then she counted to ten, not for her own equilibrium but for that of whoever worked in the office to her right; then she entered.

Fundamentally, it was a graceful room, but its agreeable proportions were somewhat obscured by banks of filing cabinets that nearly hid the wainscoted walls, by three desks holding the inevitable computer monitors, and by the frown on the face of the occupant of the nearest desk. A small triangular block on the desk identified the frowning woman as Edith Parsons.

"Yes?" she said. "Can I help you?"

Martha judged that the frown did not indicate specific displeasure; those furrows had been harrowed into that skin by many years of a life that its liver deemed to be unsatisfactory. The most effective approach, she guessed, would be earnestness, possibly tempered by the merest touch of helplessness. "I hope so, Ms. Parsons," she said. "I'm trying to locate a couple of people who might once have been students here."

"We can't give out addresses," said the woman.

"No, I understand that. I just need to know whether they were ever students here, and if so, whether there's anyone around who might remember them."

The frowning woman took a moment to answer. Martha guessed that she was considering which would be more economical of her time, attending to this interloper or trying to brush her off.

A sigh announced that she had decided. "Names?" she asked.

"The first is Kent Reed. R-E-E-D. I believe he was here three or four years ago."

"Degree program or outside student?"

"He was probably in the degree program."

Ms. Parsons turned to her keyboard. Clickety-click-click. "Kent Reed. B.F.A. 1995."

"Oh, thank you. The other one may be more difficult. I don't know if she was using her married name or her maiden—her birth name. Try Gianni. G-I-A-N-N-I. Lucy. She would have been here in the same time frame."

"Degree or outside?"

Something in Eileen's characterization of her stepdaughter led Martha to suspect that Lucy had been more dilettante than devotee. "Probably outside," she said.

Once more keys clicked, and clicked, and clicked. Presently the frowning woman said, "I've gone back six years. We haven't had any outside student named Gianni in that time."

"Would it be too much trouble to try degree students?" asked Martha.

A sigh. More clicks. "No Gianni. What was the married name?"

Throughout the clicks and the sighs, Martha had been silently scolding herself. If she had put her mind to it, she could surely have learned Lucy's husband's name before heading out on this quest. But uncharacteristically, she hadn't, and here she was, ill-prepared and embarrassed.

But the rule in this sort of situation was to push on until one exhausted the possibilities. "I don't know her married name. She might have used her birth name as a middle name. Would the records…"

She had reached the limit. "If a student registers with a middle name, naturally we have it on the records," the frowning woman scolded, "but finding it would require a manual search." She inclined her head toward the back of the room, where another middle-aged woman was busy at her computer and a rather stringy, much younger man was stealing surreptitious glances at the discussion in front. "As you can see, we're very busy. We're in the middle of end-of-term records, and even if we weren't, we don't have the personnel for wild-goose chases."

"Just so. I understand how busy you must be. This is my last request, I promise." Martha reached into her handbag and took out the photocopy. "I wonder if you might recognize this face."

The frowning woman barely glanced at the paper before shaking her head. "There are so many."

"Then..." Martha looked toward the back of the room. "I wonder, do you suppose one of your colleagues..."

Before the frown could deepen, the young man, all but panting and wagging his tail, got to his feet and started forward. "Let me have a look," he said.

Martha handed him the drawing.

He gazed at it for what seemed like a long time. "The world is full of soulful maidens," he said at last, "but I do think she looks like somebody." He held the portrait at arm's length, squinted, tilted his head from side to side. "I mean, you know, it's a type, but I think I may have seen this particular example. Not to speak to, but, you know, like wafting around the night sessions with a sketch pad under her arm?" He handed the portrait back. "Why don't you try the alumni office. That's where the yearbooks are. Maybe you'll find a match."

"Oh, what a good idea," said Martha.

"Next office back. Danny Osborne. He should be here, I just saw him."

THE NEXT DOOR BACK was labeled Daniel Osborne, Director of Placement and Alumni Affairs. It was open, revealing a fiftyish man with receding straw-colored hair and a forthright sandy mustache, seated at a desk making marks on a spreadsheet.

Martha rapped on the frame and he looked up. His face had its own permanent furrows, but these were smile lines, running from the corners of his nose to the ends of his mustache and fanning out from the corners of his eyes. "Hello," he said. "What can I do for you?"

"I'm Martha Patterson," she said. "Someone in the registrar's office said you might be able to help me learn something about a former student."

"Well, then, come on in, and let's see what we can do." He waved to a chair beside the desk. "Do you have a job to offer?"

Martha settled herself in the chair. "I'm afraid not," she said.

"Too bad. The rule book says I can only give out addresses in a placement situation. But other than that, I'm at your service."

"I understand. The truth of the matter is, I'm not even certain the young woman in question was actually a student here." She took the portrait from her handbag and laid it on the desk. "Her name was Lucy. Her birth name was Gianni, but the registrar's records don't show anybody in attendance under that surname, so if in fact she was here, it must have been under her married name, and..." She had to pause for breath. The stress of confronting her mistake was making her loquacious. "And I don't know what that was." Having brought that run-on sentence to a conclusion, she closed her mouth and leaned back.

Daniel Osborne picked up the photocopy and studied it.

Martha allowed herself further speech. "I'd like to find someone who knew her."

"You're not looking for the young woman herself?"

"No. My information is that she died recently."

"Oh, I'm sorry. I'm very sorry. And your interest is..."

"I'm a friend of her father. He's divorced from her mother and feels he rather lost touch. Now he'd like to know more about her life after he was out of the picture."

"For closure. Understandable. How long ago would she have been here?"

"Her attendance probably coincided with that of a student named Kent Reed. The registrar says he took a degree in 1995."

"Kent…" Daniel Osborne looked at her sharply.

"Reed," she said.

"Yes, I understood that. Did you know he'd died?"

"I see the news has reached you," said Martha.

"I read it in the *New York Times*. He was—it said he was murdered?"

"Just so."

"It's hard to get my arms around it. And now…" He touched the portrait of Lucy with the tips of his fingers. "Is there a connection?"

"I don't know."

"You aren't with the police, I take it?"

"No."

"But you're investigating."

"Informally, in an amateurish sort of way, and quite off the record."

"I see." He seemed to study her face. "Kent was a good-looking young fellow."

It might have been a non sequitur. Martha believed that it was not. She held her tongue.

He picked up the portrait. Much as the young man in the registrar's office had done, he squinted and tilted his head from side to side. "Is this drawing his work?"

"Yes, but I don't know for sure that the subject is Lucy."

"I see. He was quite good with the pencil, as you can see."

"Just so."

"Well," said Daniel Osborne, "be she Lucy or be she not, if this young lady was in attendance here, my guess is that she didn't take a degree. If she had, her picture would have been in the yearbook, and I don't forget those faces.'' He laid the photocopy down and swiveled to a bookshelf. The bottom shelf was filled with tall, slim, yearbook-shaped volumes. ''Ninety-five? Let's see what we can find.'' He pulled out a book, swiveled back to his desk, and opened it. ''Index, index, here we are. R...Reed, Kent. Page ten, page thirty, page sixty-three...'' He picked slips of paper out of an open-topped box, turned pages, and inserted them as bookmarks; then he handed the book to Martha.

It was open to a double spread of graduation photographs. It took her a moment to recognize Kent Reed, in cap and gown, halfway down the left-hand page. She must have given some sign of discomfort, for Daniel Osborne made a sympathetic noise in the back of his throat.

She turned to one of the bookmarks farther back. A photograph of five men and two women clustered around a computer filled the top of the page; it was captioned ''The Bytes of the Future.'' Kent Reed was sitting in front of the keyboard. Neither of the women resembled the putative portrait of Lucy.

''Yes, I've heard he was interested in computer-generated art,'' Martha said.

''Oh, yes, bits and bytes turned out to be his medium,'' said Daniel Osborne. ''In the beginning, they had quite a time getting their little club recognized. Our trustees are a conservative bunch. But we've managed to get into the stream, and recently I've had several inquiries from potential employers. A couple of them seemed quite interested in Kent.''

''One of them must have come through with an offer,'' Martha said. ''I understand he was about to start working in the field.'' She opened to the other bookmark and found a double spread, a wide-angle photograph of a classroom filled with people sitting at easels. A lightly draped female model stood in the front of the room in the classic pose of Botticelli's *Venus;* in the far rear corner, a bearded man leaned against the wall with his arms folded. Most of the faces were visible, and after a moment, Martha spotted Kent Reed standing behind one of the students, reaching over his shoulder to point to something on the easel. It was a male student. The caption read, "Gordon Zenz's life-drawing class. Kent Reed makes his point."

"Was he a teaching assistant?" asked Martha.

"He was," said Daniel Osborne. "It was one of his work-study jobs."

Martha studied the photograph. The model in the front of the room wasn't Lucy. Well, of course it couldn't be that easy. She had to study the faces of the students one by one before, at last, near the back of the room on the far side, in front of the bearded man, she spotted a face that seemed to match the drawing.

"Find something?" asked Daniel Osborne.

"Maybe." The image was slightly out of focus and she feared her preoccupation with the search might be causing her to see Lucys where no Lucys were. She pointed.

He took the book and held it directly under the desk lamp. After a moment, he pulled open a drawer and took out a magnifying glass; he peered through it and then picked up the photocopy and held it next to the book.

At last he nodded. "I think you've found her."

TWENTY-TWO

Bernard

"Now," SAID Daniel Osborne, "let's just double-check." He swiveled to face the computer, laid the portrait and the book beside the keyboard, and began typing and muttering, "We'll just…" *click* "…pull up the course offerings…" *click-click-click* "for ninety-four—ninety-five." *Click-click-click.* "We might as well be chronological about this, so we'll start with the fall semester." *Click-click-click.*

Lists appeared.

"Okay," he said, "this one looks promising. Drawing X101, exploration of the medium, introduction to techniques, blah, blah blah, Instructor, Gordon Zenz." *Click-click.* Another list. "Okay, class roster, that's my baby. Atkins, Martin; Bardwell, Georgia; come on, let's have a Lucy here. Lucy, Lucy, who's got the Lucy? 'She dwelt among untrodden ways,' but let's not be *that* untrodden. Carswell, Kathy; Cohen, Shirley; Fletcher—here we are! Fletcher, Lucy." He turned a grin on Martha. "How's that?"

"Assuming it's our Lucy," Martha said; but she took her notepad and pen from her bag and scribbled *Fletcher.* "Is that the only Lucy?"

"We shall see." Osborne returned to the computer. "Any more Lucys hiding in here? Come out, come out, wherever you are…" The keyboard clicked; the class list scrolled down the screen. "Thornton, Linda," he muttered. "Underhill, Bernard; Zander, Elspeth." He swiveled back to Martha. "Fletcher is the only Lucy. Now the question is, is *this* Lucy *our* Lucy. Maybe we can find a picture with name attached.'' He picked up the yearbook and opened it to the index. "No luck. No Fletcher got her name in the ninety-four—ninety-five annual.'' He closed the book. "Do you know if she attended for more than the one year?''

"No, I don't,'' said Martha.

"Well, we'll give it a try.'' He reached to the shelf and took down another book, flipped it open, and thumbed pages. "No Fletcher.'' He closed the book, replaced it, and tried another. "Not in ninety-three—ninety-four, either. Well, that doesn't prove anything. It's doubtful that an outside student would make the yearbook by name unless she did something remarkable. We're just lucky she was in a class that got photographed. But don't despair. We will now proceed to tap another of our boundless resources. It's called live conversation in real space. Just hold on while I print this.'' More clicks. The class list oozed from a printer. Osborne picked it up, collected the yearbook and the photocopy of the portrait, and stood up. "We will take this up to Gordon and ask the muse to take ten while we plumb the depths of his memory.''

"Gordon?''

"Gordon Zenz, the instructor of the class.''

"He's here?''

"Guaranteed. End of term in the solarium is his favorite time and place. No students, no phone, and the May light is to die for, as the students used to say. Maybe they still do, I sometimes forget to notice.''

MUSING UPON the sheer niceness of this man and the amount of time he was devoting to her search, Martha accompanied him up the grand staircase and along the second-floor corridor past what had once been seven bedrooms (she counted) that had been converted into lecture rooms and studios, and a bathroom that was now a unisex restroom. A youngish man and a younger woman were lounging on a dilapidated sofa in one of the studios and another man was perched on the windowsill. They were arguing in the same tones in which the filmmaker Ian Rosenbaum's friends argued, about what seemed, from the fragments reaching Martha's ears, to be closely related subjects.

Just past the foot of a narrow flight of stairs that led up to what had surely once been servants' quarters, Osborne guided Martha into a narrow corridor. It turned left and right and left again and terminated at the open door of a room smelling of oil paint. One wall of the room consisted almost entirely of windows; the ceiling was a frosted-glass skylight. It was a bright room but not a sunny one; oddly for a solarium, but splendidly for a painter's studio, the window wall faced north.

A collection of stools and folded-up easels had been shoved into a corner. A thick-set brown-bearded man, palette and paintbrush in hand, was perched on another stool in front of an open easel near the window wall. Martha did not need Daniel Osborne's introduction to recognize Gordon Zenz, the bearded man in the back corner of the room in the yearbook photograph.

With assistance from the yearbook and the partial photocopy of Kent Reed's drawing, Osborne explained their enterprise. When he finished, Zenz stood the brush upright in a jar full of brushes, laid the palette on the windowsill, picked up a rag from the windowsill, wiped his hands, and took the photocopy. He flicked a fingernail against the blank area where Martha had clipped paper over the model's nude body. "Fig leaf?"

She smiled. "I didn't want viewers to be distracted."

Zenz blew out a breath through his nose that might have been a laugh.

"Do you recognize her?" asked Daniel Osborne.

"Oh, sure. Had her in Drawing for Dabblers a couple of years ago."

"Drawing X101," said Osborne.

"Whatever. Pretty little thing. You know the type, teeny-tiny little talent, wants to *be an artist,* and doesn't have a clue. Decorates the family Christmas letters with little Disney sketches and all her friends squeal *'Ooh, you're so talented, I just love your letters.'"*

"Would your memory extend to her name?" asked Osborne.

"Oh, lord. Something girly and curly." He closed his eyes; his eyebrows drew together. "Big curly capital. S? No, L." His eyes opened. "Lucy. That's it. Lucy, with a swirl back under the whole thing from the tail of the Y. If she'd had an I in her name, she'd have dotted it with a circle. Or a heart, thank the lord for small mercies." He looked at the photocopy again. "That's her. Lucy."

Martha's reaction surprised her. She had found what she had traveled to Philadelphia to look for—a Lucy who matched the drawing, in a situation that made acquaintance with Kent Reed a likelihood—but what she was feeling was not satisfaction but dismay.

Still, she could be jumping to an erroneous conclusion. Lucy's connection with Kent Reed might have been quite innocuous.

"Tell me," she said, "do students ever serve as models for the classes?"

"Oh yes. It's a work-study job, or sometimes a student just wants to make the odd buck. Your Lucy didn't model in my class, if that's what you're getting at."

"Might she have modeled in some other class?"

"I doubt it. Those jobs go to degree students. Is this Kent's work?" Once more Gordon Zenz peered at the photocopy. "Could be."

"The original is signed with his initials," said Martha. "Might she have modeled for him privately?"

"Looks like she must have, doesn't it? He's dead, by the way."

The matter-of-factness jolted her. "Yes, I know."

"Murdered, of all things." Gordon Zenz looked up from the photocopy. "Is that what this is about?"

"I really don't know. I've heard he . . . liked the young ladies."

"Who doesn't? You think it went beyond modeling? It's possible. She wanted to *be an artist* and amateurs think that means *la vie de Bohème*. Faculty, and that includes teaching assistants, aren't supposed to screw students, but how are you going to stop them? We don't hide under beds with mikes."

"So you wouldn't have known if a relationship developed?"

"Not if Reed wanted to keep his job, I wouldn't."

"Did she have any particular friends in the class?"

"I didn't notice. You may not like this, but I don't pay any more attention to the teeny-tiny little talents than it takes to keep my job."

AT THE FOOT OF the main staircase, Daniel Osborne headed back to his office and Martha, having thanked him, made for the front.

She had succeeded in linking Lucy with Kent Reed, but so what?

And what business was it of hers anyway? Hannah was recovering and so was the maquette.

She looked at her watch and discovered that it was nearly three o'clock. Breakfast had been many hours ago and she hadn't had lunch. No wonder she was experiencing this sense of futility.

She stepped into the registrar's office. The frowning woman looked up. "Help you?"

"I want to thank you for your help," said Martha.

The frown furrows deepened. "You're welcome."

MARTHA HAD WALKED perhaps a hundred yards when she heard running feet behind her. A male voice cried, "Hey!"

New Yorkers in unfamiliar surroundings do not respond to anonymous shouts.

"Excuse me! Miss! Uh, ma'am!"

Hey was ambiguous, but *ma'am* carried no threat. She turned.

The stringy young man from the registrar's office was pelting up the street behind her. "I remembered her," he said when he caught up. "That girl you were asking about? In the drawing? I finally remembered who she was. It was, oh, like two or three years ago. Something like that. Maybe more. I don't remember her last name, but I remember seeing her around. You were looking for somebody who knew her?"

"Indeed I am."

"Well, I used to see her palling around with a guy named Bernard. Bernard Underhill." He put a hand in his pocket and dropped his voice to a murmur. "I pulled his phone number for you. Don't tell anybody or I'll get canned. I'm not really out here, I'm down in the snack bar getting coffee." He took his hand from his pocket. Astonished, Martha held out her own hand; a slip of paper made the transfer from his palm to hers.

"Thank you very much," she said.

"No problem. Listen, gotta go. Don't tell anybody where you got this. Maybe, you know, it was her. You know, it was Lucy who told you Bernard's phone number."

MARTHA DISCOVERED a sit-down deli a block from the hotel. By the time she had eaten, it was too late to visit a museum. There were two or three in the neighborhood, but they closed at five, and it was now after four. Contrariwise, it was too early to reach anyone who had a conventional job.

However, Bernard Underhill might be supporting himself as an artist. It wouldn't do to try to predict his working hours. She returned to her room, obtained an outside line, and punched in the number on the wrinkled slip of paper.

Four ringing tones, then a man's voice reciting the standard answering-machine message that avoided giving his name.

Asking an unknown man to negotiate a hotel switchboard in answer to a message from a strange woman was likely to be yet another exercise in futility. She hung up before the beep and went back downstairs and filled time with a walk in Fairmount Park.

AT SEVEN, she tried Bernard Underhill's number again. The same voice, but live this time, said, "Hello, this is Tom."

"Hello," Martha said. "My name is Martha Patterson. I'd like to speak to Bernard Underhill, please."

A brief pause. "Sorry, Bernard isn't here anymore."

She had contemplated the possibility; the number, after all, was two or three years old. "Could you tell me how to reach him?" she asked.

Another pause; then, "Maybe a séance."

"I'm sorry?"

"I mean, he really isn't here. Bernard died three months ago."

TWENTY-THREE

Thom

"I'M TERRIBLY SORRY," Martha said. "I had no idea."

"Thanks." The word emerged slowly, as if working its way out from under something heavy. Martha recognized the feeling; at times after Edwin's death, she had felt as if she were buried under a pile of earth. "Did you know Bernard?" he asked.

"No, I didn't," she said. "I've been trying to find out something about Lucy Fletcher's time at the Liberty Institute of Art, and someone there told me that Bernard Underhill was one of her friends."

Another heavy hesitation. "Yes," he said finally, "he was her friend."

"Did you know her too?"

"Sort of." A slight lift in his voice let her hope that he had decided to make a conversation of it. "He used to bring her around now and then, for dinner sometimes, and we'd sit around and talk."

Yes, it could be construed as an opening. Cautiously, Martha said, "I don't want to impose, but I would be grateful if you'd be willing to sit around and talk with me for a while."

"I haven't seen her for ages." Yes, his speech was looser; some of the piled earth seemed to have been dislodged. "She moved on, oh, quite a while ago. Before Bernard...before he was terminal. I don't know what happened to her."

"You didn't know she'd died?"

"Lucy?" She had startled him; the name emerged with more force than anything he'd said before. "Oh, hell. How?"

"I don't know."

"Oh, hell. Don't you get sick of people dying? What is it you wanted to talk about?"

"I'm afraid it's a bit vague. I'm acquainted with her family. Her father, actually. He rather lost touch with Lucy after he and her mother were divorced, and he feels a need to learn more about her last years."

"He does, does he? Now that it's too late."

"Better late than never, I suppose, if one may be forgiven a cliché. If you could see your way clear to talking about her for a bit, I'd be very grateful."

"What is it you want to know?"

"Anything you feel like talking about would probably be helpful."

"Well..." Another hesitation; but when he spoke again, the timbre of his voice remained tolerably unburdened. "I don't know how much help my fragmented memories will be, but I wouldn't mind getting out of here for a while." An exhalation whiffed in her ear; it might have been the ghost of a laugh. "Beats sitting in front of the tube and pretending I'm working."

THEY MET in the lobby and talked in the bar. Even in her student days, which, though diligent above the average, had not lacked for entertainment, Martha had not been much for bars, but this one was convenient. It was a sports bar, and the Phillies were playing baseball on a wall-sized screen; there was no need to lower one's voice for conversation to remain private.

His name wasn't Tom, he told her as soon as they had carried their drinks—something draft and dark in a heavy mug for him, a glass of white wine for her—to a table as far as possible from the TV screen. It was Thom: *T-H-O-M*. Thom Vandamm. He was a man of medium height, in his early thirties, with thinning light-brown hair; a little soft around the waist and jawline but not, really, what Martha would call fat. He was wearing jeans and a blue work shirt. He told her he was a copywriter for an advertising agency whose name she did not expect to, and in fact did not, recognize.

Having identified herself as the retired New York attorney she actually was, Martha took the photocopy from her handbag.

"That's the girl," he said at once.

"Lucy Fletcher," said Martha.

"Good likeness." He handed it back. "So what are you asking?"

Martha repeated that her interest was that of a friend of Lucy's father, who wanted to fill in the blanks in his scanty knowledge of her life as an artist-in-training.

"Artist." Thom raised his eyebrows.

"I detect skepticism," said Martha.

"Well, that's good, since I intended to convey skepticism." He drank largely from his mug, wiped his mouth on the sleeve of his shirt, and said, "Maybe the long-lost father would be happier if the blanks didn't quite all get filled in."

Martha took an abstemious sip of her wine, set the glass down, and said, "I wouldn't worry about that. Some of them are already filled in."

"Who've you been talking to?"

"One of her instructors."

"You mean somebody in that clip joint actually told the truth?"

"He said she wanted to *be an artist*."

"Emphasis on *be?*"

"I understood him to be distinguishing between being an artist and producing works of art."

"*Be an artist,* emphasis on *be.* Good phrase. I wish I'd thought of it. Oh, well, originality escapes me yet again." He moved his mug in a small circle on the table, pushing around the pool of condensation. "At this point, Bernard would give me that look of his and go *meow.* He wanted to take her seriously." He took another long swallow. "But truth is truth. I know artists. The ad game is full of artists. And writers, God help us. We write copy, they do layout, the rent gets paid, and life begins at half past five. If you stay away from the remote. I know artists and Lucy was no artist." He looked up. "How happy will that make the long-lost father?"

Having invoked the long-lost father only as a mask for her own interest, Martha merely said, "Truth is truth," and sipped a bit more wine.

"Tautology."

"Yes."

"And truth isn't necessarily kind, is it?"

"Thom," said Martha, "we could fence about this for the remainder of the evening."

"True."

"Which would be a waste of time, wouldn't it?"

"Speak for yourself. Keeping me away from the tube is not a waste of time."

"Well, actually, enjoying your company is not a waste of my time, either."

"Hey." His face muscles shifted in the direction of a smile, and then his eyebrows rose as if the shift surprised him. "Do you think you could keep that up? It's been a while since anybody's enjoyed my company. Maybe I'm getting a handle on this grieving process."

"One does."

"So I'm told. It isn't a skill I'd choose to cultivate, if I were granted a choice." Another large swallow of beer. "But who gets a choice about the things that matter? So. Truth or kindness?"

"Truth, please. I'd be very grateful if you could see your way clear to telling me what you know about Lucy without worrying about what anyone wants to hear. Then, if it seems advisable, I will temper the wind to the shorn lamb."

That brought a snort that was first cousin to a laugh. "From what Lucy said, the old man was no lamb."

"She was angry with him?"

"Pissed as hell."

"Because of the divorce?"

"Because he was the kind of guy who made divorce an attractive option. *And* warped her development, *and* gave her a twisted view of men and marriage and what constitutes the good life."

Joe? It seemed a judgment out of keeping with what she knew of the man. But after all, how much did she know of him? "Was he abusive?"

Thom drained the last of his beer, leaned out of the booth, and waved the mug toward the bar. "He was tedious."

Martha found that charge credible, but it seemed a passive sort of vice to generate such venom as Thom had described. She said as much.

"Well, call it mental absence. Emotional abandonment. What Lucy cared about, Daddy didn't, and vice versa." A bar waitress appeared, picked up the empty mug, looked at Martha's half-full wineglass, and departed. Thom said, "Little Lucy had her problems. But look, I wasn't the friend, I was just the friend's partner. Bernard wasn't generally one to keep the lid on particularly tight, but he kept her confidences. All I got was what fell from Lucy's own pretty lips."

"Whatever you have will help."

He folded his forearms on the edge of the table, and leaned forward. "Ms. Patterson..."

"Martha."

"Whatever you say." The waitress returned with a full mug. Thom drank, set down the mug, and said, "Martha, I think there's more to your interest than you've said."

There was no point in trying to maintain the cover story; this man, although edging toward drunk, was clever. She sipped her wine.

"I've been a little slow making the connection," he said. "You're a lawyer."

"Retired," she said.

"Whatever you say. My guess is, once a lawyer, always a lawyer. Is Lucy's old man looking to sue somebody about something?"

"I have no reason to think his interest is anything but personal. Are you aware of anything he might think actionable?"

"Hell, I don't know what's actionable and what isn't." Once more Thom resorted to pushing the pool of condensation around with the beer mug. "And actually, I don't know why I should care, as long as he isn't suing me. I ask myself, 'Do I want to know what his interest is?' And I answer myself, 'Why should I give a flying fuck?' Sorry."

Martha smiled.

"Bernard was the one who cared about little Lucy, and that was in another country and anyway the wench is dead. As is the confidant. Inappropriate reference; fornication, of course, was out of the question. So truth is truth, and forget the long-lost father. What, exactly, do *you* want to know about little Lucy Locket?"

"Was she married while she was studying here?"

"The old man doesn't even know *that?*"

"I believe we've agreed to forget the father. I'm just trying to orient myself."

"For obscure purposes of your own. Yes, she was married. After her night classes and whatever else, little Lucy went home to the 'burbs, where her lawfully wedded cardiologist, plus two—I think it was two—little bitty children eagerly awaited her return. I'm making up the *eagerly*."

Martha sipped her wine.

"One more reason to be pissed at her father. Her birth father, not her stepfather, who was a whole nother story. What I'm saying in this graceless manner is that one of the ways the old man pissed her off was by leading her to think that husbands were of necessity tedious, so when in the normal course of events she married, she married a tedious man."

"That's what she called her husband? Tedious?"

"Actually, that's my word. I think she said 'boring.'"

"And it was the tedium that led her to covet the life of an artist?"

"Probably."

"Did her concept of the life of the artist include extramarital sexual activity?"

"Don't most lives?" More beer. "Yes, there was somebody."

Progress at last. "Do you know who he was?"

"Never heard."

"Do you know of any identifying characteristics?"

"Nothing. There was a lot of dodging around. Bernard offered them the use of our place when we were both at work, but they were always gone by the time I got home."

"So the affair wasn't a matter of general knowledge."

"On the contrary. This, unfortunately for your purposes, was one of the things whose lid Bernard was careful about keeping on." He drained the last of his beer. "Honestly, I don't remember all that much about any of it. To tell you the truth, and I'm ashamed of myself, I was a little jealous of Bernard's interest in the wench so I blanked out a lot of what he said about her, and then he went down with pneumonia and my mind was on something a lot more important than Lucy's tedious little affair.''

TWENTY-FOUR

Confusion

FOUR MESSAGES awaited Martha when she got home the next afternoon. Before listening to them, she made and drank a cup of tea, unpacked, and changed into a much-laundered pair of jeans and a frayed white shirt that had once been Edwin's. Then, with a second cup of tea, she settled on the chaise beside the answering machine and punched Play.

Two client firms had research jobs they hoped she could work into her schedule. A friend whose hobby was nurturing fledgling playwrights had passes to the opening, the next weekend but one, of a new play so far off Broadway as to be in another borough altogether: Queens, actually, a church basement in Flushing, way out beyond Shea Stadium. Martha resolved to give it a shot; even if the play proved dreadful, *especially* if the play proved dreadful, the friend was reliably amusing.

The fourth call was from Florence Appleton.

Oh, bother Florence Appleton. Martha had no interest in what Florence Appleton might have to say. Be it the legal risks posed by the medical use of marijuana, or lurking women in red miniskirts, or even some altogether new subject, Martha didn't, did not, want to hear about it from this client.

It had been a long couple of days. The frowning woman's *wild-goose chase* was a reasonably accurate characterization of her trip. Yes, the subject of Kent Reed's nude drawing was surely Lucy Fletcher, née Gianni; yes, during her time at the Liberty Institute of Art, Lucy had had an affair with someone unidentified who was probably Kent Reed.

So what?

Martha had been involved with violent death once before. She had undertaken, independently of the police, an amateurish sort of investigation of her own, in the course of which she had made some inaccurate guesses and bad decisions. The result had been a bad scare and a broken ankle that still bothered her in cold weather, and she was well aware that she was lucky to have escaped with no worse damage.

She would not make that mistake again. Hannah was recovering, the maquette was safe, and brutal though the thought might be, Kent Reed's loss was Henry Reed's, not hers. She had her own work; it was Detective Sharpman who was paid to investigate homicides and associated assaults and vandalisms.

IT WASN'T UNTIL well into the evening, after she had contracted for the two new jobs, accepted the invitation to the new play in Flushing, called out for Chinese, received and consumed an order of sweet and pungent shrimp, and tidied the kitchen, that Martha mustered the resolve to return Florence Appleton's call.

"Oh, thank you for calling back," said the precise voice of the retired math teacher who, at least according to Hannah, had kept most of her marbles.

"You're welcome," Martha lied. "What can I do for you?"

"I must apologize for deceiving you."

"Oh?" Aware that her voice had edged toward iciness, Martha drew a breath and summoned neutrality. "In what way?" she asked, although of course she knew.

"I told you the young woman you brought to my atten-

tion was not the young woman I saw on the night Hannah
was injured. That was not the truth. The women were one
and the same.''

Oh, my. "I see."

"And I must tell that to the police."

"Have they questioned you?"

"No. I avoided them once and they have not been back.
Now I must come forward with the information."

Oh my, oh my. "I expect you would like someone to
accompany you." Martha reached for her Rolodex. *H,
I…Irish, Brian…*

"No," said Florence Appleton, "thank you."

"No?"

"I have sinned and I must atone. I will walk hand in
hand with the Lord in the path of righteousness and fear
no evil."

Oh my, oh my, oh *my.* "Miss Appleton…"

"Excuse me." The precise voice overrode Martha's. "In
this world, your advice would probably be sound, but I am
not long for this world and I must not follow worldly advice. How can I tell the children to follow the path of righteousness if I do not? The Lord sends suffering for his own
purposes. It is not for me to question."

Martha had been dismissed. Nothing remained but to
bring the conversation to an end.

But having of necessity acquiesced and hung up, she still
wasn't entirely out of it. The part that remained to her,
however, was both small and simple. Assuming Florence
Appleton actually carried through (and given her experience with this client, Martha had no idea what she would
actually do), it would of course be Detective Sharpman to
whom she eventually told her story of the lurking woman.
And Sharpman would then ask Martha what young woman
it was with whom she had walked down the street under-
neath Florence Appleton's window, and all Martha would

have to do was tell him who it had been. And then he would have evidence that when Olive Quist and Dennison Simm had said they had been together without interruption during the night of the attacks, they had lied.

Well, at least Sharpman would not have grounds to accuse Martha of withholding evidence: after the experiment, Florence Appleton had told Martha that Olive was *not* the lurking woman, and it was not for Martha Patterson to contradict her own client's statement.

It was all quite simple.

She must be even more tired than she thought, for it was only then that she realized that she had a further obligation. She was also obliged to show Sharpman those accursed nude portraits and tell him everything she had learned in Philadelphia.

Which was confusing. Florence Appleton's identification of Olive seemed to have nothing to do with the Philadelphia story. Just what did Kent Reed's *vie de Bohème* art school affair with Lucy Gianni Fletcher have to do with Olive Quist's lurking about the corner of Hannah's street on the night of his murder?

Martha rose from the chaise. The train ride had stiffened her back. She bent three times to touch her toes, and concluded that it wasn't just the train ride that was stiffening her up, but the meddling in matters that weren't her business. Answering all those questions was Sharpman's responsibility. None of them had anything to do with her. Hannah was recovering. She repeated it like a mantra: *Hannah was recovering.* And the maquette was safe, and Kent Reed was no loss to her.

She yawned and stretched. What she needed—well, one of the things she needed—was a good night's sleep in her own bed.

TWENTY-FIVE

Olive

WILD-GOOSE CHASE or not, the Philadelphia trip must have righted some wrong or other, for Martha slept without dreaming until nearly nine o'clock. Or at least—since it is claimed that all sleepers dream, whether they remember or not—without dreaming any dreams worthy of recall.

It was nine in the morning, and it was Sunday. Martha's postretirement contract with herself prohibited weekend work except in a genuine emergency, and further provided that if a genuine emergency occurred, she was entitled to compensatory time off at the first available slack day.

There was no emergency on her calendar. There was no scheduled entertainment, either; the song recital and the aspiring playwright's fledgling flight were, respectively, one week and two weeks in the future. She breakfasted on toast and orange juice; then she went out and replenished her supplies; then she drank a cup of tea; then she went for a walk.

She believed herself to be walking at random, but when she found herself at the door of the Friedland-Carabelli Gallery, she suspected that the belief might have been an illusion. Once more she went into the building and climbed the stairs.

THE FIRST EXAMPLE of Dennison Simm's "miniature period" was now displayed to more advantage than it had been at the opening: a couple of the big pieces had been shifted far enough so that there was room to move around it.

Martha moved around it. The openwork of its slender components reminded her of the cat's cradle games of her childhood, or of three-dimensional cobwebs—not the repellent, clingy things of Miss Havisham's parlor, but the delicate dew-spangled networks dear to Sierra Club photographers. The caption, *Untitled*, freed one to make one's own associations.

Its pedestal was still free of red dots and Martha guessed that no one was likely to spring for it in the next few minutes; the six or seven people wandering about the Friedland-Carabelli gallery were focused on the big stationary mutant robots.

Yes, she still liked it. Actually, removed from the distraction of the crowds and the irritation of Olive's huggermugger, and a week further removed from the violence in Hannah's studio, with Hannah recovering and the maquette safely on its way...under the influence of those tranquilizing developments, she liked it even more than she had at the opening. It would look extraordinarily satisfying standing next to *Euclid*.

But what did it say about her psyche, that the possibility of the sculptor's having murdered and assaulted and vandalized failed to lessen her response to the work?

Oh, bother her psyche. Any number of good artists had less than admirable characters. Benvenuto Cellini, for instance, had been a murderer; had that fact diminished appreciation—art historians' appreciation, at least—for *Perseus with the Head of Medusa?* Of course not. What a question.

Recognizing that she was contemplating an impulse purchase, Martha walked away and spent half an hour giving serious attention to the big works. Then she went back.

Yes. Whatever Dennison Simm had or had not done outside his studio, he had done something inside it that greatly appealed to her. She wanted this piece. She wanted to see this cobweb/cat's cradle standing next to *Euclid* whenever she glanced toward the corner of her living room.

But, but, but...

There was only one sensible way to deal with this sort of ambivalence. She must go away and let the mental dust settle. And if someone else bought the thing while she was dithering, so be it; the universe would have decided that Martha Patterson was not to have it.

She made for the door.

BUT THE UNIVERSE had evidently decided to kick up more dust before letting it settle. When Martha pushed through the entrance door, Olive Quist was just mounting the step from the sidewalk.

Martha produced a smile and said, "Hello, Olive."

"You!" said Olive. The exclamation did not sound friendly.

Martha raised her eyebrows. "Just so," she said. "And you as well."

"Oh, don't...don't...oh, please. Please don't be such a hypocrite. You let me trust you, and then you went running to the cops."

Ah. Sharpman had confronted Olive with the Maya Angelou book. Back to third grade and the dreadful accusation of tattling.

But Martha was an adult and the crime was not the copying of arithmetic test answers. It was homicide, and violent assault, and destruction of a labored-over work of art. "Strictly speaking," Martha said, "a cop came walking to me."

"And you spilled your guts," said Olive.

Oh, bother this woman. "If that is what you call answering truthfully the questions put to me by an officer of the law, yes, I did spill my guts.''

"It was over," Olive said. "There wasn't anything left between us. That's why I wanted the book back. It was all..." Her voice cracked and tears gathered in her eyes. "It was all over, and Dennie was...we were okay. And then you had to give the book to that damn cop so he could drag it all up again."

A couple, approaching with the obvious intention of entering the building, looked at them curiously.

Martha edged past Olive onto the walk to let them enter and then rummaged in her handbag for a packet of tissues. "I doubt that you really want to stage a scene right outside your husband's gallery," she said. "My intention was not to cause you distress, but if distress is a by-product of truth, I can only say 'so be it.'"

She thought for a moment that Olive was going to break off the encounter, but the moment passed Olive accepted a tissue, wiped her eyes, and blew her nose.

In the moment it took to tuck the packet of tissues back in her handbag, Martha made a decision. "There's something I suppose you'd better know," she said. "If you'll walk with me and keep your voice down, we can talk without drawing attention."

"What..."

Martha patted the air: *keep it down.*

With an obvious effort to subdue her voice, Olive said, "What should I know?"

"Come." Martha began to walk.

Olive hesitated, then quick-stepped to catch up. Her voice rising a tone, she demanded, "What is it I'd better know?"

Martha said, "You were seen."

"What do you mean?"

"The night Kent Reed was killed," Martha said, "after

the reception, when you said you and your husband were together, someone saw you at the corner of Hannah's street. Just you, alone."

Silence for three or four paces. "Who says?"

"I don't think it would be wise to say," said Martha.

"You mean…oh, my God, you think…" Olive's voice rose. "Oh, *God*."

"I'm not sure what I think," Martha said quietly, "but I'm afraid you're in deeper trouble than you realized."

OLIVE HAD REACHED the limit of her capacity for hugger-mugger. As they walked north along Greene Street, the story poured out.

Florence Appleton's identification of the lurking woman was accurate. Olive had been on that corner, at that time, alone. "But I didn't go down there. If anybody says I went down there, they're lying."

"Why were you there?"

"Oh, God, I don't know. It was over. I *knew* it was over, but I just couldn't believe it. One day it was wonderful and the next day…" She dabbed at her eyes with the wadded tissue. "Before I knew it, it was over. He quit Dennie and went to work for Hannah, and it was over. I don't know why I'm telling you this. I feel like such a fool."

"You're not the first, you know, and you won't be the last." Kent Reed's last, to be sure; but lovers had thrown one another over since the beginning of time and would continue to do so until the sun exploded and reduced the earth to a cinder.

Olive said, "It doesn't even seem real anymore."

"His death?"

"The whole thing. It was like being drunk. Stoned. Whatever. And now he's dead, and I can't believe *any* of it happened."

"What happened that night? You were seen there . . ."

"We'd been to the reception. I knew he'd have to be there, he was working for Hannah, he was *living* there, for God's sake. That was how much he wanted to get away from me, moving into that miserable little apartment. I had a key to his old apartment, and what good was that going to do me now? But I was still...still dreaming...Dennie knew. He had to know, it was going on right under his nose, but he never said a thing. Not while Kent was still working for him. He didn't want to know, and if he didn't say it, it wouldn't be true. He's like that."

"And not unique."

"I guess. But I did something dumb. At the reception?" Stroking the sculpture. "Just so."

"Oh, God, you saw it too. Everybody saw it, he said."

"Your husband."

"It pushed him over the line. He marched me out of there, and as soon as we were in the van, he started in."

"Physically?"

"Not while he was driving. It was the first time he said anything, not until then, not until after it was all over. He went crazy. He never hits me, but he was so crazy, I didn't know what he'd do when we got home. I never saw him that mad. What got him going, at the reception, there was a crowd."

"I see."

"He's big. Dennie's big. It was...exciting, I guess, when I first met him, how big he is. But that night he was so mad I got scared. We got back to Canal Street, we were heading for the tunnel and you know how the traffic can get. It was just gridlock, and I opened the door and jumped out. I thought, well he couldn't do anything there. He couldn't just leave the van in the middle of all that traffic and come after me."

"And you went back to Williamsburg?"

"Not right then. I found a phone that was working and

tried to call Wendy, but she wasn't home. I didn't know what to do. I walked around for a long time, and all the time I was thinking—still dreaming, really—that if I could just talk to Kent, tell him I'd stay with Dennie and not say any more about moving in with him, just go on the way we were, everything would be okay. And I got tired walking, so I went in a bar and spent a long time drinking a couple of beers. I mean, a *long* time. And finally, when it looked like they were getting ready to throw me out, I left, and I'd had two beers, and *that's* when I went back to Williamsburg.''

"How did you go?"

"I went up to Fourteenth Street and took the L train."

"Do you know what time it was?"

"I wasn't thinking about time. I didn't get home until way after midnight, I know that much."

"So there you were, more or less in the middle of the night, on the corner of Hannah's street."

"And that's as far as I got. I got to the corner and I was about to start down the street, and then, oh, I don't know. Maybe the beer was wearing off, I don't know. The whole thing began to seem crazy. I was standing there, sobering up, I guess, and then I saw somebody—" She broke off. "Oh! That's who it was!"

"Who?"

"Some filmmaker Wendy knows. Adam, Ivan, something like that. He was way down at the other end of the block. That far away, I don't know how he could tell who I was, but I could tell it was him. He's tall, I mean really tall, and he wears that big long ponytail, and he had a movie camera over his shoulder, on a tripod, you know how they carry cameras. I guess if I could recognize him, he must have recognized me."

Martha said nothing.

"And then I guess I really sobered up, because I realized

I was being a real fool, and I went back to the subway and went home. That's who told you I was there, isn't it? That filmmaker. I didn't even know he knew my name." Olive stopped dead. "Oh, my God, that's why you were trying so hard to get me into that deli that night. He didn't know my name, but he hangs out there, and you wanted to show me to him so he could say it was me he saw."

"Olive, you're imagining things."

"Listen, after my Maya Angelou book, I wouldn't put anything past you. But I'll tell you this, he didn't see me go any closer to Hannah's than the corner, because that's as far as I got."

Perhaps. "The reason I told you this," Martha said, "is that the person who saw you is going to tell the police that you were there."

"Or you will."

"Well, *someone* is going to say you were there, and if I were in your position, I'd want to get my own version of the events on record voluntarily, rather than wait until Detective Sharpman came to me."

It was advice that Martha would have given a client of her own, but that wasn't why she had given it. The police should know, but there was no guarantee that Florence Appleton's change of heart would last.

"You think so?" said Olive.

"Yes, I do."

"I didn't see anybody," Olive said. "Just that filmmaker with the ponytail down at the other end of the block. I didn't see anybody go into Hannah's. That's what they're going to ask, isn't it? If I saw anybody go into Hannah's. I didn't see anybody."

WALKING NORTH toward Houston Street, once more alone, Martha wondered.

The story was both plausible and consistent with Florence Appleton's account. But Florence's observations did not cover the whole of Olive's stay on the corner; Florence had not seen Olive arrive or depart.

What if Olive had not been alone in Williamsburg? What if she and Dennison had come back together and Olive had been lurking at the corner, not because she was trying to decide whether to have a go at mending things with her ex-lover, but because she was standing guard while Simm did the dirty deed.

Dirty *deeds*. Three of them: killing Kent Reed, destroying the maquette, and bludgeoning Hannah.

And therein lay the kicker. Martha could imagine—could just barely imagine—that Dennison Simm and Olive Quist might have conspired to destroy the maquette. But killing? *Conspiring* to kill? As Robert in his teens had been given to declaring, it didn't compute. Martha could, just barely, imagine that either of them individually might, just possibly, have had a motive to bludgeon Kent Reed to death— Olive out of rage because the affair was over, Dennison out of rage because it wasn't—but the two motives rather canceled each other out, didn't they?

So if they had conspired, most likely it was only to destroy the maquette. The theory, then, would be that Kent had caught Simm, and he had seized the sculpture and lashed out.

This hypothesis required them to have supposed that Kent wasn't there. Perhaps they had known about the dinner in Chinatown and expected Kent to be part of the group. But that supposition raised another difficulty: there was no sign that anyone had broken into the studio. This fact implied either a key or admission by someone inside. The hypothesis required them to suppose that no one was inside, and Olive denied having a key. Nothing, of course, guaranteed the truth of the denial. Olive could have had a key, given it to Dennison, and stood watch at the corner while he used it to enter the studio and destroy the maquette, only to be surprised, first by Kent and then by Hannah...but if Hannah had arrived while Olive was lurking and Dennison was vandalizing and killing, wouldn't she remember having seen Olive? No, not necessarily; there was that postconcussion amnesia . . .

This theory suffered from a flaw common to conspiracy theories: it contained too many improbabilities to be credible.

So what if Olive had been alone, and had gone down the street after Florence stopped watching, and—

The light at Houston Street turned red, interrupting both Martha's physical progress and her mental floundering. The ratio of hypothesis to fact in this maundering was far too high. She must stop speculating. Let it be. Let Florence, or Olive, or both of them, tell Detective Sharpman about Olive's lurking, or dithering, or whatever it was she had been doing, and let him test hypotheses against evidence. That was his job.

Which, of course, would be impeded if neither of them chose to tell. If they both kept silent about the lurking (or dithering), he would be lacking a critical fact...

Wait. Stop. Think.

She herself could tell.

She was under no obligation of confidentiality to *Olive*. If she left out Florence Appleton, she could relate Olive's story to Detective Sharpman without violating the lawyer's Code of Professional Responsibility. As to her own sense of honor . . .

Someone had assaulted her best friend. She had already tattled about the Maya Angelou book. This was not an arithmetic test.

She would give Olive a day or two to follow her advice, if she was going to, and then she would call Sharpman herself.

The light turned green and she crossed.

AND WHAT, she wondered as she put the kettle on for tea, did any of this have to do with that nude drawing of Lucy Gianni Fletcher?

TWENTY-SIX

Ian

THE APARTMENT was stuffy. The tea tasted like mud. Martha had finished *Persuasion* and none of the other books on her shelves, nor any of the new ones, whether praised or panned in the reviews, which she could purchase if she wished at the chain bookstore down the street, tempted her.

She was not in a weekend mood. Nor was she in a weekday mood; she didn't feel like working.

The problem, of course, was that she didn't really trust either Florence Appleton or Olive Quist to tell Sharpman about Olive's lurking, and although professional ethics did not constrain her from repeating Olive's admission, she found that, now that she had obtained Olive's confidence, she was nearly immobilized by a protest of *Why me?*

Why wasn't there some other bystander who could do a little of the dirty work?

Wait a minute.

Ian.

Ian, the filmmaker, with his tripod over his shoulder. Olive had seen him down at the end of Hannah's block that night, while she was lurking/dithering up at the Bedford Avenue end. Could Ian conceivably have looked up the street and seen Olive?

The Wong Gallery's telephone number was on the flyer in the letter holder on the back of her desk.

SURE, AMY WONG remembered Martha. How was Hannah? Good, they'd been missing her. Ian? Sure, Ian was there.

He was in the cutting room; no, no problem, she'd get him.

She got him.

First having been thoroughly assured of Hannah's well-being and then having listened to Martha's question, Ian agreed that at some point during the night in question he had been working in the street that crossed Hannah's, down at the other end of the block from the corner where Olive had been lurking. He'd been scouting for a background that would supply texture without distraction, and he was pretty sure he'd spent a little time—not a lot, but some—actually on the corner of Hannah's street.

"Do you remember seeing anyone up the street?" Martha asked.

"Hannah's street? I don't think so. It's really empty at night."

"What about at the other end of the block?"

"Up at the avenue? I wasn't really looking. I mean, even in the middle of the night there's traffic on the avenue, and I guess I saw some bodies coming and going out of the corner of my eye, but, you know, it's a long block. You probably wouldn't recognize anybody that far away."

"I see."

"I guess this is about finding the creep who beat Hannah up, and everything?"

"Yes, it is."

"Well, rats, I wish I had. The problem is, when my head's in the film I'm working on, I don't register much else. That creep could be right up the street and I'd never see him."

"Or her."

"Oh, hey, you think?"

"Well, Ian, right now, I don't believe I can be said to be actually thinking. I just have some disconnected shreds of information that I'm trying to fit together."

"Oh, yeah. I know that feeling. I really wish I could help."

"Well, what about this notion? I think I heard you say the other evening that your camera was, so to speak, running itself without a separate cameraperson?"

"More or less. One of my friends rigged up a radio-controlled remote so I could turn it on and off from wherever I was." He laughed. "Ian's ego trip."

"If only all ego trips were so entertaining. My notion is this: do you think your camera could have caught something on film while you were concentrating on your performance?"

"Maybe. If it was going on behind me, I guess it's possible."

"So the film might possibly show something that was happening up Hannah's street, even though you weren't looking there yourself?"

"Maybe. It would have to be on the outtakes, because none of the footage I showed was shot on the cross streets. But even if it did, you know, that's a long block. I don't see how you'd be able to pick out anybody a block away up at the avenue. Not to know who it was. But, look, if you think this is important, I could look at the outtakes."

"Would you?"

"Sure, anything that might help catch that creep. Or, look, I have a better idea. How far away are you?"

"In the Village. Eighth Street."

"Oh, great. I was afraid you might be miles away, out in the 'burbs somewhere. What I'm thinking, if you could come over here, we could look at the outtakes together and see if there's anything that helps."

THE WONG GALLERY was lighted up. From the street, Martha could see the unframed paintings on the walls. Large red dots were affixed to the wall next to three of them;

someone—or three someones—had actually paid out good American dollars for works that Martha wouldn't cross the street to view.

The door was locked, but a sign taped to it said, "The Gallery is open, please ring." She rang, and presently saw Ian emerge through a door at the back and come forward to let her in. "Amy had to go out," he said, "so we may get interrupted if somebody shows up."

"For profit's sake, I'm sure an interruption would be welcome," said Martha.

"Yeah, well, we're not quitting our day jobs anytime soon."

THE CUTTING ROOM was behind the gallery. It was a windowless space that must have been the storage area for the retail shop the gallery had replaced. Steel shelves now held books and papers and round cans of movie film reels and a collection of odd-shaped objects whose use Martha didn't even try to guess. A projector in one corner was aimed at a screen the length of the room away.

Ian shut the door behind them. And as he did so, Martha experienced a frisson. She was alone, she realized, with a man she barely knew, a stranger who had been in the near vicinity when Kent Reed had been battered to death. And the gallery's front door was locked.

A man with a motive?

Wendy: *"Did you see how Kent was hitting on Amy?"*

A man who had wanted to know where Hannah had got to.

She gave herself a mental shake. Amy had given no sign of interest in Kent Reed's almost laughable seductive advances, everyone wanted to know where Hannah had got to, and Hannah herself had declared, *"Ian's all right."* And he would have to be an excellent actor to convey his outrage at the violence—*"Goths and Visigoths!"*—so convincingly.

Well, he was a performer.

Of sorts.

Martha, cut this out. He had not locked the cutting-room door behind them, and the passage to it was clear.

SHE HAD EXPECTED to view the outtakes—the footage Ian had cut from the film—projected on the screen, but Ian explained that he preferred to run the reel through the viewer of the editing table; the splices he had applied to hold the outtakes together were quick and dirty jobs that he didn't want to subject to the stress of the projector, and the viewing-table method would work better for their purposes anyway; he could fast-forward through the irrelevant parts, and slow the film, run it backward, and freeze the frame at the parts they wanted to look at in detail.

"You're the doctor," said Martha.

This was her first view ever of an editing table, but each part resembled something she had seen before in another context. The table itself was about the size of an office desk; its top was studded with a number of little gray spools that resembled the bumpers of a pinball machine; at each end were a couple of disks that looked like the turntables of a record player; and the viewing screen, mounted at the back of the table, looked like a small television monitor.

Ian dimmed the room lights at a rheostat next to the unlocked door from the gallery, took a seat in a scuffed swivel chair facing the table, and waved Martha to a bar stool just behind his left shoulder. This arrangement would have been all very well if she had brought the old pair of reading glasses that were the right focal length for viewing her computer monitor, but since she had expected to view the film projected on a screen, it hadn't occurred to her to bring them. She was wearing her bifocals: perching on the stool would oblige her to crick her neck.

So be it. She perched.

Ian took a reel of film from a can, set it on one of the turn-tables, and unwound a length of film. "Kent laughed at this setup," he said.

"It looks impressive to me," said Martha.

"It's a Model T. Video and electronics are the thing now." He threaded the film in an intricate pattern around the pinball bumpers on the right, through a device below the viewing screen, around the bumpers on the left, and onto a yellow disk on one of the left-hand turntables. "He was full of up-to-date advice, but I like the physicality of real film and silver halide. Now, I haven't rewound this, so it'll take a minute to get back to it." He manipulated a toggle switch, the screen lighted up, the reels started turning, and flickering images ran backward at high speed. Martha hadn't watched film running backward since the audio-visual programs of her high-school days. She had often found the backward action more interesting than those films.

Eventually numbers flickered on the screen, and then it went black. Ian worked the toggle; the numbers repeated themselves in reverse, and the action began to move jerkily forward at normal speed: brick walls and shiny wet street surfaces and puddles in gutters, the images flashing on and off without sense or continuity. Martha leaned closer over Ian's shoulder, her right ear inches from his ponytail. She recognized the setting. It was the street that crossed Hannah's at the far end of the block—the street she had walked along the other day to avoid passing Florence Appleton's building on the way back to the subway. None of the clips showed Hannah's street itself.

The end of the film rattled and flapped through the bumpers and Ian switched off the viewer. "Sorry," he said. "I really wanted to catch that creep."

"It was a long shot," said Martha. "No pun intended."

"That's good," he said. "Well, so long as Hannah's okay. She really is all right?"

"I'm inclined to believe so. She's planning a new piece in black velvet called *Concussion.*"

"All of a sudden everybody's working in black."

"Perhaps it's the millennium," Martha said. But she spoke absently, because her mind was flittering off again...

Black...

and she really wasn't paying attention to what she was saying.

Black.

Black art. Black dreams.

"Ian," she said, "I just had a wild idea. Would you have time to run the film for me? The work-in-progress version you showed the other night?"

"Why not?"

"If it wouldn't be an imposition. I'm afraid it's a very wild idea."

"Hey, the wilder the better."

THE RERUN, in miniature on the viewing screen:

Black street, empty of everything but brick walls and pools of radiance from the steetlights and the puddles; then suddenly, without fade-out or fade-in, Ian dancing far off. Cut. Ian closer. Cut. Ian—

"Stop!" she cried.

The action froze.

There it was, what she had remembered: a black figure, barely visible, far in the background against the faint texture of the brick.

"Hey." Ian worked the toggle and the black figure walked jerkily backwards until suddenly, at another cut, it was not there. Ian stopped the film, then ran it forward frame by frame until the image reappeared. He froze the action. The figure, in a hat and a black coat and black pants, was silhouetted against the wall.

"You didn't know he was there?" Martha asked.

"I saw him when I was editing, but I didn't make the connection. I just liked the visual. It looked like some kind of a symbol. Of what, God only knows. Decide for yourself." Ian advanced the film in slow motion. The figure walked forward, jerking from frame to frame as far as the cut; in the frame that followed the cut, the sidewalk was empty. Ian ran the film to the end, but the figure did not reappear.

"Do you know where he went?" asked Martha.

"I never saw him at all until I started editing," said Ian, "but maybe the camera did." He reached for the outtake reel.

BUT THE CAMERA hadn't seen where the black figure went. When at last, after searching backward and forward through the outtake clips, they found the black figure, the film showed no more than did the part Ian had included in the exhibited film: a figure deep in the background, wearing a black coat and hat, walking along the sidewalk in front of a brick wall until it passed out of the frame. Where it went after that, the film didn't show.

But now they knew that someone who was neither Olive nor Ian had been in the neighborhood of Hannah's studio that night.

TWENTY-SEVEN

Thom Again

THEY PEERED AT the walking black figure until Martha's eyes ached. They studied it at normal speed, in slow motion, and frame by frame. Then Ian projected the finished film on the screen; again, now in full size, they watched the figure's jerky walk until the cut banished it.

The exercise provided no additional information. No matter how often and in what form they studied it, the face of that coated and hatted figure was obscured by darkness. In the end, they were able to agree that the hat, coat, and pants, and possibly the walk, looked masculine; but even that assumption was open to contradiction.

Finally Ian switched off the projector. "Sorry," he said.

"What about computer enhancement?" asked Martha.

"I sort of doubt it. The image is so small and there's so much grain, I wouldn't think there's much of anything to enhance."

"Still," said Martha, "technology keeps advancing."

"No argument there. And I keep resisting. If you think there's any chance those clips might help, I can turn them over to the fuzz."

Martha considered.

It had been a little past eleven-thirty when Florence Appleton had seen Olive lurking and dithering, and it was while Olive was lurking and dithering that she had seen Ian with his camera. And it was around twelve-thirty when Hannah's call had awakened Martha.

The times seemed to be right. Martha reached in her handbag for Detective Sharpman's card.

ON THE WAY HOME, she detoured a few blocks to a recently opened Thai restaurant, waited half an hour for a table, and treated herself to shrimp and peanuts. The meal satisfied her taste buds but proved only marginally successful as a remedy for frustration.

At home, a message was waiting. "Ms. Patterson, it's Thom Vandamm?" said the voice on the answering machine. "From Philadelphia?" A rising, querying inflection, as if she might have forgotten.

As if.

He had come across something he'd like to tell her about, said his recorded voice. She might call him any time until midnight, or any other day between, say, six or seven and twelve. Six or seven p.m., he added with a small laugh—a very small laugh, but a laugh just the same.

It was half past nine.

"FIRST OFF," Thom said. "I want to thank you. When Bernard died, I just shoved all his papers in a box and stashed it on a closet shelf. Talking to you shook me loose. I'm finally going through them."

"There comes a time," said Martha.

"Time, right. Time wounds all heels. Mortally, as you tell me." Martha inferred a few beers in the recent past. "Anyway," he said more soberly, "I found something you might be interested in. Are you interested? I warn you, it's a mess."

"If it's important enough for you to call about, it is surely important enough for me to hear about," she said. "Yes, I'm interested."

"That's what I thought. I mean, it was important enough for you to come to Philadelphia about, so I thought it was important enough for me to call you about. Okay. While I was sorting Bernard's stuff, I found a packet of letters from Lucy. They corresponded after she left art school. I didn't even know. Lots of pouring out of the wounded heart. First of all, the guy in question was named Kent. That could be a first name or a last name, but the way she was using it, my guess is first.''

"That's an accurate guess.''

"You know who he is?''

"We've met.''

"Will you be offended if I express the opinion that the guy's a real piece of work?''

"Not at all.''

"It sounds like you do know him. How the affair started I can only guess, but what she wrote to Bernard after it blew up makes him sound like what our ancestors would have called a bounder. I know young women are supposed to be able to take care of themselves in all possible situations these days, but if you'll pardon just the tiniest little bit of sexism, every now and then you come across one who would justify reviving the institution of the chaperone.''

"He seduced her.''

"I didn't know that word still had a use. Very good. The way I read it, she was bored with suburban wifehood and motherhood—wifedom and motherdom? Anyway. She was pretty, you know that. What I read between the lines is that Kent, the bounder, came on to her with guile and charm, and down she went. She conceived—oops, bad pun. She came up with the hare-brained idea of leaving hubbie and the two little ones and moving in with this bounder.''

"Whereupon,'' said Martha, "he ran like a rabbit.''

"Why did you waste a day in Philadelphia if you know the story?''

"I didn't know Lucy's story, I only know a similar story set in New York."

"He makes a habit of it? I hope your New York lady came out of it better than Lucy."

"What happened to Lucy?"

"Guess."

"No games, please, Thom."

"Sorry. You're right. It was all just too, too Victorian. He got her pregnant."

She would have guessed correctly.

"She didn't discover her shame—this story does bring out the archaisms, doesn't it—she didn't find out she was pregnant until after he decamped. She aborted, of course, but the cuckolded cardiologist had already cut her adrift. Apparently he had a piece on the side and was pleased to have an excuse. He was allowed to hang onto the kids and Lucy came apart. The last letters in the packet were full of remorse and breast-beating, whether for the abortion or the affair is confused. No doubt all of the above. Eventually she was hospitalized for clinical depression, and there the letters stop. My guess is, that's what she died of."

"Suicide?"

"Yes, ma'am. Here she was pouring all this out to her dear helpless friend Bernard, and I didn't know the whisper of a word about it. I wish I hadn't been such a jerk about their friendship. God, I'm tired of people dying all over the place."

"Thom, I share your weariness."

"Shit happens. Tell me, what do *you* know about this Kent creature?"

"He's dead."

"You're serious?"

"Perfectly."

"*He* didn't do himself in, I suppose? Somehow he didn't

come across as somebody likely to be overcome by fatal remorse.''

"The diagnosis is homicide.''

"You're serious?''

"Someone fractured his skull with one of his sculptures.''

"Holy shit. Who?''

"Unknown as yet.''

"Oh, hell, don't tell me you're a cop.''

Surprised into an inappropriate laugh, Martha said, "No, I'm just nosy.''

"Well, if you find out whodunit, maybe you ought to give him a medal. Or her. I'd say that *her* is a valid possibility.''

"I'm afraid I wouldn't be so inclined. The culprit also did some serious damage to a friend of mine. Tell me, Thom, how many people might have known about Lucy's involvement with this man?''

"Besides Bernard? Well, the husband had to know, since he used that as the excuse to throw her out. And the divorce court had to know, since that seems to be how he got to keep the kids. And I'd think she'd have told her shrink.''

"Perhaps.''

"You think maybe somebody wreaked vengeance on this Kent creature?''

She didn't answer.

"I don't think it could be the cardiologist. It sounds as if he was grateful for a way out. He married the side piece and moved to San Diego before Lucy was hospitalized.''

"Thom, I don't know what I'm thinking,'' she said. "Thank you very much for calling.''

BUT OF COURSE she knew what she was thinking. She just didn't think it would be wise to express to Thom Vandamm a conjecture that, however strongly suggested by the circumstances, could even so be both erroneous and defamatory.

But the circumstances certainly supported the conjecture. As Thom had surmised, Lucy's adultery would almost surely have been part of the divorce-court record. And if the fact was a matter of public record, the name of the other party to the adultery would be as well, would be available to anyone interested enough to go to the courthouse and look it up.

Martha had entered Detective Sharpman's number on her Rolodex, but when she turned the number up, she got no further than placing her hand on the telephone. Even tattling on Olive Quist, who was nearly a stranger, had caused her qualms; setting Sharpman on Joe Gianni, who for decades had been, if not a friend, certainly far from a stranger, seemed beyond her powers. Surely the police would themselves be examining everyone's background and life history, including Joe's former marriage and his deceased daughter. Why should it be up to Martha to fill in details that the police themselves should be—surely would be—discovering? Had surely *already* discovered, and followed up, and found to be purely coincidental.

Circumstantial, all of it. Feathers, really.

If only she could lay the whole mess before Edwin's agile mind...but she knew what Edwin would say.

Edwin would say *"Sleep on it."*

Which would be excellent advice if her mind would agree to put sleep on the program. It was a dreadful night.

TWENTY-EIGHT

Conversation by the Fire

THE MORNING was better. Not a great deal better, but better. Having given up on sleeping, Martha had, after all, slept; opening her eyes, she had to squint in the venetian-blind-slivered light to read the bedside clock.

It was 7:52.

Well, all right. The last time she remembered looking, it had been 3:01. Four hours and fifty-one minutes of sleep, while not enough to make a day really easy to navigate, would make it less difficult than no sleep at all. And as Edwin had repeatedly assured her it would do, sleep had cleared her mind.

She had been carrying on this amateur investigation long enough. She would make just one more phone call, which might or might not turn up one more link in the chain of circumstance her mind was assembling, and then it would be time to go to Detective Sharpman.

She showered and breakfasted and dressed, and at 9:05 went out to the telephone by the chaise in the living room.

Daniel Osborne, the placement officer of the Liberty Institute of Art, remembered her instantly. He hoped she had had a safe trip home. She said she had. He asked how he could help her. She said, "I believe you said you'd had a number of inquiries from potential employers about Kent Reed."

"I believe I did," said Osborne.

"Would you be able to tell me if any of those inquiries came from accountants?"

"Now that's a really interesting question," he said. "You wouldn't ordinarily expect accountants to look for staff in an art school, would you?"

"No, I shouldn't think so. I imagine a query from such a source might attract your attention and stick in your memory."

"I imagine it would. And I imagine you have a good reason for asking this interesting question."

"It is a reason that seems good to me," Martha said. "Are you able to answer it?"

"As it happens, I am, because it did attract my attention and it has stuck in my memory. If you think your reason for asking is a good one, that's good enough for me. Yes, somebody from a New York accounting firm did call a few weeks ago, and asked about a particular student named Kent Reed. I took it upon myself to ask why they were looking for an accounting employee in an art school, and the caller said they needed a graphic designer for some brochures they planned to issue. On its face, the explanation seemed reasonable enough, so I passed on Kent's address. Addresses, actually; he had given instructions to provide both home and work addresses."

"Would the work address be in care of someone named Hannah Gold in Brooklyn?" she asked.

"I don't think so. As I recall, it was a New Jersey address."

"Dennison Simm in Jersey City?"

"Well, if I say that's a good guess, I'm not giving out classified information, am I?"

She tried one more question. "Do you have the name of the person who called?" She didn't expect a useful answer; even if the answer weren't regarded as confidential information, Joe—if it was Joe—would surely have covered his tracks.

"It should be in the files," Osborne said. "Hold on a

minute; that isn't one of the details that has stuck in my memory.'' Faintly, Martha heard the sound of a file drawer being rolled open. After a moment Osborne came back. ''I don't seem to have recorded the name of the individual, but the firm was Anderson, Gianni, and Zolov, in New York City. Does that help?''

Help? It depended, didn't it, on what one meant by *help?* She said, ''Yes, thank you very much,'' and terminated the call.

ALL RIGHT. Sharpman.

No. Not yet. Not quite yet. She was obliged to tattle, yes, but her own sense of herself obliged her first to tell Joe what she was about to do.

And there was always the chance that Joe could provide her with a coherent and innocent explanation. He had, after all, not tried to conceal the source of the inquiry to Daniel Osborne.

She resisted her impulse to go to the kitchen for another cup of tea and turned her Rolodex to A. Accountant: Joseph Gianni. Anderson, Gianni, & Zolov.

AT A QUARTER to six that evening, Boris buzzed her to say that Mr. Gianni had arrived.

She had not, of course, told Joe why she was requesting this appointment, only that she would like to see him that evening after they had both finished the workday. (She had not been surprised to find herself working effectively; she had nearly always been able to submerge her private concerns in her work.) If Joe supposed that she wished to inquire about the advisability of some investment or other, good.

''Thank you, Boris,'' she said. ''Please tell Mr. Gianni I'll be right down.'' She pocketed her keys and billfold and took the elevator to the lobby.

She had given some thought to choosing the site for this encounter. She was not fool enough to confront Joe Gianni in her apartment, alone, with evidence tending to support a conclusion that he had battered a young man to death, grievously injured an elderly woman, and destroyed a work of art. Equally, but for different reasons, she had not regarded a restaurant, a bar, or a coffeehouse as an appropriate venue. She had considered meeting him outdoors in some public space, but had rejected the idea for one of the reasons she had opted against the eating and drinking establishments; she would not feel comfortable walking home alone, even through the populated streets of Greenwich Village, after the conversation she intended to initiate. The weather, chilly and wet and predicted to continue so for the next twenty-four hours, had provided an excuse (in her opinion a lame one, but evidently acceptable to Joe) for remaining at home and meeting him at her building rather than traveling to his office.

When she got down to the lobby, nodding to three neighbors who were waiting to enter the elevator as she left it, Joe was standing midway between Boris's podium and the little grove of ficus trees that screened the elevator and the mailboxes, staring out the glass wall at the rainy street, his briefcase at his feet and his hands in his pockets pushing back his unbuttoned raincoat. A new raincoat, a tan one. Something that looked like the brim of a matching hat was peeking out of one pocket.

"Hello, Joe," she said.

He turned abruptly, began to speak, broke off, and cleared his throat.

His appearance startled her. The last time she had seen him—the day of the elder-law seminar in Queens, that was, just last Tuesday—that day she had observed that he looked fined down, his cheekbones prominent, as if he had lost weight. She had supposed then that he'd been working out.

But this evening his face was more than fined down; it was gaunt, and the skin around his eyes was dark and puckered. He looked decades older.

The change was so obvious that ignoring it would be disingenuous. "Forgive me if I'm intruding," she said, "but you don't look well. Have you been ill?"

He shrugged stiffly, as if his shoulders ached. "I picked up a case of Lyme disease and it's taking a while for the antibiotic to kick in." His smile was weak and brief. "Damn deer. It isn't enough that they eat everything you try to grow."

Lyme disease? For someone living in northern Westchester, where infected deer ticks were endemic, it could be the truth. She said, "I'm sorry. I believe that can be serious."

"Well, penicillin is supposed to knock it out if it's caught in time. Thank God it waited until after tax season. I just don't see how I could have been outdoors enough to pick up a tick."

"I'm sorry to be bothering you when you're ill." She nodded toward the far side of the lobby, where a sofa and two easy chairs formed a conversational box in front of a fieldstone fireplace. Here she would feel secure. Boris's sense of the unseemly, which as a rule annoyed her, would be useful tonight; Boris would detect any hint of trouble before it could escalate. "Let's sit down," she said.

The gas flame had been lighted in recognition of the weather and was licking cozily at the fake logs. Martha took the chair to the right of the fireplace, leaving Joe a choice between the other chair and the sofa, both of which were obliquely visible from Boris's podium. He chose the sofa, facing the fireplace and at right angles to her, set his briefcase on the floor in the angle between the sofa and the chair, and said, "What can I do for you, Martha?"

Martha couldn't remember being this nervous since her

very first appearance in court, now half a century behind her. At least in court, a ritual *"Good morning, Your Honor"* was available to bridge the gap between silence and speech.

Begin.

"Joe," she said, "you didn't tell me your daughter—Lucy—knew Kent Reed."

Clearly he hadn't been expecting this: the question froze him. He stared at her while the silence lengthened. At last he said, "I didn't know you knew Lucy."

"I didn't. Eileen mentioned her."

"She...died. Lucy. Did you know she'd died?"

"Eileen told me."

"Eileen doesn't—" He stopped and started over. "Why do you say Lucy knew...that young man? I didn't know that."

"I talked with people in Philadelphia. People who knew her. They told me Lucy knew Kent Reed very well."

"I didn't know that." The repetition had a desperate edge.

"Joe," she said.

"Martha, I didn't know that."

"I think you did, Joe." A part of her mind seemed to be floating outside this scene. *You sound like a cop in a cop show,* it commented. *A hostile cop.* The comment didn't quite stop her. She said, "I think you must have found his name in the divorce papers."

"Divorce?"

"Lucy's divorce. Her husband's complaint in the divorce action would have named the man with whom she had the affair."

He shook his head. "I never...I..." His voice sounded normal, but he could not control his body language: his head went on shaking back and forth, almost mechanically, as if a switch were stuck in the on position.

His discomposure, validating her surmise, dismayed her even as it emboldened the hostile cop. "You knew his name," she said. "You knew it was Kent Reed who had..." the cop had no trouble with an archaic vocabulary..."had betrayed Lucy. You tracked him to Dennison Simm's studio through the school's placement office." He hadn't covered his tracks; had he wanted to be caught? To be stopped?

Did the unconscious really work like that?

Still his head went back and forth.

"You used me," she said. Trying to force down anger, she drew a deep breath and let it out. But anger was as strong as a rising tide and would not be dammed. "I suppose Dennison Simm told you Kent was working for Hannah, and you used me to put you in touch with her so you could meet him and"—one might as well let the cop say it his way—"avenge her death."

She folded her hands in her lap. The silence grew. His hands resting on his knees, Joe stared into the fireplace. His head was motionless now; only his sunken eyes moved, flickering up and down as they followed the flames sweeping over the fake logs.

A chilly draft brushed the back of her neck and voices sounded at the front door; more of her neighbors were coming home. Martha turned her head to look over her shoulder. Even as Boris greeted the people who were entering, the set of his head told her he was aware of the tension by the fireplace.

She turned back.

As if her movement had broken a spell, Joe stirred and looked at her. "Martha," he said, "I don't know what has given you these ideas, but you're mistaken. Even assuming that I had any reason to—and, Martha, I had no idea Lucy even knew—" He cleared his throat. "Why on earth would I do any damage to Hannah's maquette? That has to have been the work of that black man, that black sculptor. He's the one with the grudge. A double grudge, if I'm not mistaken. It's the only reasonable explanation—unless it was just a random attack. Somebody breaking in..."

He was floundering.

"There was no evidence of a break-in," she said. "Kent let someone in. Let *you* in. Maybe you told him you wanted to buy that sculpture of his. Maybe that's why he let you in. Maybe that's how you were able to pick it up without arousing his suspicion."

And it was Martha, wasn't it, who had showed him how? Martha's imp, as much a part of her as her rational brain, had treated that steel column like a baseball bat, and Joe, full of rage at his daughter's seducer, had been watching. "You picked up the sculpture and battered him to death and then went on to ruin the maquette. You kept trying to put the blame on someone else. You tried to implicate Dennie; and when I said I had doubts, you tried the people at the gallery, and when that theory didn't hold water, it was Dennie again. You came back with the keys you found in the desk drawer when Henry Reed was there, and you destroyed the maquette again. Blaming Dennie again, or Olive..."

Another draft tugged at her attention; another jumble of voices faded as the speakers passed behind the ficus trees to the elevators. The everyday sounds nudged her toward reasonableness. There was no reason to be hectoring Joe like this; she had summoned him only to give him notice of her intention.

Almost gently, she said, "It doesn't matter, Joe. I didn't ask you here to argue. I just wanted you to know what I'm going to tell the police."

"The police?" His voice was incredulous, as if he'd been confronted with a wholly new idea.

"Joe, we're talking about homicide. I have to give the

police this information. I'm going to tell them that people who knew Lucy in Philadelphia, people who knew her well, say she had an affair with Kent Reed. They'll subpoena the divorce papers. They'll learn that she became pregnant, and that when Kent broke it off, she fell into a suicidal depression.'' Anger flickered again. ''And I'm going to tell them how you used me to bring you into contact with Hannah. I'm furious about that, Joe. But because we've been acquainted for so long, I didn't want to do this behind your back.''

After a moment, Joe said, ''That's all?''

''For what it's worth. And for what it's worth, they'll learn that a man in a black coat was seen approaching Hannah's street that night.''

He looked down at the raincoat lapped over his knees. The new tan raincoat. His victims' blood would have splashed on the black one. Had he dumped the coat somewhere on the way to Grand Central? It probably wouldn't have looked like blood on the black fabric; could he have worn that coat, still bloody, all the way home and disposed of it there?

A new image, like a scene from Ian's fast-cut film, flashed in her mind: once more she saw the sludgy, granular puddle in the gutter that Sharpman had stepped around that night. No, Joe wouldn't have kept that bloody coat on. ''The police will learn that blood nauseates you,'' she said, ''and they'll have noticed a pool of vomit in the gutter in front of Hannah's studio, and they're trained to take samples of things like that.'' *Granular.* ''Vomit that contained rice,'' she added, ''and they know we went to Chinatown for dinner.''

He stared at her. One hand moved to touch the lapel of his coat. He jerked it away. His lips, already taut, thinned to a slit.

Martha moved her feet to one side. ''And Joe, when they

find out what I've learned about Lucy, they'll go to that sample and they'll look for a match with your DNA.'' Now she was guessing; she didn't know whether DNA would be present in vomit. Perhaps, she thought, only the DNA of the rice would turn up.

The flame of rage had consumed its fuel and died to a spark. She hadn't needed to tell him all that. She had been showing off. Simply showing off. The spark died, and all that remained was emptiness and a terrible sadness.

The gas flame in the fireplace hissed quietly.

Finally Joe spoke. "I wasn't planning to..." His voice was barely audible; she had to hold her breath to hear him. "I just wanted to see what he was like. He was the father of my grandchild. My grandchild who wasn't allowed to be born, and I wanted to see what he might have been like. And then I did. I met the father of my dead grandchild—and what did I find? A smarmy, womanizing *black* man."

Martha held her breath.

"There was something Hannah said, how what you do never comes up to the concept you started with. Do you remember that?" He stared at her as if her answer was important. "Do you remember?" She must have nodded, for he went on: "When I picked up that thing he had made, I expected it to feel good. Like hitting the tee shot square on and seeing it fly a hundred yards straight down the fairway." He rubbed his face again. "It wasn't like that."

She let her breath out silently.

"I didn't expect Hannah so soon. I heard her at the door, and I was afraid..."

It was the blood that had done it.

It will have blood: they say blood will have blood...

(Hamlet? Macbeth? Shakespeare, certainly; no one else wrote so compellingly of revenge...)

Her mind was trying to escape into tangents.

"I stood behind the door, where Hannah wouldn't see

me when she opened it. I didn't mean for her to be hurt. I felt terrible..." He dropped his face into his hands. "Oh, God, can this be me?"

I, not me, you dolt. It's a predicate nominative: Can this be I?

But pedantry provided no escape from the emotions that were mobbing her. "Joe," she said, "you need a lawyer."

He raised his head from his hands and stared at her.

"Your firm must have an attorney on retainer," she said. "Call them. Get a referral to a competent criminal defense attorney. Right now, tonight."

Still he stared. She wondered if he had taken in what she'd said.

She said it again: "You must get a lawyer, because I'm going to tell the police everything I've said to you." She glanced at Boris. He was alert to the tension.

"Police," Joe said. "Oh, God, this can't be happening. Oh, God, the boys. And Eileen."

You should have thought of them before.

But she didn't say it, of course; and after another silence, Joe planted his hands on his knees and drew in and expelled a series of deep breaths, and even produced that twisted caricature of a smile. "Well," he said, "gotta do what you gotta do." He pushed himself to his feet, staggering a bit but catching himself with a hand on the back of the sofa. For a moment he stood slumped; then, without looking at her again, he squared his shoulders and made for the door.

She twisted around in her chair and watched him pass Boris's podium. He shook his head at whatever doormanly remark Boris offered and pushed out through the door. Through the streaks of rain on the glass front wall, she saw him head east.

She must get up out of this chair and go upstairs and call Detective Sharpman. She felt made of lead.

From the front, Boris said, "Ms. Patterson?"

"Yes?"

"Your friend looks very bad."

And so would you if you were on your way to confess to murder. "He has Lyme disease," she said.

"He shouldn't be out in this weather, but he didn't want me to call a cab."

The weather was the least of Joe's problems. "You're right," she said, "but we aren't his keepers." *Call Sharpman.* She pushed herself to her feet, felt her foot bump something, and looked down. Joe had left his briefcase standing against the end of the sofa.

She picked it up, her body adjusting automatically to its heft, and turned away from the fake fire.

How rattled must one be, to walk off without one's briefcase?

Gotta do what you gotta do.

She skirted the end of the sofa and started, not toward the elevators, but for the front door. Boris exclaimed as she hurried past his podium, but she ignored him and, the briefcase still in her hand, shoved through the door and bolted down the shallow steps to the sidewalk.

Joe was no longer in sight.

Gotta do...

Dodging raincoated pedestrians, Martha ran east through the rain.

TWENTY-NINE

Uptown Local

BEFORE MARTHA HAD gone half a block, the rain had soaked through her hair to her scalp, plastered her shirt to her shoulders, and set off a spasm of shivering. A corner of her mind questioned the sanity of this race through the rain. No rational response presented itself, but still the impulse that had sent her out the door kept her half running along the walk, and presently the movement warmed her blood and she stopped shivering.

Rush hour had begun to wind down, but a substantial trickle of people was still converging on the subway station on the far side of Broadway. A red light held her up at the corner; confirmed New Yorker though she was, she judged that jaywalking among these aggressive cabs and delivery vans would require an agility of which her aging knees were no longer capable. But while she waited, she was able to see, across the clots of traffic and through a gap between hurrying bodies, a tan-raincoated man half a block ahead of her, striding eastward. Something in his walk and the set of his head convinced her that he was Joe. He had bypassed the station for the R train; apparently he meant to continue another block to the Astor Place station on the Lexington Avenue line. If he meant to go home, that choice made sense; the uptown Lex would take him directly to Grand Central.

The light changed and she crossed. He was walking at a good clip; even dodging past the foot traffic at a pace just short of a run, she was unable to shorten the distance between them. She thought of shouting, but some lingering sense of dignity, combined with the realization that traffic noise would drown anything less than a scream, kept her silent. She was, however, able to keep him in view, and when she reached the complex intersection where Eighth Street, Astor Place, Lafayette Street, and the Bowery converge, she saw him, across the stream of traffic, just starting down the stairs to the uptown local. Once more the light held her up. By the time she reached the top of the stairs, he had passed around the landing and was no longer in sight.

She descended amid a swarm of home-bound commuters, gripping the handrail against the risk of an unexpected buckling of her knees and clutching the handle of Joe's briefcase with her free hand. At the bottom of the stairs, she transferred the briefcase to an under-arm grip and fished out her billfold, grateful for the inexplicable impulse that had caused her to shove it into her pocket when she left her apartment. She extracted her Metro-Card and buried the billfold in her pocket again. She joined the line in front of the turnstile; her turn came; she swiped the card through the slot and pushed through onto the platform.

It was well populated; obviously some time had elapsed since the last train had passed through. At first she despaired of locating one man among the many, but then the crowd shifted and opened a bit and she saw him, standing at the end of the platform, close to the edge, staring down the tunnel, as one does, in the direction from which the train would arrive.

Martha sidled through the crowd. When she supposed herself within earshot, she said, "Joe!"

Two or three people glanced at her, but Joe continued to stare down the tunnel.

She edged closer. "Joe?"

This time he turned. His forehead was creased as if he

were trying to work out the solution to a puzzle, and his eyes seemed to focus on something not detectable by ordinary vision.

She raised the briefcase. "You forgot this."

His eyes moved to the briefcase and back to Martha. With a surge of dread, she wondered if he even knew who she was.

A distant rumble from the depths of the tunnel announced that the train was approaching. Joe looked back down the track again.

She moved closer to him. "Your briefcase, Joe," she urged. "You forgot it."

Again his gaze returned to her, but he neither spoke nor moved to take the briefcase, and after that glance, he looked away again, back down the track.

The rumble grew, and now light glowed on the tunnel wall from the headlights that were still out of sight on the far side of a curve. A draft pushed ahead of the train through the confines of the tunnel, struck a chill through her wet hair and shirt. And then the twin headlights cleared the curve and swept into view, the draft freshened to a wind, and the rumble grew into a clattering roar.

Joe moved to the brink of the platform and leaned into the wind and the roar...

Metal screeched on metal. A scream raked Martha's throat. She grabbed for his arm, but he had already overbalanced and her clutching fingers missed his arm and locked on the slick fabric of his wet raincoat sleeve. His weight pulled at her and she let go, but she had put too much weight on one knee...

"Hey, watch it!" someone shouted, and hard fingers closed on her arm and hauled her backward, and she must have shut her eyes, for all she could remember afterward was the *screeeeech* of metal sliding on metal, and, not quite drowned out, a dreadful squashy thud...

Then for a moment, an eerie silence.
Then the screams.

IT WILL HAVE BLOOD: they say blood will have blood.

THIRTY

Cat's Cradle

SHARPMAN STARED at her with the hard face of the street cop he must have once been. "Martha Patterson," he said, "I ought to book you for hindering prosecution."

Martha had told the officer who took her statement on the subway platform that the victim was involved in a case under investigation by Detective Sharpman, of whatever precinct it was that covered Williamsburg. She had refused medical attention, and had finally been sent home. A long phone conversation with Hannah, a great deal of hot tea, and a surprisingly sound sleep restored most of her wits. When Sharpman phoned at nine o'clock the next morning and arrived at her door half an hour later, she was ready with a coherent account of almost everything she had learned and everything she had guessed, beginning with that sludgy granular puddle of vomit in front of Hannah's studio and finishing with her chase through the rain after Joe Gianni. Even without including Florence Appleton's sighting of Olive—for until Martha heard otherwise, the Appleton story was still confidential, and Sharpman didn't say whether or not she had talked to him—the interview took up most of two thirty-minute audiotapes.

Sharpman didn't say whether he had heard from Olive Quist or Ian Rosenbaum, either, and she didn't ask. If he hadn't heard from them, Martha had no doubt that they would be hearing from him.

"I assume," she said now, "that hindering prosecution is a criminal offense."

"That's right."

"Criminal law isn't my field," she said. "I'd appreciate your informing me of the elements of the crime."

His face didn't soften. She surmised that the suicide of a suspect was not the ideal way to close a homicide case. "The part I'm talking about," he said, "is warning a person you believe to have committed a crime that he's about to be discovered or apprehended."

"Thank you. I suppose my conversation with Joe could be said to fit that characterization. But it seems to me that there must be more to it than that. In order to be a crime, mustn't an action be carried out with criminal intent?"

He took in a breath and let it out and said, "The warning must be intended to prevent, hinder, or delay the discovery or apprehension of that person."

"Then with all due respect," she said, "if charged, I shall plead not guilty."

"Naturally," he said.

"You recommend that I tell it to the judge?"

He didn't answer.

"My intention was purely social," she said. "I've known Joe Gianni a long time and I didn't want to go to you behind his back."

"Social," said Sharpman. "Social."

"Under the circumstances, the word sounds absurd, doesn't it?"

"It's sounds asinine."

"I was on my way to call you when I stumbled over Joe's briefcase. That sent me tearing out to stop him."

Sharpman's expression seemed to ease a little. "Did you know what he was going to do?"

"I was apprehensive. He looked dreadful, and there was the example of his daughter."

"A little late thinking of that, weren't you?"

"Yes."

Sharpman stared at her for another long moment. Then he muttered, "Social," shook his head, and began packing up the tape recorder. "You know something that burns me up?" he said. "The crappy way he picked to do it. Do you know what a man on the tracks does to motorman's nerves?"

"He wasn't thinking of motormen," she said. "Or anyone else. If Joe Gianni had been thinking, he'd have remembered that suicide would void his life insurance."

"OH, YES," said Hannah. "Yes, it's good."

It was Friday in late June, warm enough for the air-conditioning in the Friedland-Carabelli Gallery to be turned on. Nell and Paul Willard had persuaded Hannah to stay another two weeks for a proper vacation after the stress of reconstructing and dispatching *Love.* She had returned bearing a sheaf of sketches for the new black velvet work, *Concussion,* and had been nearly incommunicado in her studio ever since.

But when Martha had requested that they meet at Dennison Simm's gallery so that Hannah could take a look at the cobweb/cat's cradle, she had consented to emerge. She had walked around the little work. Then she had walked away to study the mutant robots. (A second one had been sold, Martha noted.) Then she returned to the cat's cradle and said, "Yes, it's good."

"I think I want it," said Martha.

"It doesn't give you bad feelings?"

"Not that I'm aware of. Does it bother you?"

"The man wasn't my friend."

"Well, not mine, either."

"But you knew him a long time." Hannah walked around the piece once more. "By me it isn't bother, it's surprise. A kinder, gentler Dennie Simm. Is it an aberration

or does he have some more in him? The market for aber-
rations isn't so big.''

"Olive said it's the first work of Dennison Simm's Miniature Period.''

"Oh, Olive. She was selling. When Dennie sells something, Dennie acts human. I only wonder, does he have any
more like it in him?''

"Actually, I don't care,'' Martha said. "If I buy it, it
will be because I want to look at it for a long time, not
because I want a capital gain. What I want you to tell me
is if you think it will really work with *Euclid.*''

"It will work. It just shouldn't give you bad dreams.''

"I don't see why it should. The matter is resolved, and
Dennison Simm is an innocent bystander.'' Martha circled
the piece one more time. "Hannah, I really don't think this
piece is going to give me a problem.''

As MARTHA WAS signing the Visa slip in the gallery office,
she heard Dennison Simm's voice, out in the exhibition
space, booming, "Hey, Miz Gold. Good to see you up and
about.''

Barney Friedland, the gallery's co-owner, picked up an
envelope from the desk, said, "Excuse me a minute,'' and
went out the office door. Martha laid down the pen and
followed him.

Simm was standing next to the cat's cradle with Hannah.
"Had me an idea the other day,'' he was saying. "How
about we collaborate?''

Hannah looked wary.

"How about I make me a crazy big lady,'' Simm said,
"and you make her a crazy big dress?''

Before Hannah could answer, Friedland said, "I've been
trying to call you, Dennie. You've got mail.''

Simm took the envelope, looked at the return address,

turned it over and tore it open, extracted the single sheet, unfolded it, and took a long time reading it.

Finally he looked at Hannah and said, "You get this too?"

"Get what?"

He handed it to her.

Hannah scanned it, looked at Simm, and shrugged. "Mine will be in the mail at home," she said, and handed the letter to Martha.

It was from the sponsor of the Minneapolis competition. In standard rejection prose, it thanked Simm for his excellent entry, said the selection committee had been gratified by the outstanding quality of all the submissions and grieved that all could not be winners, declared that making the final selection had been difficult, but...

But they had settled on a piece by a Chicago sculptor; Martha had seen photographs of the man's work. He went in for fourteen-foot figurative bronzes of seated family groups.

"It'll be another rip-off of those Henry Moore things from the forties," said Hannah.

Martha handed the letter back to Simm. He crumpled it in his fist and put his big arm around Hannah's shoulders. "So after all that shit," he said, "all's happened is, we both of us get our butts whipped."

THE HIRELING'S TALE

JO BANNISTER

A CASTLEMERE MYSTERY

Detective Inspector Frank Shapiro and his two chief investigators, Liz Graham and Cal Donovan, probe a murderous conspiracy, which may rob Castlemere of more than one of their finest.

A young prostitute is found dead on a boat in the Castlemere Canal. Adding to the puzzle, there's a hired killer on the loose, making target practice of farm animals—before taking aim at the real mark. But the hit misses—and Shapiro takes the bullet. Now it's up to a shaken Graham and Donovan to sort out a complex crime that will lead to another fatal confrontation in the lonely English countryside.

Available March 2001 at your favorite retail outlet.

WORLDWIDE LIBRARY®

WJB377

DEAD AND GONE
DOROTHY SIMPSON

AN INSPECTOR LUKE THANET MYSTERY

During a small and decidedly uncomfortable dinner party, Virginia Mintar, wife of a prominent lawyer, disappears, only to be found hours later, stone dead in the garden well of the rustic cotate.

Virginia's scandalous behavior had earned her the rage of family, friends and lovers alike. Who had been finally driven to kill her? As Inspector Luke Thanet and his partner, Sergeant Mike Lineham, begin to unravel the tangled threads of dark family secrets, bitter hatred and devious intent, not even they are prepared for the final, ghastly discovery in what emerges as the most poignant and disturbing case of their careers.

Available March 2001 at your favorite retail outlet.

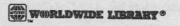

WORLDWIDE LIBRARY®

STEVEN F. HAVILL

OUT OF SEASON

AN UNDERSHERIFF BILL GASTNER MYSTERY

Sheriff Martin Holman didn't like flying. Much less at night, with bad weather. So why he took a plane ride over a nearby mesa under those dangerous conditions are questions as disturbing as why somebody shot the pilot dead from the ground—causing the plane to crash.

Undersheriff Bill Gastner, just months away from retirement, now has a murder on his hands. Following his sharp instincts and a tenacity born of long years as a cop, he uncovers a scheme of illegal doings and nasty buried secrets. Unfortunately it could make his biggest case his last.

Available April 2001 at your favorite retail outlet.

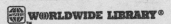
WORLDWIDE LIBRARY®

WSH382

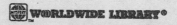

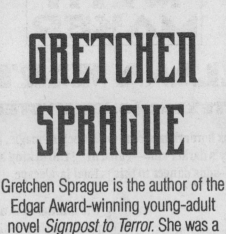

GRETCHEN SPRAGUE

Gretchen Sprague is the author of the
Edgar Award-winning young-adult
novel *Signpost to Terror.* She was a
legal services attorney in Brooklyn,
New York, for eleven years.

W3781BC